PRIZE OF PAIN

Two women kneel on the seats to either side of me, locking my head between their hands as blonde Harriet, stripped to the waist, smiling thinly, leans forwards over me, lifting her closed hand to my mouth. Sperm is oozing slowly between her fingers and I feel droplets of it land on my thighs. The women on either side tighten their grip and Harriet murmurs.

'Open and swallow it.'

I try to shake my head but can't move it.

'How is it going, Harriet, dear?' the inspectrix calls from behind her.

'He refuses to open his mouth, Miss.'

'Pinch his nostrils shut and wait. We will bear this disobedience in mind as we deliberate over his next punishment.'

By the same author:

DISCIPLINED SKIN
BEAST
PALE PLEASURES
SIX OF THE BEST
VAMP

PRIZE OF PAIN

Wendy Swanscombe

This book is a work of fiction.
In real life, make sure you practise safe, sane and
consensual sex.

First published in 2004 by
Nexus
Thames Wharf Studios
Rainville Road
London W6 9HA

www.nexus-books.co.uk

Typeset by TW Typesetting, Plymouth, Devon

Printed and bound by
Clays Ltd, St Ives PLC

ISBN 0 352 33890 3

Those who find themselves in Hell will be chastised with the Scourge of Love. How cruel and bitter this Torment of Love will be! For those who understand that they have sinned against Love undergo greater sufferings than those produced of the most fearful tortures. The sorrow which takes hold of the heart that has sinned against Love is more piercing than any other pain. It is not right to say that sinners in Hell are deprived of the Love of God. But Love acts in two different ways, as suffering in the Reproved and as joy in the Blessed . . .

St Isaac of Nineveh

And after his wives, on the same side, sit the ladies of his lineage yet lower, after that they be of estate. And all those that be married have a counterfeit made like a man's foot upon their heads, a cubit long, all wrought with great pearls, fine and orient, and above made with peacocks' feathers and of other shining feathers; and that stands upon their heads like a crest, in token that they be under man's foot and under subjection of man. And they that be unmarried have none such.

The Travels of Sir John Mandeville (1366), Chapter XXIII: 'Of the Great Chan of Cathay. Of the Royalty of His Palace, And How He Sits At Meat; And of the Great Number of Officers That Serve Him.'

You'll notice that we have introduced a set of symbols onto our book jackets, so that you can tell at a glance what fetishes each of our brand new novels contains. Here's the key – enjoy!

cp (traditional)

cp (modern)

spanking

restraint/bondage

rope bondage/hojojutsu

latex/rubber/leather/enclosure

fem dom

willing captivity

medical

period setting

uniforms

sex rituals

One

He picked up the paper and began to read:

> You have two hours to complete the examination.
> Answer all questions writing on one side of the paper
> only. *ANY GRAMMATICAL AND ORTHOGRA-
> PHIC MISTAKES WILL BE PUNISHED*
> SEVERELY *ON A RISING SCALE OF TORMENT.*
> Do NOT touch or read the examination paper until
> your Mistress gives you permission to do so.

He blinked and swallowed, allowing the paper to slide
from his fingers, and looked up to see her violet eyes
fixed on his, smoky with anger. She shook her head
slowly, a wing of her hair sliding across her left cheek,
then across her right, and her lips were pursed with
threat. Then her eyes closed slowly, and when she
opened them again she looked away from him, at the
clock on the wall to her left.

'You may begin,' she said.
He swallowed, picked up his pen, and began to write.

Question 1: Describe your favourite masochistic fan-
tasy. *ANY GRAMMATICAL AND ORTHOGRA-
PHIC MISTAKES WILL BE PUNISHED*
SEVERELY *ON A RISING SCALE OF TORMENT.*

1

I'm on the Underground. It's high summer and it's hot down there. Very hot. Strangely, it's deserted, and I get down to the platform for my usual station without seeing a soul. I walk along the platform, enjoying the silence and the emptiness, but finding them strange and a little disturbing too. I hear a whisper of sound in the distance, then feel the wind on my face as the train pistons down the tunnel. But even the wind is hot. When it slides into the station I see there's no one on it, and I don't even see a driver. I get on and sit down on the far side, facing the platform. Just across from me there's a notice about fare-dodging, warning of on-the-spot punishments at the discretion of the ticket inspectrix. I read it as the train slides out of the station, feeling sweat start to trickle under the hair on my forehead. For a moment I think the next station is deserted, but then a young woman slides past, left twenty or thirty feet behind me. The doors slide open and the young woman walks along the platform towards my carriage, low-heeled shoes tapping crisply and regularly, and steps inside. She's a slim, coldly attractive blonde in a light grey business suit, expensive-looking laptop hanging from one pale short-nailed hand. Her eyes pass over me without any change of expression and she sits on the opposite side up the carriage from me, opens her laptop and starts typing. I watch her covertly, feeling my cock begin to stiffen a little at the crisp efficiency with which she attacks the keys. We're at the next station almost before I realise it, and the platform's definitely not empty this time: there are three or four more women standing on it. Our carriage travels past them but they walk on down to it, more low-heeled shoes tapping crisply and regularly, and step inside as the doors open. They're more coldly attractive young businesswomen – a redhead, another blonde, two brunettes. Four pairs of eyes pass over me without expression, and they sit down opposite me. Another laptop is opened, another pair of carefully manicured hands starts to attack another set of keys, and my erection thickens and lifts. The other three women stare across the carriage without expression, avoiding my eyes.

We reach the next stop and the platform here is quite full: fifteen or twenty young women stand waiting for the train. Our carriage travels past them again, but they walk on down to it, low-heeled shoes tapping crisply and regularly, and get aboard as the doors slide upon. More blondes, brunettes and redheads in light summer business suits, more laptops, and the eyes that pass over me without expression feel like flicks from the lightly frozen tassels of a whip. The row of seats opposite fills up almost at once, and women start sitting on my side. The new laptops click open and more keyboards start to rattle, one only a couple of seats down from me, and I casually put one leg over the other, feeling my erection push up hard against my thigh. The air has started to feel hotter, filling with perfumes and powders, and I can detect light tendrils of female sweat.

As the train slides out of the station I start to count the number of trim, coolly efficient, narrow-lipped pussies sitting between slim businesswomen's thighs, moving my eyes, not my head. I'm only at thirteen when we slide into the next station and my heart starts to thump like a bass speaker inside my chest and throat. The platform is crowded three or four rows deep, and they're all young, coldly attractive businesswomen, all walking down the platform to reach our carriage. *My* carriage. The sound of their heels on the platform outside is like the sound of busy typing inside, and when the doors slide open and they start to pour on, dozens of them, I can barely

3

suppress a groan. It's already hot and there's not going to be an inch to spare and (my cock throbs a second before the thought forms) they are . . .

He stiffened in his seat, suddenly aware of how hard and solid his cock was in his trousers. His Mistress had moved from the front of the deserted examination hall, her stiletto heels clicking as she walked down the aisle towards him. He realised that he had stopped writing and blinked, trying to regain the thread of his thought. But then she was passing him, then past him, her perfume washing over him for a moment, then her heels had clicked down the aisle to the far end of the hall and he heard the door open and shut. He gathered his courage and looked behind him. He had been left alone in the hall. He turned back, looking at the page he was writing on, the nib of his pen still paused halfway through a word, then blinked and continued.

. . . going to *sweat*.

The seats on my side are filled before even a third of them are aboard, and I can feel my cock throbbing thickly beneath my thigh, a marrow bloated with hot juice as the sea of legs sheathed with pale silks floods in, filling the aisle. Their skirts all finish at the same height, two or three inches above the knee, and all of them, strangely, seem to be the same height, about 5 foot 6 to 5 foot 7, slim but with well-rounded breasts and hips and buttocks. The disturbed air is full of light, summery, creamy scents, tickling my nose, seeming to float on the increasing heat without contributing to it, veiling but not masking the thickening tendrils of sweat. The doors slide shut and I'm sealed in with what must be – let's think: about fifty young women, eight stones each – yes, two-and-a-quarter tons of female bone and blood and meat sealed in clean, smooth, dry skin. But it's not going

4

to stay dry for long. Not in this heat. Not with this overcrowding. There's a sea of legs below, and a forest of arms above, raised to the roof-straps, and I imagine the shaved armpits beneath the suits, smooth clean depressions starting to shine with moisture, starting to weep musky tears of sweat. Despite the heat I shiver, anticipating another crowded platform at the next stop, another ten or twenty women packing into the carriage, another ten or twenty smooth bodies radiating warmth, turning the carriage into a sauna, a steam-bath, and then next (God deliver it) there might be a breakdown on the line, a twenty- or thirty-minute halt, with just me and three tons of sweating young female flesh, all trapped deep and dark beneath sun-blasted London.

There's a burst of light from ahead that hangs and grows and I shiver again. Next stop. I can't see out because of the bodies between me and the window, but I can imagine the platform we're about to slide along, crowded three or four ranks deep, and maybe when they start pushing onto the train they'll jostle one or two of the crowd onto my lap. I surreptitiously uncross my legs, allowing my erection to bulge upwards under cloth, releasing an involuntary sigh that's half a prayer of thanksgiving. We slide out of the darkness, slow, stop, and after a second the doors slide open. I can feel the hot air inside the carriage flood out into the warm air of the platform. Anyone standing there would feel a breeze of it, almost enough to lift the hair, but the thick little pulses in my throat and groin slow and thin, because I can sense that there is no one there to feel it. No one at all. The platform is empty: the sound of it and the way the women already aboard are reacting tell me that. So what are we waiting for? We're losing heat inside the carriage, leaking it fast, and that's not good. We need to be sealed in, sealed in so that my sea of legs and forest of arms and mountain range of breasts and buttocks can sweat properly, can begin to glisten and trickle. No one speaks; no one has spoken, but the tap of the keyboards carries on, hurried but relaxed, admirably efficient. Then, over the platform speakers, there's a sudden spurt of static and a single huge clap of sound. It sounds like the crack of a whip.

And now, trickling into the carriage like a thread of sweat trickling beneath a light summer suit, comes the sound of feet descending a distant stair. Feet in sharp-heeled shoes or boots. And, as soon as the sound enters the carriage, the sound of typing stops and women in the crowded aisle are twisting their bodies and heads to look out onto the platform and see who is coming. Are they whispering to each other, discreetly lipsticked mouths put to pearly little ears? Are there gasps of excitement and anticipation running up and down the crowded carriage? I think there are, but why am I reacting like this? Because I can feel the thick tube of my erection beginning to deflate and shrivel. What is going on? What is happening? Whose are the boots descending the stair? They're getting louder, nearer, neither hurrying nor dawdling. Purposeful, self-confident. Moving, I now begin to realise, with an unmistakable nuance of menace. And I now know what the whispers are, and as though in confirmation a woman standing almost right in front of me puts her mouth to the ear of a woman standing next to her and whispers it with minute but perfect clarity, spacing the syllables almost with a chuckle. 'The inspectrix.' Not the inspector, *the inspectrix*. As on the warning poster.

When the boots reach the bottom of the stairs and begin to stride on the level, moving a little faster now, as though the woman – the inspectrix – is becoming a little impatient, I realise that my cock is fully deflated. I try to rouse it with the thought of the carriage full of moistening skin, those dozens of square feet of it sliding smooth and pearly over breasts and buttocks, bellies and thighs, but it's no good. My attention is fixed too firmly on the approaching boots, and I'm getting anxious. More whispers, and the boots suddenly get much louder, as though the inspectrix has rounded a corner and is almost in sight of the platform. The carriage suddenly, collectively, releases a sigh of delighted recognition, and the boots are on the platform, striding down it towards the carriage. I can't call it my carriage any more, not now, not when the real owner is here. I'm trembling, glad that I'm sitting down, because my knees wouldn't hold me up if I weren't, and the boots are right outside the carriage now, approaching the open doors. Suddenly they stop. Then, cutting with perfect timing through the perfect silence that settles for two or three seconds (the young women seem to have held their breath as they wait) comes the sound of a woman's voice. Low, deep, vibrant, with a trace of central European accent, full of authority, cruelty and threat.

'Tickets please.'

For a moment I think my bladder and bowels are going to let go, that I'm going to pollute the scent-and-sweat-seasoned female air with the harshness of male piss and shit, but I somehow manage to retain control of my spasming sphincters and force my terror back into the visceral lair from which it's sprung. My heart is hammering and my body is running all over with sticky sweat and when the boots scrape on the platform and step forward, lifting their invisible owner into the carriage, I almost cry out with dread. The sea of stockinged legs before me sways as the inspectrix works her way down the seats along the opposite side. No more words are spoken, there's only a shuffling and the click of a ticket-punch. Sweat is prickling all over me now and I can feel my terror mounting again in my belly. I don't have a ticket. I know I don't have a ticket. I'm on the tube without a ticket and the inspectrix is working her way towards me. But I notice that with the mounting terror blood is seeping back into my deflated cock, that it's starting to stiffen and bulge the cloth at my crotch again, and the young women before me, crowding the carriage, screening me from the inspectrix's gaze, seem suddenly insubstantial. They are nothing, nymphic mist before the hot and heavy numen of a goddess.

She's worked her way to the end of the seats on the opposite side now, and started on the women in the aisle. It won't be long before I catch a glimpse of her through the legs. Maybe her boots first. Her sharp-heeled boots. Black and glistening, that's the way they'll be and I can just imagine them – and then the shriek is back in my throat and I've so nearly soiled myself that for a second I can feel a thick pool of moisture sitting beneath me. But it's only sweat, cooling sweat that suddenly feels icy in my arse cheeks and in my crotch and on my chest and back and beneath my arms. Because the veil of young women has opened unexpectedly in front of me, as though she stalked through it, through the sea of legs like a shark, through the forest of arms like a tiger, to surprise me where I sit, ticketless. In the first seconds my vision is blurred, darkened with my terror, and I can make out only a vague impression of her but, as she licks her lips (I know, though I don't see it, that she licks her lips) and hisses that phrase again, this veil of darkness parts and I see her clearly, in all her icy perfection.

'Tickets please.'

And she adds with an ironic, spine-shivering, ball-shrivelling purr: 'Sir.'

My gaze travels up her body. Her sharp-heeled boots are black and glistening, as I imagined them, reaching up her legs as far as the hem of her knee-length black skirt, which fits snugly around her heavy thighs and swelling waist. My heart and belly sink as my gaze rises over her boots, over the pleats of her skirt, over her thick glistening leather belt, her tight-cinched black leather basque, bursting with the bounty of her breasts, over her bare shoulders, her arm-length black gloves, and oh God, oh God, that round, heavy, heart-shaped face beneath the peaked black cap, those full red lips and smouldering amber eyes. She puts one arm forward, holding out her hand for my ticket, and I see the heavy curls of moist black hair slip from a cleft of her glistening armpit. She's waiting, but I haven't moved or spoken and I realise that the young women standing around her in the crowded carriage are all staring at me with dislike, their faces surrounding hers like soft white lilies around a heavy black rose. I jerk with fright as she speaks again.

'Tickets please.'

She works the jaws of the ticket-punch in her other hand. The hand she's holding out at me is steady, unshaking, firm and strong. The expressions on the faces around her are hardening into disgust and disbelief. Why do I not speak? Why do I not answer her, produce my ticket, let the train carry on its way? But I can't. I don't have a ticket, and those smouldering amber eyes, locked on mine, are beginning to brighten and glow. Those ripe red lips part again, almost panting with anger, and she grinds the words out.

'Your ticket, sir. At once.'

When I try to swallow it's as though an iron band has tightened around my throat. I open my mouth, trying to answer her, but no sound comes out. My whole body is drained of strength, as though I'm

9

trying to slide into the seat, through the seat, through the floor of the train, to the track, then down, down, through the earth, escaping the horror and humiliation that await me. A tale-bearing whisper sounds in the carriage behind the inspectrix, sharp with Schadenfreude, the vowels rich and rounded.

'He hasn't got one, Miss. He hasn't *got* a ticket.'

The inspectrix shudders and hisses like a great cat and her eyes widen on mine, suddenly blazing with fury.

'Iss . . . iss this true?'

A squeak escapes me and a tear, cool against my burning skin, slides down my face. Her strong white hand snaps the ticket-punch shut, as though she were operating a castrator, and I jerk again. Then her strong white teeth snap shut too and she purses her lips musingly, pondering my fate. The fires of her amber eyes are banked now, burning deep and steady, fuelling her will for the tortures she is about to inflict, seeming to scorch my face despite the sweat that trickles down over it. She turns her head back for a moment, saying, 'Girls, what shall we do with him?'

The white lilies stir with glee, as though a breeze has passed among them, and that sharp, Schadenfreudian whisper sounds again, saying something I don't catch properly for a moment, until it's taken up and repeated, whispered in public-school accents from a carriageful of discreetly lipsticked mouths, again and again, getting louder and louder, until the whole carriage is chanting it, over and over, emphasising the middle syllable with a stamp of feet on the floor, until my ears are ringing with it and my hard-on has almost burst through the crotch of my trousers.

'Cock-*frost*-ers. Cock-*frost*-ers. Cock-*frost*-ers. Cock-*frost*-ers. Cock-*frost*-ers. Cock-*frost*-ers. Cock-*frost*-ers.'

The inspectrix, her head still turned from me, begins to smile, then suddenly the hand she has held out for my ticket swings up vertically, clenching into a fist, and the carriage is silent again in the same instant. Her face turns back to mine, her smile broadening, her scarlet-painted lips flattening and tightening.

'Cockfrosters it is.'

The door slides shut behind her and the train shudders and begins to leave the platform. The inspectrix draws in a long breath, allowing her heavy breasts to rise and fall, then says, 'Prepare him, girls.' She steps to one side, dropping the ticket-punch into a pocket of her skirt, letting the sea of legs gush towards me. Slim hands, individually light and fragile, collectively overwhelming and irresistible, clutch at my body, at my head and hair, dragging me off my seat, pulling me up and into the midst of them. They back off a little, leaving me in a small circle as whispers hiss through the sea, women being summoned for the task that awaits. The sea eddies and swirls, parting then resealing as the summoned women push out of it and surround me, faces stern and merciless. They slip out of their jackets, before dropping them carelessly to the floor with soft rustles of soft, expensive cloth and then, eyes still on my sweating face as I turn and turn within the circle, looking hopelessly for escape, start to unbutton their white shirts, slim hands climbing down silken ladders. The shirts gape, exposing light bras on firm breasts, then, unbuttoned, are tugged off and dropped to the floor with rustles of soft, expensive cloth.

Are they going to advance on me now for the stripping that awaits? No. They stand still for a moment, as though steeling themselves for their task, but I realise that small slim hands are busy behind them, unclipping their bras one by one in a sweep that

11

runs around the circle. My mouth dries and knees tremble as I turn on the spot, hearing odd snaps of rubber from behind me as I watch the bras jerk loose and the firm breasts bounce free, shining with sweat, nipples sternly erect. The last bra jerks loose and the last pair of breasts bounces free, and I suddenly see what the snaps of rubber were: as the bras were unclipped and tugged free, the strippers have held their hands up, flat and vertical, and surgical gloves have been tugged down over them. Now, surgically gloved, stripped to the waist, they are ready and they advance on me, rubber-sheathed hands reaching out to clutch and grip, wrenching at my tie, dragging my suit off, tearing at the buttons of my shirt, undoing my belt and beginning to drag it loose. They work in silence but the women behind them, peeking over their bare shoulders, peering between their smooth flanks, are whispering a commentary on the stripping, hissing their disgust and disdain.

'He's sweating like a pig. Just look at him.'

'I know. And doesn't he stink? Stink like a pig.'

'He is a pig.'

'Pig-pig-piggy.'

'Piggy-pig. Grunting, stinking, sweaty pig.'

'Yes, a grunting, stinking, sweaty pig, but remember *why* he's a pig. Because he *chose* to be one. That's why he must be punished. Punished hard.'

'Very hard.'

'Very, very, *very* hard.'

'Very, very, very, v–'

But the whisperer breaks off, because they've started to pull my trousers down and the giggles have started. Then the whispers start again.

'Very, very, very, very, very, *very* hard. Just like . . . *that*.'

My trousers are down, pooled around my ankles, and cool fingers tug at my underpants, sliding them down.

'Like what?'

'Like *that*. Like his . . . *thing*. Just *look* at it.'

Women are bouncing on tip-toes, trying to see over the shoulders of the stripping circle, pushing their heads between the smooth flanks, to see my straining, bulging cock. Two of the strippers look back as they're almost pushed forwards on top of me. One of them tuts angrily.

'For heaven's sake, girls, be careful. Take *turns*. There's plenty of time for everyone to have a look. It's not as though it's going to shrivel up and drop off. Not just yet, anyway.'

More giggles, more whispers as they organise a rota, as heads slide between slim flanks, eyes widening with shock and delight at the sight of my straining, bulging cock. We flash past a station, but no one turns to look at it. I'm being clutched by my arms and shoulders, my hair and ears, turned and turned to be exhibited to them, to be needled by the contemptuous whispers.

'Just *look* at it. Isn't it disgusting?'

'Yes. Yuck. And just look at the state of it. He's obviously got his hopes well up, the foolish little pig.'

'Hope springs eternal in a piggy's breast.'

'But for this piggy, hope is hopeless. You're not going to get to use that thing, piggy. Not a *hope*.'

'Not a hope in *hell*, piggy. Pig-pig-piggy-wig.'

'But is he a pig? I mean, just look at all that hair. A pig doesn't have hair like that around its . . . *thing*. Does it?'

'I suppose not. And it's all over his chest and his arms and his legs too. Maybe he's not a pig after all.'

'Then what is he?'

A pause, then sniggers.

'He's a chimpanzee.'

'*Yes*. You've got it. A chimpanzee. That's why he stinks so much and why he's got all that hair everywhere. He's a chimpanzee. A dirty little chimp.'

It's taken up and flicked from mouth to whispering mouth as I'm turned and turned, exhibited over and over to them. I'm starting to feel dizzy. Another station flashes past.

'A chimp. Chimp. Chimp. Chimp.'

'Chimp-chimp-chimp.   Chimpy-chimpy-chimp-chimp.'

'Yes. A chimpy-chimpy-chimp-chimp. But an *undersized* one. Because it's not very big, is it? His *thing.*'

'*Its* thing. But you're right. It *is* tiny. Disappointingly tiny.'

'Yes. We expected much better than that, even from a chimp like this.'

'A *pig* like that.'

'A pig-chimp.'

'A chimp-pig. Chimpigganzee. Even from a chimpigganzee we expected much better. Much bigger. Much bigger from the pigger-wigger-pig-wig.'

'Much, much, *much* b—'

'Squeece hiss balls.'

The inspectrix's voice cuts through the whispers, and there's a sudden silence. The train is starting to slow, ready to draw up along a new platform.

'Squeece them. It is a remedy for an undersized cock.'

A rubber-sheathed hand slides between my thighs from behind, cool and slick on my sweating flesh. It closes on my balls, clutching them loosely.

'Squeece them. Squeece them *hard.*'

The hand closes sharply, tightening agonisingly on my balls, and I groan aloud, barely aware that the train is slowing, slowing, stopping.

'Stop. Let go.'

The hand releases my balls, slides back between my thighs.

'Hass it vurked?'

14

My balls are aching fiercely, shafts of pain throbbing up from them into my guts.

'No, miss. It's still tiny.'

'Then he does not deserve to keep it. Or them. So we shall freeze them off him. Shan't we?'

The train has stopped and the doors slide open. I feel the overheated air inside the carriage pour out again. Where are we?

'Yes, Miss. Frost them for him.'

'Good. Then prepare the operation.'

The clutching hands release my body and I slump to my knees, the shock of contact with the floor, even through the cushion of my discarded clothing, sending another shaft of pain spearing upwards from my balls. I can hear the clatter of heels along the platform as the carriage empties. I shake my head, trying to clear it so I can look up and out, but before I can gather the will a gloved hand closes on the scruff of my neck and jerks my head upright. Cool breath puffs over my left ear as the inspectrix lowers her mouth to me and speaks.

'Look, little man. See what awaits you.'

I blink, trying to clear my blurred vision as I look out. The young women are running to and fro along the platform, heels clattering, gleefully chattering to each other as they swing open cupboards in the station walls and pull out odd pieces of equipment. One small group is standing on a bench, hoisting one woman up to the platform sign. She seems to be holding something in her hand, lifting it forwards to the sign. I feel the floor of the carriage shudder under my knees as the women start pouring back in, carrying the equipment they've looted from the station. I hear them drop it to the floor of the carriage, then watch as some of them leave, lining up along the window, putting their faces to the glass between shielding hands, peering in at me and my swollen cock with grins of anticipation and excitement. I can't see the hoisted woman properly now, only her hand as it hovers over the sign. A black mark suddenly appears near it and I realise she's using a can of spray-paint, adding something to the sign. A correction mark, and above it . . . yes, an *R*, so that the station is now called . . . *Cockfrosters*. Cockfrosters. The hand disappears as the woman is hoisted down, and between the women lining the window I see the group jump off the bench and run across the platform back to the train. They jump aboard and I feel the inspectrix lift her head from my ear.

'Good girls,' she says. 'We are nearly ready to begin.'

The doors slide shut all along the train, but we don't move. The feeling of enclosure already makes it seem hotter inside. I can feel fresh sweat break out under the clutching hand on my neck and a moment later, as though in sympathy, it starts to trickle down my spine and in the cleft of my chest. Cool breath touches my ear again as the inspectrix lowers her mouth back to me.

'Well, little man, are you ready?'

Her head lifts and she raps out an order to someone standing behind me.

'Suits and masks on. Prepare the extinguishers. And, you girls, if you pleace, there is insufficient activity aboard. Strip yourselves and let us have some *movement*. We do not want our little man – our little *chimpanzee* – catching his death of cold, do we? At least, not just *yet*.'

The carriage fills with giggles and I hear them begin to strip. Zips buzz; silk and cotton rustle; discarded clothing falls softly to the floor. Then I feel the floor begin to shake beneath my knees and hear pants of exertion. Behind me I can hear more cloth sliding, even creaking a little, but it's being put on, not taken off. The inspectrix's hand tightens on my neck and she twists my head left and right as cool breath puffs over my ear again.

'See, little man, see what they are prepared to do for you.'

Left and right the carriage is full of naked women, bending and stretching, running on the spot, breasts and buttocks bouncing juicily, the clefts of their perfumed bodies beginning to shine with sweat, their breath coming faster and harder. The air seems to be getting hotter now as heat pours from their skin. Someone outside taps on the window and as the inspectrix directs my head forwards I see the first faint haze of condensation along the glass. The inspectrix lifts her mouth from my ear.

'It is no matter,' she says almost to herself, 'we will wipe it clean for you when the time is here. As nearly it is.'

Then, lowering her mouth back to my ear: 'Tell me, little man, how are your balls? Do they ache still?'

Yes, they ache, they ache all right. The sight and the sound and the smell of those two dozen working bodies in the carriage would have guaranteed that even if they hadn't been, those few minutes before, so cruelly and expertly squeezed.

'Yes, little man, they ache?'

I don't mean to reply but I make some movement, some minute nod of the head that she reads with her clutching hand, for she hisses with satisfaction and continues: 'Ach, that is so sad. So sad that your poor balls ache so. Therefore we must do something to relieve you of your suffering, must we not? Of course we must, and we shall. Shall –' her head is lifted from mine, her voice strengthening to a shout '– shall we not, girls? Shall we not relieve our poor little chimpanzee of his suffering?'

And the answer comes, bursting from two dozen gasping mouths as the floor ceases to shudder under exercising feet:

'Yes, Miss!'

The women outside, now invisible behind the white film of condensation that screens the window, beat on the glass with the palms of their hands, acknowledging the inspectrix's words and the hearty reply.

'Then,' says the inspectrix, 'we shall relieve him.'

Her leather-gloved hand releases my neck and she steps away from me.

'Operations squad: prepare him for cockfrosting. Exercise squad: prepare the buckets.'

A dozen new hands are suddenly on me, gloved in smooth rubber, gripping my neck and shoulders, slipping under my upper arms to drag me back to my feet and turn me to face the women who have been sitting along the row of seats behind me all the while. The women are dressed in firefighter's gear, absurdly suited in shiny asbestos suits in this steamy heat, small delicate heads hidden beneath the vast swine-masks of breathing apparatus, sitting well forward because of the tanks of oxygen that hang down their backs, holding two-foot red fire-extinguishers erect on their laps like giant phalluses. Odd sucking noises have begun to left and right, but I can't turn my head and the inspectrix is delivering a new order.

'Frost his cock, girls.'

The hands grip me tighter, locking me in place as my legs are dragged apart and a hand slips between my thighs from behind, pushing my aching balls forward beneath the jutting bar of my cock. The row of seated firewomen stands in sequence, hefting their huge fire-extinguishers. One steps forwards, staggering a little under the weight of the suit and the oxygen tank, adjusting the nozzle of her extinguisher to the height of my cock. I can hear glass squeaking behind

18

me. Someone is wiping the window clean of condensation so that the women outside can see in, can watch my buttocks tighten in agony as the extinguisher blasts icy breath over my cock and balls. The firewoman has paused, as though waiting for a signal, the black mouth of the nozzle presented squarely to my crotch. The signal comes, a nod of the head or a flick of a black-gloved hand, and the firewoman triggers the extinguisher. I howl with anguish as searingly cold chemical blasts over my cock and balls. The firewoman swings the nozzle slightly from side to side, then drops and directs it slightly upwards, making sure my balls are well sprayed. As palms patter on the glass behind me, signalling the glee and approval of the audience through the laughter of the women inside the carriage, the blast of spray cuts off and the firewoman steps aside, instantly replaced by firewoman number two, who swings the nozzle of her extinguisher to my cock and balls, waiting for the signal from the inspectrix.

It comes and the searingly cold chemical blasts again at my cock and balls, provoking me to another howl of anguish. More laughter, more pattering palms on the glass behind me, but I'm getting worried. My cock is turning numb and my balls have burrowed up hard against the fork of my crotch, trying to drag themselves up and away from the fierce, penetrating cold. The blast stops and firewoman number two steps aside, instantly replaced by firewomen number three. The signal comes at once this time and I hear rather than feel the blast of searingly cold chemical: my cock and balls are frozen numb, and only the fierce, gut-lancing ache in my balls tells me anything is still there. The blast stops, leaving my ears feeling slightly hollow, and firewoman number three steps aside, replaced instantly by firewoman number four, who triggers her extinguisher the moment its nozzle is lined up on my cock. I'm not howling now, I'm begging for mercy, babbling that they're going to give me frostbite, castrate me with cold.

'Silence!' the inspectrix commands. 'You must take your punishment like a man, even as you cease to be one.'

Firewoman number four steps aside, instantly replaced by firewoman number five, and for the fifth time an extinguisher discharges over my cock and balls at point-blank range. They're truly numb now: frozen solid and even my balls have started to ache a little less, as though the cold is anaesthetising them even as it destroys them. Firewoman number five steps aside but the inspectrix must be shaking her head or gesturing for a stop, for firewoman number six remains where she is.

'Enough. Turn him and exhibit him. Let us see how his little cock is faring under your tender attentions.'

The clutching hands drag roughly at me, turning me to face the row of grinning faces along the window, jerking me up and off my feet so that my splayed thighs and frozen cock and balls are on open display. Palms patter with delight and I feel tears of rage and humiliation start to leak from my eyes.

'Is he well frosted, girls?' the inspectrix asks. 'Araminta, examine him and report.'

I feel only the pressure of the hand probing my still rigid cock, but jerk and cry out with pain as it squeezes my balls individually between forefinger and thumb, then hefts them on its palm and squeezes them together, cruelly, lingeringly. The hand leaves them.

'Yes, Miss,' says Araminta. 'He is well frosted.'

'Then you may tip the buckets.'

The buckets? Then, as two naked woman advance on me from left and right, small aluminium buckets dangling from their right hands, I remember those soft sucking noises. What were they? What was going on? A bucket is lifted and poised above my crotch. The air in my nostrils is thick with my own sweat but even through that I can smell the aroma rising from the bucket. Girl-sweat. They've filled a bucket with the sweat of those exercising women, sucking it from their naked bodies somehow, running a small nozzle between breasts and buttocks, into armpits and knee-hollows, drawing off the heavy film of sweat, the trickles and beads of it, from forty or fifty bodies, filling two small buckets. Which are now about to be tipped over my frozen cock and balls.

But no: the second woman crouches and holds her bucket beneath my cock and balls, ready to catch the sweat tipped from above. I'm going to be basted. Blasted and basted. Blasted with cold, basted in girl-sweat. That inaudible signal comes and the first woman slowly tips her bucket, the tip of a pink tongue protruding from a corner of her mouth as she concentrates on releasing the thinnest possible trickle of it over my cock. And there, it's falling, the thinnest possible trickle, pouring over the head of my cock, then, as she moves the bucket nearer me, down the shaft, then over my frost-caked pubes. I try to restrain my gasp of pleasure at the warmth of it, and the thought of it. Warm female sweat trickling over my frozen genitals, then splattering as it falls to the bucket held beneath my crotch. The trickle thickens, turns to a stream, and I can't restrain my gasp of pleasure now. It's so warm and seems thick, almost syrupy, heavy with salt and skin-secretions, basting my cold-blasted cock and balls.

I close my eyes and savour the feeling of it and suddenly I'm gasping again, much louder, half with pleasure, half with surprise. A pair of gloved hands has taken hold of my cock and balls and begun to rub the sweat well in, slowly massaging the cold out of them, peeling my foreskin fully back, polishing the purple gem of my glans with sweat. I shudder and jerk, snorting like a horse, but the hands are well practised and read the onset of orgasm and slip away from my glans, moving down the shaft of my cock again, catching the falling sweat and delaying its drop to the waiting bucket below a second or two. Then the hands slip away. My cock pulses with frustration and my balls tighten, aching hard. I open my eyes. The bucket above is nearly upside-down now, the last of the sweat pouring from it, but the bucket below has caught almost all of it and the last of the falling sweat lands now with a splash and churn, not a splatter. There. The first bucket is empty. The women change places, the first crouching on the floor ready to catch the sweat tipped by the second, who holds her bucket poised for the inspectrix's signal. But it doesn't come just yet. Instead: 'No. Wait a moment. I fear very much we are not having the salutary effect on our fare-dodging chimpanzee for which we hoped. It is evident that he iss . . . *enjoying* it.'

・ I hear gasps of incredulous disgust from the women crowding to my left and right.

'Yes,' continues the inspectrix, 'he is enjoying it. He is a pervert as well as a criminal. He is enjoying the sensation of this sweat poured over and rubbed well into his pathetic cock and undersized balls. Perhaps – we must give him the benefit of the doubt – it is in part the warmth of it, for he was no doubt in some pain from the cockfrosting, but certainly there is too an element of *perversion*. Of *fetishism*. But fortunately we have a remedy. He may enjoy sweat-pouring and sweat-rubbing, but he will not enjoy . . . sweat-*drinking*. Clara, there is a beaker in your pregnancy-testing kit, is there not? Then you will lend it to us for use on our perverted little chimpanzee.'

I can hear murmurs among the woman and a zip being pulled. Clara is opening her kit and taking out the beaker.

'Yes,' says the inspectrix. 'Good girl. It hass been cleaned, of course, since last you used it? What, it has not? Well, no matter. Fill it from the bucket and force it upon him. Pinch off his nostrils if he resists you. He will drink some sweat as we baste his genitals, and we will have removed this perverted enjoyment of his.'

I hear a scamper of bare feet, and then another of the naked women is dipping a small plastic beaker into the bucket poised above my cock and balls. She raises it and swings it dripping towards my mouth. I turn my head aside, but rubber-gloved hands are instantly clamping on my temples, forcing my head back, wrenching at my jaw. That inaudible signal comes again and the bucket is tipped, beginning to trickle sweat over my cock and balls again as my tormentrices struggle silently and ferociously to open my mouth and force me to drink warm female sweat. The inspectrix watches the contest in silence for a few moments, then issues her order.

'Nostrils.'

Small fingertips pinch my nostrils shut and I feel my defrosted cock pulse beneath the warm stream of sweat now sliding up and down it. I try to lock my jaw, try to summon the will to lose consciousness rather than submit and open my mouth, but my cock knows my secret desire and pulses again as rubber-sheathed fingertips peel my lips roughly apart and begin to lever at my jaw.

'Tilt his head back. He will submit soon. Very soon.'

My head is pulled roughly back as I hear the last splash of sweat drop into the lower bucket. Clara's smooth white hand poises the beaker above my mouth, ready for the moment when the inspectrix's

23

prophecy is fulfilled and I submit, open my mouth, and allow the sweat to pour inside. My vision is starting to blur and there is a muffled roaring in my ears.

'And he will orgassm, girls. He will orgassm the moment your delicious sweat touches his foul little tongue. He will not even need to –'

My mouth comes open, gasping for air, and the poised hand tips the beakerful of sweat neatly inside. And God, she's right. The taste of it on my tongue is enough, the thickness of it, the thick saltiness of it, the thick salty muskiness of it, and the thought of where it's come from, the streaming breast- and buttock-clefts, the glistening armpits and knee-hollows, the inner thighs and pussy-lip creases, and what it's been tipped from, an unwashed piss-beaker from a pregnancy-testing kit. I splutter, choking on it, feeling it burn the back of my throat and fill my sinuses like acrid, liquid smoke, and in the centre of my body my rigid cock is jerking rhythmically, firing off shaft after shaft of another thick, salty, musky fluid. I can hear it land against the window with a soft splatter, as though replying to the palms that beat there a few minutes ago, and the horrified silence that surrounds me, beating on my ears with silken hammers, strengthens and lengthens my orgasm. I gulp gladly at the sweat in my mouth, knowing that the sensation of it sliding down my throat will add another shaft or two to the volley my cock is firing. The sweat sears down, burning the back of my mouth, acrid and bitter and ambrosial and my cock and balls do not disappoint me, my cock jerking another inch higher even as it ejaculates, my balls delivering their hottest and thickest sperm for the final three shafts.

Then it's over. Silence and stillness. The pinching fingertips release my nostrils and the clamping hands let go of my head. I bring my head forward, gasping and blinking at the window in front of me. There's a broad circular patch of splattered sperm on it, gathering and slowly sliding downwards in thick white tears, and through it, blurred and shadowy, I can see the faces of three of the female spectators standing outside along the platform. Then the silence is broken: the inspectrix snorts with disgust.

'Filsy. You filsy, filsy, filsy little beast. Well, you shall pay for that. You shall pay for soiling the company's property with the loathsome exudate of your pathetic little balls. Girls, let us have some suggestions for a suitable punishment. Come now. Put your horror aside and make some suggestions.'

Hesitant at first, then quicker, more eager, the suggestions come.

'Frost his cock again, then . . .'

'Then make him drink the whole bucket of sweat.'

'Then stretch him on the floor and we'll all piss on his face.'

'Then make him suck Jennifer's tampon.'

'And then lick her pussy clean.'

'And Louisa's tampon too.'

'And Naomi's.'

'And mine.'

'And mine.'

The women outside have their ears pressed to the glass of the window, listening to the debate that is obviously taking place within the carriage. Now one of them lifts her head away, taps on the window, and puts her mouth to it and licks at it as though she's trying to taste my sperm through the thickness of the glass.

'Ah,' says the inspectrix. 'An excellent idea, little Maria. He can lick the glass clean himself, and then we will vote on a suitable further punishment. Come on, little chimpanzee, you have soiled the window;

now you must clean it. Put the buckets to one side for now, girls, and show him the path of duty.'

The buckets are set aside and those rubber-gloved hands seize me again, lifting me onto the seat and pushing me forwards to the window, pressing my face against the sticky patch of sperm.

'Lick, little chimpanzee,' the inspectrix commands. 'Lick. Force him, girls.'

My face is ground at the window, my nose painfully flattened against it, full of the sour stink of my own sperm.

'Lick!' commands the inspectrix, losing patience. 'Harriet, on my word of command, squeece his balls until he obeys. Show him no mercy.'

I jerk and stiffen. A rubber-gloved hand has reached between my thighs from behind and taken firm hold of my balls.

'Squeece.'

My cry of pain is muffled against the smeared glass and as my face slides upwards a little sperm is caught inside my lower lip.

'Lick, you disobedient little beast. Lick. There are further delights awaiting you and we grow impatient to bestow them upon you. Harder, Harriet. Show him no mercy. Squeece till they pop if that is what it takes.'

Harriet pauses, cruelly allowing me to anticipate the coming shaft of pain she is about to deliver, then squeezes suddenly harder. I jerk upwards, trying in vain to drag myself away from her hand. My whole groin is glassy and brittle with pain.

'Lick. Lick, you little beast! Squeece harder, Harriet . . . Ah, he obeys. At last he obeys. No, Harriet, do not release them yet. But do not squeece them now. Do not be cruel to them. Rub them. Soothe them. He is still suffering considerable pain, I am sure, and his poor balls will be bewildered at sudden gentleness. Perhaps we can provoke him to another discharge, if we bewilder his balls sufficiently. Cruelty and kindness, sowing confusion and repentance. It is always the best way, with balls. Yes, that is the way. Girls, look. Do you not see how he shudders as Harriet strokes and soothes them? And do you not see how eagerly he obeys, now that he receives kindness? He is a good boy at last. But make sure he licks away every last drop. Yes. Direct him to them. Very good. Very good.'

At last, my stomach rolling with nausea and disgust, my mouth thick and sour with the taste of my own sperm, I'm dragged back from the window. Harriet's rubber-gloved hand is still stroking and kneading gently at my balls and my semi-softened cock is beginning to re-erect.

'There,' says the inspectrix. 'Do you see what a good boy he is? Do you see how eagerly he obeys when we hold the key to his obedience? No? You do not? I see scepticism around me. Amanda, do you not see what a good boy he is? How eagerly he obeys? No? Then what of you, Louisa? Jennifer? Charlotte? You demand more proof? Ah, then we must supply some for you. Harriet, take hold of the head of his cock for a moment. It will be hard to find, it is so very small, but if you reach forwards from his balls you may have the luck to come across it without too much delay. Yes? You have found it already? Then give it a twist. First clockwise. Then anticlockwise. Then again clockwise. And anticlockwise. Th– what, it has happened already? Yes? And you have caught his foulness in your hand? That is very good, for now that he has finished on the window he will need something to occupy him while we vote on the next stage of his punishment. You, Harriet, you will feed it to him while we vote. Tessa and Marjorie, you will assist her. Very well? Good.'

My face is dragged away from the window and I'm twisted, tugged forwards, pushed back and planted on the seat beneath it. Two women kneel on the seats to either side of me, locking my head between their hands as blonde Harriet, stripped to the waist, smiling thinly, leans forwards over me, lifting her closed hand to my mouth. Sperm is oozing slowly between her fingers and I feel droplets of it land on my thighs. The women on either side tighten their grip and Harriet murmurs.

'Open and swallow it.'

I try to shake my head but can't move it.

'How is it going, Harriet, dear?' the inspectrix calls from behind her.

'He refuses to open his mouth, Miss.'

'Pinch his nostrils shut and wait. We will bear this disobedience in mind as we deliberate over his next punishment.'

Harriet grunts softly with satisfaction and reaches for my nostrils with her free hand, cradling her sperm-hand against her breasts. She pinches my nostrils shut and then puts her face forward close to mine, gazing deep into my eyes.

'There,' she says. Her eyes are green and shining with pleasure. 'You can't breathe, you little chimp. And it's going to hurt soon. Very, very soon.'

As she speaks the puffs of her breath are cool and scented against the sweating skin of my face. Behind her, the inspectrix claps her hands together. The first sediment of pain is beginning to settle at the base of my lungs, slowly beginning to thicken and rise. My ears are starting to buzz and the inspectrix's voice seems faint and echoey, as though it's coming from a long way away.

'So, girls! The second punishment. What were the suggestions? Katharine, did you suggest that we frost his cock again?'

28

'Yes, Miss.'

'And you, Belinda, you suggested . . .?'

'That we make him drink the whole bucket of sweat, Miss.'

'Ah, yes. And your suggestion, Jessica, was that we stretch him on the floor and piss on his face?'

'Yes, Miss.'

'Right. And finally, what was it? That we make him suck Jennifer's tampon and then lick her pussy?'

'Yes, Miss. And then Naomi's and Louisa's.'

'Yes. And also yours, Amanda?'

'Yes, Miss. And Philippa's.'

Their voices are getting fainter and fainter, drowned in the thunder of blood in my ears. Harriet's eyes are sparkling as she watches the pain gather in my eyes.

'Open,' she whispers, and the puff of her breath feels cooler than before. 'Open, chimp.'

I close my eyes and try to force my attention out of the shell of pain I'm locked into, trying to concentrate on the inspectrix's voice, on the vote.

'Excellent,' I can just hear her saying. 'So we have cockfrosting, sweat-drinking, face-pissing and tampon-sucking.'

If only I could breathe pain. My lungs are full of it.

'Let's have a show of hands. First, cockfrosting . . . Very well. And sweat-drinking . . .? Uh-huh. Face-pissing . . .?'

Full of pain. My lungs are full to the brim with a thick, burning sludge of pain.

'Good. And tampon-sucking . . .? Right. Can I see the hands for tampon-sucking again . . .? Thank you. And face-pissing . . .? Good. It seems we have a win–'

I surrender, opening my mouth, gasping in breath, feeling my heart battering at the bars of its cage.

'*Good* chimp,' Harriet says. She lifts her gloved hand from her breasts and puts it to my mouth, carefully opening her fingers, releasing the sperm that fills her closed palm.

'Swallow it, chimpy.'

I'm still struggling to control my gasps for air, still feeling my heart hammer against my ribs, but I obey, licking at the thick trickle of sperm she's releasing into my mouth, sucking it in with obscene pops and splutters.

'Good chimp. Good, good chimp. Now lick it clean. All of it.'

She's pressing her gloved hand to my mouth now, forcing me to lick it clean, watching as I run my tongue between her fingers, licking hard at the smooth rubber.

'Nearly finished, Harriet?' the inspectrix asks from behind her. She nods, not looking back.

'Yes, Miss. *Very* nearly. He's been a very good little chimp. Swallowed all that nasty stuff and wasn't sick even a little bit, were you, chimpy?'

'Don't get carried away, Harriet, darling. He *has* been good, I will agree, but we cannot yet say that it is habitual to him. He does not obey without question. Far from it: he resists, and must be forced to the obedience that he owes us by right. That is why his punishments are not yet over.'

Still licking at her gloved fingers, I see Harriet's nose wrinkle with annoyance at the rebuke.

'Yes, Miss. Sorry, Miss. I think he's finished now.'

She pulls her hand away from my mouth and examines it, back and front.

'Yes, he's finished now, Miss.'

She pushes herself away from me, pauses for a moment to smooth her face, then turns to the inspectrix.

'Good,' the inspectrix says. 'Then now you can supervise—'

She breaks off.

'Oh, Harriet, *what* is that on your breasts?'

Watching her from behind, I can see the smooth bell of Harriet's hair tilt forwards as she looks down at her breasts.

'Oh!' she says. 'Yuck. I was holding my hand there, Miss, when it was full of his come. Some of it must have dribbled out.'

'Make him lick them clean. You can't supervise the face-pissing when your breasts are soiled.'

Face-pissing. So that's it. The next punishment. Harriet turns, her face creasing momentarily into a scowl as soon as she's sure the inspectrix can't see it, and lowers herself over me.

'Lick, chimp,' she says, pushing her breasts up hard against my face and mouth. I lick. Her breast-skin is hot and sweaty and tastes of salt and perfume more strongly than of sperm, as though my sperm has submitted to her the way I myself have, acknowledging her superiority, her power and female strength. Her breasts shiver as I lick and suck at them, and as though to disguise her pleasure she pushes them harder against my face, entombing my nostrils in soft flesh. I can't breathe again, and I can feel my softened cock begin to stir. But it doesn't last: I've soon licked them clean and she pushes herself off me with a sniff and turns to face the inspectrix again.

'Clean now, Miss.'

'Good girl. Now, please supervise the face-pissing. Tessa and Marjorie and you three others, let us have him on the floor, face up. By the door, to save time. For I'm afraid we've overrun a little and most of you are going to be late for work. Get dressed again, leaving knickers off until you've pissed on his face and have left the train.'

As I'm being lifted off the seat and dragged to the nearest door I hear it slide open so that the women on the platform can get back aboard. They push

31

roughly past me as I'm forced to my hands and knees, made to lie flat to the floor, then pulled over onto my back. Then my manhandlers kneel on my hands and feet to keep me in place. I can lift my head a little and watch what's going on down the carriage. Women are getting dressed again, bumping into each other as they crouch to the litter of clothing on the floor, pawing through it, picking up items, unfolding them, calling out descriptions to their neighbours, exchanging, until they've got what they want and can stand to slip back into shirts and skirts and suits, then squat to slip their shoes back on. My cock's erect again, jutting up from my supine body, and one of the women kneeling on my feet slaps at it with a snort. She twists her head and looks back at the inspectrix, who's watching the dressing women further down the carriage with a fond smile.

'It's up again, Miss.'

The inspectrix looks towards her, puzzled. 'Eh?'

'His . . . *thing*, Miss. It's up again.'

'Oh. I see. Just about. It's hard to catch when the light's wrong, something that size, but I see what you mean.'

Some of the women further down the carriage are dressed now and have begun to queue for the face-pissing, knickers tucked into pockets. Four or five of them are checking their make-up, peering into the mirrors of pocket compacts, working quickly with lipsticks. The firewomen have climbed out of their asbestos suits and left them neatly folded along the row of seats, helmets on top. The blank eyepieces seem to watch the nude and semi-nude women still dressing in front of them, reflecting pale images on dark glass. My hands and feet are beginning to hurt under the knees pressed on them, and the woman who slapped at my cock is still staring at it in disgust. She twists her head again.

'Miss?'

'Yes?'

'Can't we do something about it? It's getting on my nerves. The way it sticks up like that. And look: it's starting to twitch.'

And it is too. Women in the queue are watching and whispering to each other, laughing.

'What do you propose?' the inspectrix asks.

She's going to say she wants to tug me off. I know it. Tug me off, so that my cock softens and she can push it down and out of sight between my thighs. I know she is. I pray she is.

'Tape it, Miss. Tape it up against his stomach.'

'Very well. In fact, that is an excellent suggestion. Girls, has anyone got any tape? Marjorie would like to tape our little chimp's ... *thing* up over his stomach. Out of harm's way for when you all piss on his face. Yes? You have, Rosalind? Good girl. Hand it to Marjorie.'

One of the women in the queue comes forwards, holding out a small roll of tape to Marjorie. The queue's lengthened, doubled back on itself, more women standing ready to piss on my face and get off the train, knickers tucked into their pockets. The woman kneeling on my other foot pushes my cock up and flat to my stomach with her gloved fingers, then holds it in place with a fingertip just under the glans. Marjorie peels a hanging strip from the roll, bites it off with small white teeth, and leans forwards. She tapes my cock down halfway up the shaft, leans back, peels another hanging strip from the roll, bites it off, leans forwards to add it to the first. After she's taped the third strip into place the other woman lets go of my cock and it stays down, taped hard to my belly. Marjorie adds three more strips, then takes hold of my foreskin with gloved fingertips and tugs at it, gently at first, then harder, testing whether the tape is strong enough. My cock shifts a little and she purses her lips, not yet satisfied. She peels, bites off and adds two more strips, tugs experimentally at my foreskin again and nods with satisfaction.

'It's done, Miss!' she calls out. 'Here you go, Ro. Catch.'

The roll of sellotape flies across the carriage, caught neatly by Rosalind in small, slim hands.

'Good girl,' says the inspectrix. 'Then I think we are now ready.'

Behind my head the door slides shut again and through my naked back, pressed hard to the floor, I catch the vibration of the engine a moment before the train begins to move. Then we're moving, sliding out of Cockfrosters, back down the Piccadilly line.

'Right, girls. Who's for Oakw–

He shuddered and stopped writing, his pen halfway through a word again, aware suddenly that he had heard the door open behind him a moment before and that her heels were clicking their way up the aisle. Now that they had been given their chance, the sensations in his body were clamouring at him: the ache of hunched concentration in his shoulders, the pain in the fingers and wrist of his writing hand, the dull gnawing in his balls and the pre-come oozing thickly from the head of his cock. The heels clicked their way up to him and stopped, and a moment later he smelled her perfume again. The gnawing in his balls sharpened. He tried to see her out of the corner of his eye but she had stopped just behind him.

'How many questions have you completed?'

He couldn't think what she was asking for a moment, then he realised.

'One, Mistress.'

'Let me see.'

Something moved in his peripheral vision and he realised she was holding her hand forwards. He put down his pen and picked up the sheaf of paper he had written on, surprised at its thickness, but pleased at it, because she would be pleased at it. At his energy, his industry. His eagerness. He added the final page to it, then held it out to her and jerked as she plucked it from his fingers. Then he listened hard. She was leafing quickly through it, then pausing as she reached the final page.

'This isn't finished.'

He opened his mouth to reply.

'No . . .'

'You said you had finished one question.'

He opened his mouth again, but couldn't think what to say.

'You lied to me. Didn't you?'

'Yes, Mistress.'

'You haven't even finished one question. Have you?'

'No, Mistress.'

'And how long have you had?'

He looked up at the clock and had to blink and shake his head. Three-and-a-half hours? Had he really been writing for three-and-a-half hours? His heart started to beat faster and he could feel his throat thicken with fear.

'Three-and-a-half hours, Mistress.'

'How long were you given?'

'Two hours, Mistress.'

'For how many questions?'

He looked at the examination sheet.

'Five questions, Mistress.'

'What is your explanation?'

'I . . . I got carried away, Mistress.'

Silence.

'You got carried away.'

Her voice was icy with contempt and disbelief. He licked his lips.

'Yes, Mistress.'

It had barely been a whisper. He jerked again, as though she had struck out at him, but she had merely

35

walked past, her heels clicking on the floor as she carried on up the aisle to the desk that stood waiting for her underneath the clock. He kept his eyes fixed on the surface of his desk, listening as she walked. She paused for a moment when she reached the desk and he heard something rattle as she laid it on the surface of the desk. Then her heels clicked again for a few steps, then he heard her pull back her chair and sit down.

'Come here.'

He looked up and his cock jerked in his trousers as he saw what she had laid across one corner of the desk. A cane. She sat upright in the chair, the sheaf of paper sitting in front of her, overhung by the heavy shelf of her breasts. He pushed his own chair back and started to stand up.

'No. On your hands and knees. Crawl to me.'

He pushed the chair further back and went down on his hands and knees, then crawled to her. When he reached the front of the desk she said, 'Hands on head.'

He put his hands on the top of his head.

'Squat.'

He squatted, his eyes just above the surface of the desk, looking directly at her breasts. They quivered, flattening to the surface of the desk and the sheaf of papers as she reached down and slid open a drawer, before lifting something out. A pen. She put it on the surface of the desk and pushed the drawer shut, breasts quivering again. Then she picked up the pen. He blinked. It was red. He watched as she started to read the first page of his fantasy, the pen hovering above it like a bird of prey in her left hand, the forefinger of her right hand tracing the line she was reading. Then her forefinger paused and the sharp red nail descended to tap twice on the paper, then slid back as the red pen in her left hand swooped. His cock jerked and pain gnawed sharper again in his balls as she circled a mistake and wrote something in the margin, then began to read again, tracing the line with her forefinger.

She turned over the final sheet and put it on the pile, then turned the pile over so that the pages were in order again, top to bottom, first to last. He waited, eyes still fixed on her breasts.

'It's full of mistakes,' she said.

'Yes, Mistress.'

'You will be punished for each of them.'

'Yes, Mistress.'

'On a rising scale of torment.'

'Yes, Mistress.'

'And your attitude to women is still in severe need of correction.'

'Yes, Mistress.'

'In severe need of *severe* correction.'

'Yes, Mistress.'

'You are still labouring under the misapprehension that they exist for your pleasure, when the truth is quite the opposite. Isn't it?'

'Yes, Mistress.'

'Then what is it?'

He raised his eyes to hers for a moment, frowning. She frowned back.

'The truth, you fool. What is the truth?'

'That I ... that I exist for their pleasure, Mistress. Solely for their pleasure.'

'Then at this moment you exist solely for *my* pleasure. Is that not so?'

'Yes, Mistress.'

'Like a dog.'

'Yes, Mistress.'

'And whose dog are you?'

'Yours, Mistress.'

'Then you must fetch and carry for me.'

'Yes, Mistress.'

'So fetch that stick for me, little dog. Fetch that cane.'

As he went back on all fours and crawled to the corner of the desk on which she had balanced the cane, he heard her push her chair back and turn it to face him. He reached the cane and raised his head to it, trying to take it between his teeth, knocking it with his nose for a moment and thinking with a sudden sick rush of fear that he had pushed it onto the floor. But it was OK: he managed to stop it rolling with his chin and then lower his mouth carefully to it. He closed his teeth gently on it, fearful of marking the golden bamboo, and lifted it off the desk, crawling backwards a few inches so that the cane would not bang against the legs of the table when he crawled around it to her chair. Then he crawled, carrying the cane to his Mistress, ready to suffer at her hands whatever she demanded of him.

'Thank you, little dog. Now, while you are trained, I am going to tell you a story.'

Two

Her agents are everywhere. In libraries, in banks, in restaurants, serving behind counters in delicatessens and patisseries, working the tills at supermarkets and news-agents, clutching clipboards or trays of poppies in shopping arcades and on street corners. Hundreds of them, all over the country, watching and waiting. Waiting for the right men. The men whose secret desires are, to the trained eye, as plain as the words on a page. The men who can be read like a book.

The first contact will be very discreet. So discreet that some of the men will never know it has been made, will never know what they have missed. It will come on a strip of paper slipped into a book or bag of shopping or into a pocket. Her agents are highly skilled and many could earn their living as professional pickpockets. Some did so, before they were hired by Her, and will do so again, when they have left Her service. It is very easy for them, planting a strip of paper somewhere on a man's person or purchases or possessions without being seen by him. For the strip is, after all, no longer and no wider than a woman's little finger. And bears something so innocent. Nothing but a telephone number.

But the strip will not wait to be discovered by chance. Within a few minutes after it has been planted it will begin to call for attention, softly at first, then louder and louder. For it will begin to leak perfume. A close, heavy perfume specially blended, specially tested, specially designed to appeal to a certain class of man. A disturbing perfume. A delighting perfume. A dominating perfume. And the men who smell it as it begins to leak from the strip will remember where they have smelled it before. They will remember the woman who, that morning or yesterday or the day before, served them in a restaurant or questioned them on a street corner or stamped their books at a library. How attractive she was. And that heavy, close perfume she wore. That disturbing, delighting, dominating perfume. The same perfume they can now smell leaking from the strip.

Though sometimes, of course, it calls in vain. A book is put down and left unread for a week or two or three, and when at last it is opened the perfume has faded to nothing and the strip that flutters finally from the pages is picked up and examined and found to be completely blank. Or some shopping is unloaded quickly into a refrigerator or cupboard and the strip that accompanies it is jammed between jars or packets too tightly to release its siren-song or falls to the floor and is swept up and goes out with the rubbish the same day. Sometimes, simply and mundanely, the man has a cold. If it lasts more than a week he has lost his chance, for the perfume and the number are both designed to fade to nothing within a week.

But at other times the perfume does not call in vain. The men notice it almost immediately and hunt it down. How their fingers tremble when they have found the source of it and hold the strip stretched between left thumb and forefinger and right thumb and forefinger, reading the number printed thereon! For they think, of course, with that pitiable, pathetic, perennial male sexual optimism, that it is an invitation from the woman who wore the same perfume. The perfume that is leaking from the strip stretched between their fingers and that now, in the privacy of their own home or office, is provoking the reaction it was specially tested, specially blended, specially designed to provoke.

The reaction of cock-stiffening. But cock-stiffening of a particular kind. The cock-stiffening of the submissive male in the presence of his Mistress. The cock-stiffening of those hungry for pain and humiliation. How their fingers tremble as they think their cocks are not stiffening in vain! For here, with the perfume, is a number to call. Perhaps if they thought a little more they would be suspicious. The telephone number is *printed* on very thin, fragile paper, not written by hand, and it should be obvious even from a single specimen that many of the strips have been manufactured for distribution in the same way. This is not a casual invitation from a woman who has been irresistibly attracted to a man she has seen at a counter or till for perhaps thirty seconds, or even at intervals over two hours in a restaurant or pub. No, this is part of something bigger. It's obvious. But not to the men who are holding the strips stretched between their fingers for the first time. They're not thinking with their heads but with their cocks, and they won't discover their mistake – their misinterpretation – until they ring the number.

When, in many cases, they discover their mistake very quickly. The quickest time is by a man who discovered the strip almost at once and was punching the digits on his mobile phone with a trembling forefinger after five minutes and thirty-eight seconds. The Domina, when the record of the call and the record of the purchase had been collated, was most displeased. She does not like the strips to be discovered so quickly, for this places Her agents at some risk of confrontation and even, in a strictly limited way, of exposure. Better for at least an hour to elapse before the call is made and the men listen eagerly to the sleepy, tigerish purr of a ringing phone. Some of them must be expecting an answering-machine for, if the strip is from the woman they think it is from, she cannot have finished work when they ring. But they don't get an answering-machine and their surprise often shows in their voices when, after the phone has rung exactly thirteen times, it is picked up and, after another carefully calculated pause, a cold female voice speaks to them.

'What do you want?'

The answer given is the first step of the screening. Some men, despite the skill of Her field agents, are unsuitable for stage two of the journey they have begun. Occasionally the strip is not discovered by the man for whom it was intended but by his wife or girlfriend and she, naturally enough, will often be the kind of woman who will wish to know for herself to whom the number on this perfumed strip belongs. Both sets of interloper are quickly and smoothly persuaded to accept a cover story though, if the women sound both suitably suspicious and suitably prepared to act on that suspicion, they are often left subtly unsatisfied: it gives the Domina and Her phone operators great satisfaction to know that they have sown the seeds of a chastisement. Sometimes, sometimes, very occasionally, the women will sound suitable for recruitment: the ranks of the Domina's agents are joined every year by women discovered in this way, though She prefers, of course, to use more conventional means.

This, however, is rare, as is a call from an obviously unsuitable male, one who answers that cold question too confidently, too cocksurely. The Domina does not want cocksure men. She wants men who stammer as they answer, whose excitement at the tone of their interrogatrix's voice is plainly audible in their voices. These men are asked further questions by that cold female voice, taken deeper into the web the Domina has begun to spin around them, and each response is carefully weighed both by the intuition of the operator and by the voice-analysis software whose results glow on the screen in front of her. In combination the two are nearly infallible, and the few unsuitable men whose answers to question number one are misleading are fewer still by the time they have answered questions two, three, four and five. By then the Domina almost always has the crème de la crème, and many of them are hoarse or almost speechless with excitement by the time they come to answer question six.

'Thank you, Mr Davies. And are you prepared to take part in our survey?'

And he is, of course. Often by question six the operator's eyes will have narrowed with cruel satisfaction and she will have reached out and tapped a single key of the black plastic keyboard in front of her. The M. And oh, how he will suffer for it, should he win through to the final stage! And then the operator's unsmiling lips will come apart and she will ask the final question, lingering on the words, finally allowing her full contempt and disgust to enter her voice, so that each syllable is like a needle of ice slipped into his ego.

'What is your full name and address, Mr Davies?'

Seven times out of ten Mr Davies will, without hesitation except perhaps for a gulp or gasp of excitement, give his full name and address. The operators love to hear that gulp or gasp, but they love more to hear the men who, on the other three times out of ten, have some excuse not to give a full name and address. For fear of their wives or girlfriends. Sometimes they admit it openly sometimes they hint at it, but it is always a very good sign. These men are ordered to arrange some secure postal address and ring again in a week's time, having committed the number to memory. If necessary they are given careful instructions on how to arrange a new address, and woe betide them if, having set about this simple task with typical male incompetence, they ring in that week's time to report not success but failure. They will be given a tongue-lashing over the phone and warned that they will not receive a second chance.

Nor do they. It is quite common for some sorry male pervert, having failed inadvertently on the first occasion, to fail by design on the second, merely to experience a repeat of the tongue-lashing over which, in the week that has elapsed, he will plainly have masturbated many times. Unfortunately for him, the Domina has no wish for Her staff to waste their time on such games, and Her staff do not do so. If a potential client is eliminated, it is his loss, not theirs and certainly not Hers, for he will be replaced with the greatest of ease. But such fools are fortunately rare, and those who are ordered to prepare secondary addresses within the week will generally have done so within no more than two days. They tell the operator so, when they ring again, but her voice loses nothing of its cold indifference as she tells them their instructions will now be despatched.

The instructions will arrive two or three days later, dropping through the doors of men all over the country in long grey envelopes. These too, though more subtly, leak the perfume of the strips and of the women who supplied the strips. Occasionally a susceptible postman will detect it as he lifts the envelope to a mailbox. He may stop and sniff, even raising the envelope to his nostrils and drawing in a deep breath. It will disturb and delight him without his knowing why, setting up a thickening in his cock and an ache in his balls, and he may even invent some excuse and attempt to deliver the envelope in person. If he succeeds and speaks to the man to whom the envelope is addressed there may be some flash of mutual recognition, each seeing in the other what he is himself, but the recipient will have been warned to discourage enquiries on penalty of exclusion from the survey, and the postman will go away disappointed, having gained nothing but maybe a fading ache in his balls from the deep sniff he took of that grey envelope whose weight and silken texture lingers yet in his fingertips. Two or three times a year one of these postmen, more enterprising or more susceptible, may even hold an envelope back to steam it open and discover from the contents what the return-address-less exterior denies him.

The blank sheet of paper he discovers inside will not enlighten him unless, enticed to greater crime by the perfume soaked into the sheet, he decides to withhold delivery altogether and keep the sheet and envelope for masturbation. If he does so, he may discover the secret of the sheet. The legitimate recipients do so far more readily, for they are already half aware, at least, of what they embarked upon and it takes little thought to deduce that the blank sheet must be printed with invisible ink. It then remains only to discover the necessary chemical to expose what is printed there, and their first experiment is generally the successful one. Splashed with sperm, the blank white sheet will begin to streak and speckle with black, and if the sperm is then smeared over the entire surface of the sheet the instructions for the second stage will soon be legible.

They will consist of an unlabelled map of a city or town with an odd, incongruous and seemingly unconnected phrase or sentence printed beneath it. Somewhere on the map will be a small arrow pointing to some point along a street. And that is all: the scale will be small, the map confusingly detailed, and it is unlikely that the panting, sweating man who has just masturbated to reveal it will recognise what he sees. He must discover where the city or town is and travel there to see what the arrow is pointing to. And the town or city is always, of course, at some considerable and inconvenient distance from the town or city in which the contestant lives. Now that Her operations are extending overseas it is even occasionally on the continent. She is weeding out the unworthy, you see: if a contestant is not prepared to make an effort for Her, how can he be worthy of even the least of Her prizes? And so men living in London or Plymouth must travel to Belfast or Aberdeen, and men living in Belfast or Aberdeen must travel to London or Plymouth, having already devoted some hours, perhaps, to leafing through atlases or clicking through CD-ROMs. When he arrives there and finds his way through dirty and dangerous-looking streets to the spot indicated by the arrow, he will often think for a moment that he has made some mistake, for the spot indicated by the arrow is always a newsagent's, and always a shabby, seedy, unsuccessful newsagent's.

Or so it will appear from the outside. He will push his way through the door, hearing a bell ring harshly somewhere at the rear of the shop, and discover that appearances have not been deceptive: the shop will be ill lit and ill stocked; there will rarely be any customers, and the male or female assistants who, always in twos, appear from the rear of the shop or are already behind the counter will be middle-aged and look tired and dirty and ill. This is the way the Domina baits Her traps. The contestant will approach the counter, confident now that he has made no mistake, because he will be about to use the phrase or sentence printed on the map.

'A packet of Tunes and a Mars bar, please.'

Or: 'A copy of the *Daily Star* and a packet of B&H, please.'

And the eyes of the men or women behind the counter, already perhaps brightened with recognition, will brighten further. If there is another customer in the shop, they will motion the contestant silently back, to wait till the shop is empty. But that, as already noted, is rare: generally the contestant will be served straight away. One of the assistants will nod and say: 'And is that all, sir?'

The contestant will say, perhaps, 'No. I don't think so.' Or simply: 'No.'

As a final precaution the assistant will repeat the digits of the telephone rung by the contestant perhaps only a week before, watching the customer's eyes closely. Even if he does not consciously remember it, there will be some trace of recollection there and he will of course guess what the numbers are intended to be. Satisfied at last, the assistant will now emerge from behind the counter and beckon the contestant after him or her to a dim corner where, almost hidden between dusty shelves of dog food or yellowing lavatory paper, there sits a small lottery terminal. A most curious lottery terminal, black and elegant, almost minimalist. Quite out of place in such a setting, and not positioned to attract or even to be seen by many customers.

The assistant will unlock and tug open a drawer or cupboard near the terminal and take out a sheaf of lottery cards. He or she will detach one and hand it to the contestant with a small gold pen, nodding at or pointing to a small shelf he can lay it on while he fills it in. The contestant – and at this moment, having accepted the card, he has truly become a contestant – may be a little bewildered for a moment, but once he has read what is written across the top of the card his expression will suddenly change and he will fill the card in with sudden energy. When he gives it back, his hand may have begun to shake. The assistant will take the card from him and enter his details into the terminal, occasionally having to query an illegible word or uncertain number, and then finally punch the key that sends everything flashing over many miles of wire to the Domina's headquarters. The assistant will then return to the counter, beckoning the contestant along, and sell him the items for which he originally asked.

And that will be it: if the contestant tries to linger, as though expecting something further, the assistant and his or her companion will soon make it apparent by their silence and blank expressions that there is nothing further to expect. It is over: he has done what he has come all those miles to do and all that remains is for him to leave the shop, return home and wait. Many contestants undoubtedly expect to find something in the packet of Tunes and Mars bar or *Daily Star* and packet of B&H they have been forced to purchase, but there will be nothing there. The shops are owned by the Domina for the black lottery terminals and nothing else, and the assistants there are employed by Her only to sell the tickets in the lottery for the prizes She has to offer. One-hundred-and-eighty are on offer every three months: a hundred one-night passes to one of the training Dungeons that She secretly maintains around the country, and which are always in need of fresh training material; fifty five-night passes for the same; twenty-five vouchers for a private session with one of the Domina's regional Secretaries; finally, for five lucky, lucky men, invitations to make their wills and attend a week of dark delights at the Dungeon over which the Domina Herself presides: *Le Cœur de Ténèbres*, the Heart of Darkness Itself.

No man, and no woman outside Her Inner Circle, knows exactly where the Heart of Darkness lies. Some say, a little banally, that it lies deep beneath St John's Wood in London. Others, more exotically, say that it was secretly commissioned as part of the drilling of the Channel Tunnel and lies exactly midway between Dover and Calais, thus, by some quirk of international law, granting the Domina legal immunity in the event of a death on the premises. Yet others say that, to the same end, the Heart of Darkness is in fact maintained on a large private jet flown high over the Atlantic. The truth is that no strangers learn the truth but those five men who thrice-yearly win the chief prizes in Her lottery, and none of them has ever returned to reveal Her secret.

Three

Let us follow one of the five men destined to win the next lottery in the week before he receives his telephone strip from one of the Domina's agents. Philip Tyndale. He's twenty-three, a postgraduate student of European literature at the University of Northchester and Julia Whipley, one of the junior librarians, has had her eye on him for more than a term. It's the books he's been taking out and (she's been in touch with one of the secretaries in his department) the essays he's been writing. Books like Mario Praz's classic *The Romantic Agony* and Jennifer M. Vilcriste's *Promethea Unbound*. Essays like '*Femmes du Mal*: the Sadistic Female Archetype in the French Decadents' and '*Tracking the Panther Slotwise*: The Femme Fatale in the Early Work of Swinburne'. And it's the way he looks at her when she's serving at the counter in the library. She can read him like a book and he, apparently, can read her. He knows what she's capable of. He knows why she wears that close, heavy perfume, and why her lipstick is that particular dark red, and why she sometimes wears black or dark purple, as though in mourning, or celebration. It is not usual that one of the Domina's agents should be so plainly a member of the Sorority, but the librarian has been Her regional secretary for nearly six years, after rising through the ranks from work for a library in one of the suburbs of Liverpool, and the Domina places an implicit trust in her. Work in the libraries and secretarial departments and canteens of universities is some of the most important Her agents do, for the Domina is hungry for young and sensitive flesh and male students can supply it in abundance.

On Tuesday evening of this week, therefore, the librarian slips one of the telephone strips into the third of the books young Philip has handed over for stamping. Joanna Whitby's *A Space of our Own: An Introduction to Separatist Hermeneutics*. She looks up at him unsmilingly, appraisingly, as she hands the books over one by one, shifting her body almost imperceptibly to waft her perfume forwards and over him. She sees his nostrils flare and knows that if she glances downwards she will see evidence that he has responded to it. She does not glance downwards, but she allows anger to glow suddenly in her eyes and almost permits a smile to touch her lips at the shiver of pleasure that runs through him. Then it is over: he pulls the books to him and – walking a little stiffly – leaves the library, aware that her eyes are following him as he pushes through the turnstile and out into the darkness that has swallowed the campus. She knows, and he knows that she knows, that he will be masturbating shortly in his room, the books dropped hurriedly on his desk amid (she can picture them easily) unwashed coffee cups and scribbled notes from a lecture.

She wonders idly, serving another student, whether he listens to music as he masturbates and, if he does, what band he chooses. A girl band, perhaps? The Domina has had a hand in two in the past three years: Medusa and vAMp. Both, as though surfing a wave of the female domination more and more evident in private and public life, have been highly successful. Perhaps too successful for his tastes, too widely known. So maybe a female-fronted indie outfit? The Opheliacs, with the shaven-headed Tara O'Donnell, already celebrated for her violent relationships with two film-star boyfriends. One had one of his famously pearly teeth loosened by her in an argument outside a nightclub in New York; the other, arrogantly stepping in to replace number one as he boasted privately that he would be the one to tame her, had been forced to take out a restraining order on her when he panicked and tried to leave her after three weeks and she reacted with displeasure. Yes, she knows that The Opheliacs are a great favourite among certain male students.

She finishes serving at the counter and goes back into her office to pour herself a cup of coffee. Perhaps he likes something even more obscure, not pop or indie but industrial or electronic. There the range is so much wider and the bands, free of the necessity to disguise or soften their true tastes for the mass market, so much clearer in their messages. Ovum-987, for example. Ah, Ovum-987. She herself has all their three albums, their two EPs and their recent *Breast of* ... greatest hits compilation, and the Domina had once sought to hire them to perform at a soirée in one of Her provincial dungeons. But they had, despite the size of the fee, refused to play if men were present in the audience, although they would, as always, have been happy to admit men backstage after their performance. Would little Philip be a fan of Ovum-987? Would he know of the disclaimers all men admitted backstage were required to sign? Of the soundproofing that their elaborate riders always insisted be installed in their dressing rooms? Of the dark rumours that circulated about two recent gigs in Holland? Or perhaps he was a fan of the mysterious, possibly French, possibly Canadian, possibly Malagasy Trinfé, whose three members always performed simultaneously in three widely separated venues linked by video. Their albums, always issued on three separate CDs, one for each performer (*Voix*, *Flûte Fémorale*, *Batterie*), could only be properly

51

played on three machines, the second set playing exactly three seconds after the first and the third exactly three seconds after the second.

She sips her coffee, pondering, as Philip Tyndale climbs the stairs to his room. His cock is poker-stiff in his trousers and, although he knows he should devote the remainder of the evening to some serious reading and note-taking, the librarian's perfume seems to linger in his nostrils and he knows the first half hour or even hour will be devoted instead to some serious masturbation. He unlocks his door, opens it and steps inside. The curtains are still open, because he has not been back there since midday, and the air is twilit with the lights of the campus outside. He drops his books on his desk amid unwashed coffee cups and scribbled notes from a lecture and goes over to the window to draw the curtains. But he stands motionless for a few moments first, staring at the corner of the library that is visible up the short hill he has just walked down. *She* is there, above him in space as she is above him in age and power and beauty and in all other ways. His cock strains harder at the zip of his trousers and that tantalising whiff of her perfume still seems to hang in his nostrils. He draws breath slowly in, wondering if he's hallucinating the smell, then exhales, feeling his heart start to thump in his chest. That distant lighted window, on the ground floor of the library. Is it the window of her office? And is its bright rectangle blurred just a little with a dark shape, as though someone is standing there and staring out, down the hill, down at the unlit rectangle of his window? Oh God, is she standing there, looking down and thinking about him as he stands here and looks up and thinks about her?

His hand drops almost involuntarily to the zip of his trousers and draws it down. He reaches inside, tugs his cock out, pauses a second and then starts to masturbate hard, feeling orgasm gathering in his balls at once. This could be a five-second tug-off, he's feeling so excited, but he forces himself to stop, closing his eyes for a second before re-opening them and staring back up the hill at the lit window. His hand resumes its work on the head of his cock, but more slowly, more lingeringly, prolonging his pleasure, taking its rhythm from a thump of music travelling up from one of the rooms on a floor below. Imagine she's standing up there and looking down, he tells himself. Imagine doing this in broad daylight, so that she can see me standing here and staring up at her. Imagine her eyes narrowing as she grows suddenly suspicious, wondering why I stand here so long, why there's that streak of white visible at my waist. Imagine that she's got a small pair of binoculars in her room, sitting in a drawer of her desk. Imagine her turning away from the window and fetching them, before returning to the window, lifting them to her eyes, adjusting the focus, then suddenly crying out with rage and disgust at what she sees.

Yes. Oh God, yes. Imagine her dropping the binoculars on the sill and turning back to her desk, wrenching the phone off its cradle, starting to punch out the code for campus security ... then stopping abruptly, one digit short, as a new thought strikes her. Imagine her putting the phone down and returning to the window to raise the binoculars again, a cruel smile beginning to brighten her face as she sees me still at work. Then imagine her unhurriedly seeking permission for an early lunch to walk down the hill to find me in my room.

The thought of it is enough: his cock jerks under his working hand and begins to spurt. The sound of his sperm striking the glass in front of him is curiously loud in the twilight inside the room. When he has finished coming he draws the curtains, leaving his sperm to trickle downwards behind them and pool on the sill, where he's wiped it up a dozen times before. He walks back down the room, his cock still sticking out of his trousers ahead of him, and switches the light on. Strumming at the head of his cock, knowing that he'll be ready again very shortly, he goes over to his bed and kneels beside it to reach underneath and pull out a flat black box with his free hand. He stops wanking to open it, revealing rows of pirated cassettes, each spine labelled with artist and album in his small, neat handwriting. The librarian would smile to see them. Medusa's *Hiss'n'Hers* and *Stone-Cold Love*. vAMp's *Bite-Sized* and *Knead to Gnaw*. Ovum-987's *Solonas* and *Castro*. Trinfé's *Et Ta Mère I, II* and *III*. He slips one of the tapes out – it's labelled *WT 2 (Various)* – and walks over to his CD player, starting to wank again, puts the tape into the deck one-handed and presses play. Her knock on the door would come in a couple of minutes. He would open it, stammering in confusion as she pushed her way inside and told him what she had just seen, lips curled with contempt and disgust as she pushed the door shut behind her. Next, ruthlessly, coldly, stomach-hollowingly, cock-shrivellingly, ball-achingly, she would tell him what she is going to do. She is going to blackmail him. He will have to submit to her cruellest desires or be exposed to the entire university as the foul and disgusting pervert he is.

The tape starts to play as he reaches his bed and lies down on it, settling himself comfortably on his back then reaching down on the side next to the wall lifts up a bottle of hand lotion. He flicks the cap and squirts some on the head of his cock, then puts the bottle back beside the wall, adjusts his hand carefully at his groin, closes his eyes and begins to wank as the vocals float through the opening bars of the song. She would force him to strip. She would . . . yes, she would have brought a camera with her. For proof of his perversion. She would force him to stand naked at the window and photograph his naked back and buttocks, then order him onto the bed, on his stomach. Then she would produce a dildo from her handbag. A large one. Force him to lie motionless on the bed as she inserted it slowly up his backside, then photograph him, taking care to ensure that his face is in shot. And she wouldn't lubricate it. Or his arsehole. It would hurt, stretching him till he felt his sphincter was going to tear, but all the while his cock would be throbbing as he held it pressed against the bed. But she wouldn't let him touch it. Wouldn't even let him expose it. *Disgusting thing*, she would say. *Keep it out of sight*. As she would keep pushing at the dildo, sliding it further in.

He stops wanking, panting, because he's about to come again and he can't, not till the third song begins. He waits, thinking of what she would do next. Yes, after she'd taken pictures of the large dildo inserted up his arse, she would tell him to slide it out. It would emerge with a pop and she would groan with disgust at the state of it. *Filthy pig*, she would say. So she would decide it needed cleaning. Still naked, he would have to take it down the corridor and wash it in the shower. Wash his blood and shit off it. For a few seconds he would protest, saying that he might be seen, that it's the middle of the day, anyone might . . . but her head would swing slowly to one side, then slowly swing to the other. *No protests. Do it*.

The second song starts on the tape and he starts wanking again in time with it, moving his hand more slowly as he imagines himself slipping naked from the room, padding as quietly as he can down the corridor to the shower, carrying the blood-and-shit-smeared dildo in front of him and the pain of his penetrated arsehole behind him. He savours the thought of his own fear. The fear that Alan might see him. That Mary might or Gillian or both. That the second-year Arab chemistry student, whose name he could never remember, might. That all of them might, appearing on the corridor in a laughing group then suddenly standing silent, eyes and mouths gaping with shock. He would be sweating by the time he reached the shower, pushed the door open and stepped inside.

But as he did so, he would hear the door of his room slam shut behind him and he would spin in the open door to see her striding down the corridor towards him, a cruel smile on her face. She would have locked him out: his keys would be in his trousers, his trousers behind the locked door. He would be locked out, naked, with an abused, bleeding arsehole and a blood-and-shit-covered dildo in his hand. But as she gets nearer she would throw something up in the air and catch it with a jingle. His keys.

'Get inside,' she would say. 'I've not finished with you yet.'

Then, fully clothed, she would follow him, fully stripped, into the shower, closing the door behind her, slide the bolt, then turn to supervise him. The air would feel cool and damp between the tiled walls and he would feel the heat of his still engorged cock rising against the skin of his stomach.

'Look at you,' she would say. 'Pathetic. Absolutely pathetic. Go on, get it washed. Now.'

He would turn the shower on and hastily begin rubbing at the soiled shaft of the dildo.

'Get under it yourself,' she would say.

He would get under it himself, twisting the shower-dial to warm.

'No!' she would say. 'You're wasting electricity. Turn it to cold. All the way.'

He would plead but she would be merciless, eyes glowing angrily on him as he stood naked beneath the shower, still clutching the dildo, cock jutting ahead of him.

'Do as you are told or you will not get your keys back. Turn it to cold and stand fully under it.'

He would have to obey her, twisting the dial till the arrow stood against five dark blue dots. For a moment or two the water would still run warm, then the first traces of cold water would appear in it, and a second after that it would be flooding down on him, a freezing stream, ice-cold, roaring against his back, spray bouncing up from his shoulders and touching and chilling his ears and cheeks.

'Head under too,' she would say. 'I want all of you under that water.'

He would hesitate for a moment, but she would lift the keys and dangle them between forefinger and thumb and he would have to obey. Head under too. Cock under, still poker-stiff, pulsing with the pain and humiliation of it. Then she would drop his keys to the floor with a clatter and step forwards, holding out her hand.

'Give it to me. Then turn round and bend over, keeping well under the water while you hold your cheeks apart.'

For a moment he wouldn't know what she meant, then he would realise she wanted the dildo. Hand shaking with cold, he would hold it out to her and she would snatch it roughly from him, licking her lips for a moment as he began to turn around.

'Bend over.'

Her voice would hiss through the roar of the shower and he would bend over under the icy stream, feeling it hammer all along his back, making his kidneys ache.

'Hold your cheeks apart.'

Shaking uncontrollably with cold, the sound of his chattering teeth echoing off the tiles, he would reach behind himself, take hold of the cheeks of his arse and tug them apart. His stiff cock would be bouncing in front of him and the glans protruding half through his foreskin would be pale purple now. Then out of the corner of his eye he would see her arm reach out above him, twisting the dial of the shower and after a moment the water spearing down on his back, torturing his skin, would be cool, not cold. In another second it would be

57

warm, or hot. The relief of it would be ecstatic, but he would gasp suddenly as he felt her put the head of the dildo to his sore arsehole.

'On the count of three,' she would say. 'One ... two ... three ...'

And he would scream as, with one swift merciless jerk, she would bury the shaft of the dildo between his buttocks, spearing it into his bowels. His cock, provoked beyond endurance by the pleasure of sudden warmth and the pain of sudden anal violation, would begin to spurt.

Lying on his bed he groans involuntarily at the thought of it, wanking more slowly still, imagining how strong his orgasm would be, wrenched out of him by the stiff shaft invading his arse as his skin sang beneath the flooding warmth of the shower. And, Christ, the thought of it is enough: he begins to come, groaning more loudly, twisting himself half onto his side so that the spurts of sperm splash against the wall. He'll have to wipe them off in a minute. And mop up the sperm pooled on his windowsill. But for the moment he lies there, hearing the chorus of the third song playing behind him, still able to detect a faint trace of the librarian's perfume, as though orgasm has sharpened his senses.

He sniffs, then sniffs again. Perhaps it has. Perhaps he really is smelling it. Perhaps there's a trace of it lingering on one of his books. He rolls over onto his other side, then slides off the bed, bending for a moment to pick a discarded sock off the floor. He mops at the sticky head of his cock as he walks over to his desk, tossing the sock aside when he has finished. He reaches the desk and puts his head down to the little tower of books, sniffing. Yes, he can smell it again, and stronger. He lifts the first book and sniffs its cover, back and front and spine, then flips through the pages, sniffing. No. He puts it down and picks up number two. The first sniff tells him that this is it: the perfume is suddenly almost searingly strong in his nostrils, and he feels his limp cock respond, jerking half upright. Was it left from just the contact of her fingers? But then he notices something sticking out between the pages. A small slip of paper. He opens the book and slides the paper out, realising it's longer than he thought, a strip of paper, not just a slip. There's nothing on one side and he turns it over, holding it stretched between left thumb and forefinger and right thumb and forefinger, and feels his heart begin to thump with excitement and fear as he reads what is on it.

Four

On the same evening, many miles to the south, another of the five men destined to win the Domina's next lottery is arriving at a television studio. His name is the Rt. Rev. William Richardson and he's due to take part in a debate on the future of the Church of England. He's a prominent traditionalist, long active in the campaign against female priests and now leading an even more vigorous campaign against homosexual marriage and female bishops. There's talk of a schism, of a breakaway church and, despite his lowly rank, he is spoken of as one of the potential leaders. He's been accused of arrogance, of spiritual pride, of rampant misogyny and homophobia, often to his face, even *into* his face, by red-faced, sometimes near-hysterical liberals on chat shows, but his massive, almost sepulchral calm remains unperturbed and the more strident the accusations grow the more he seems amused. The hooded, penetrating gaze he turns on his twitching, fleck-lipped opponents, male and female, hints that at least half of the emotion he has stirred by his outrageous comments in his slow, deep voice is in fact something far earthier than they would be prepared to admit. They may, in their foolishness and their blindness, disagree with him, his gaze seems to say, but it is plain to see that they would nevertheless be more than happy to be fucked by him.

Which in many cases is perfectly true: more than one of his fellow guests on chat shows and late-night political forums, male and female, have had to make an urgent trip to the lavatory when the discussion is over. More than one interviewer has had to. Because there is no doubt that he is a very attractive man, with the looks and the physique to appeal to all ages of heterosexual women and homosexual men. He's in his middle forties now, heavy-set, broad-shouldered, dark-haired and dark-jowled, with the face of a fleshy, slightly dissipated matinée idol. He's a well-known bon viveur and gourmet, and womaniser too in his youth, as he now freely admits, and even his most committed opponents are prepared to concede that he has performed an almost impossible feat and made the Church of England not only fashionable but sexy.

But he also has a dark secret. Very few people have ever guessed it, and perhaps he has almost succeeded in concealing it from himself, but this is the third time he has visited this studio and the second time he has sat and been prepared for the camera by one of the Domina's agents, and she has read the tension in his skin as her light fingers apply discreet make-up and her perfume enfolds him. She knows he has an erection too, the way he had an erection on the first occasion he sat there and she prepared his face, and she had shivered slightly at the thought of it, forgetting her allegiance to the Domina in the face of his dark, dominant masculinity, imagining how thick and massive his cock would be, imagining it spearing into her, liquefying her belly with its heat and solidity as it settled into rhythm and began to piston slow and relentless in her cunt or arse. She was leaking as that first session ended, dry-mouthed and thinking that she too was going to have to make an urgent trip to the lavatory, but then something had happened. Something very trivial but, she knew at once, very significant. He had cleared his throat, as though he was about to speak. As though he was about to ask a question that many men of a certain kind had asked, confirming what, in almost every case, she had already deduced. That they were suitable material for the Domina.

Some, rock-stars or businessmen, were direct: 'What *is* that perfume you're wearing, darling?'

Some, politicians mostly, were slyer: 'It's my wife's birthday next month and I was wondering . . .'

But from *him*, the Great White Hope of the traditional wing of the Church of England, she would never have expected it. She wouldn't even have expected that he had noticed the perfume, except as a faint trace of floral sweetness, coming and going as she moved around him, powdering his face, adjusting the skin tone around his eyes, leaning forwards, leaning back. Because normal men didn't notice the perfume. It spoke only to a certain class of men, but to them it spoke with the voice of the trumpet exceeding loud (Exodus 19:16) and the tongues of angels (1 Corinthians 13:1). Which is why they often cleared their throats, the way he had, and asked that question. The way he hadn't. But still, the throat-clearing put her on her guard and the next time he came to the studio she would be ready for him. Ready to pay him proper attention, recognising that she had re-learned a valuable lesson. To treat each man on each occasion as a stranger, and try to read him afresh.

So tonight she has treated the Rt. Rev. William Richardson as a stranger, never before seen, never before heard of, and she has tried to read him afresh. And what she has read in him has surprised and delighted her. To be blunt, he's a sub. He's gagging for it. His cock is stiff not at the thought of *having* her over the chair, but at the thought of being *had* by her over the chair. Of being bound over it, big balls dangling between his hairy thighs, and mistreated, abused, beaten. His cock is stiff at the thought of submitting to light, delicate, feminine her. Of being forced to drink the heady, red, foaming wine of her fornication (Revelation 17:2).

She finishes the make-up and steps back, smiling at him. He nods as though she's spoken, then says, musingly, conversationally, 'It's my wife's birthday next month, you know, and I've been wondering what to get her. She's always been a great one f–'

But he breaks off, because she's not been able to help herself and she's laughing into her hands. One dark, thick eyebrow climbs a little up his forehead, but his mouth is curved and he's smiling. One of his greatest weapons, beside his charm and his sex-appeal, is his ability to take a joke at his own expense. He has often made opponents look foolish by it.

'Can I share the joke?'

She shakes her head, recovering from her laughter.

'It's nothing, Reverend Richardson.'

'Oh, Bill. Please call me Bill.'

'It's nothing . . . Bill. It's just that so many men have asked me what you've just asked me, but somehow, till recently, I never expected it from you.'

'But I haven't asked you anything yet.'

'My perfume. You were going to ask about my perfume. Weren't you?'

He nods.

'You were going to ask where you could buy some, for your wife.'

He nods again.

'But you don't really want it for your wife, do you?'

He hesitates a moment, then shakes his head.

'You want it for yourself.'

He swallows and nods again.

'And you can have it, Bill.'

He raises his eyebrow again.

'Yes, you can. You really can. But there's one small condition.'

'What?' His voice is husky, almost strangled.

'You have to . . . submit to me.'

The sound of his gulp almost sets her laughing again

64

and she lets her eyes rest on his lap for a moment. Oh, Bill, please don't disappoint me. Please be as big as you look.

'Here?' he asks.

She purses her lips and nods slowly.

'Now?'

His voice is cracking slightly with eagerness. She shakes her head.

'No,' she says. 'Less speed, more greed. We don't have time now. After the show. Say you've left something behind and come up here.'

'All right. I will.'

'You'd better.'

'I will.'

'Say, "I will, *Mistress*." '

'I . . . I will, Mistress.'

'Good boy. Then I'll see you after the show.'

She leaves him then, laughter bubbling up in her throat again. The *risk* he was running. For all he knows she is on a retainer from the tabloids, like so many hairdressers and make-up artists, and will be running straight off after their session to sell her story for big money. Because it would be worth big money. The Rt. Rev. William Richardson, scourge of liberal decadence, defender of traditional Christian morality, not only having adulterous sex, not only having adulterous sex in a dressing room, not only having adulterous S&M sex in a dressing room, but having adulterous S&M sex in a dressing room and *being the sub*. Being. The. Sub. The fucking *sub*. The *fucked* sub. *Him*. Oh, she is sure she could get big, big money for that. And for a moment she even considers it. She considers telling him, just after they've started, that it's what she's going to do. Just to see how eager he really is. Because she suspects it wouldn't make any difference to him. Nothing lives for the next five minutes like a stiff dick. But she won't do it. The Domina would never forgive her; and, if the

65

Domina would never forgive her, she would never forgive herself.

She gets herself a cup of coffee and comes back past the make-up room, glancing in and seeing that it's empty. He's been taken to the studio, ready to perform. She goes into one of the monitor rooms to watch, sipping her coffee as she watches the last few minutes of the lead item. Then the presenter, a patronising smile on her face, introduces the discussion and there he is, sitting at the end of a row of chairs. He's up against three of his old antagonists, a militant gay campaigner, a liberal bishop and a feminist theologian. She watches carefully, sipping from her coffee as she reads body language and posture. She notes sardonically that both the campaigner and the feminist seem to sit a little forwards in their chairs when Bill's speaking, almost as though they're yearning towards him, almost as though they're hearing quite other messages in his voice than merely his words. She takes another sip from her coffee and grins. The happily married liberal bishop too does not seem immune to his opponent's heavy, dark, masculine charms, and she would be prepared to bet that he would much rather go to bed with Bill than with the scrawny feminist theologian, whose voice is beginning to crack a little as she interrupts a point Bill is trying to make in his slow, deep, rich voice. Sexual tension is crackling in the air and the female BBC presenter who is supervising the discussion is suppressing a smile as she intervenes, asking the feminist to let the Rev. Richardson make his point, aware that things are going well, that there may be a half-page story on an inside page of one of the broadsheets tomorrow. Or maybe even on the front page.

There's that habitual smile on the Rt. Rev. Richardson's face too, but tonight it's a little crooked, and there's a faint sheen of sweat on his forehead by the time the presenter thanks her guests and turns to the camera to introduce the next item. Joe Public wouldn't spot the sweat, maybe, but the make-up artist does, watching in the monitor room. It doesn't disturb her professional self-esteem, because she knows why it's there. She finishes her coffee and crumples the light plastic cup, feeling the familiar ache in her nipples and trickle in her cunt and flutter in her stomach. She calls the flutter her 'flutterfly' and she even has what she calls a framed specimen of it on the wall of her flat. When her boyfriends first ask about it, she tells them: 'Well, it might look like a butterfly to you, but it's really my flutterfly.'

And then, when they ask her what her flutterfly is, she tells them. It's the flutter she gets in her stomach at the thought of dominating a man. A flutterfly fluttering through bright air like a leaf to land on the broad, black back of a bull. And the bull shudders and snorts under the light contact of its threadlike feet. This is what it feels like for her, dominating a man. It feels like being a butterfly and making a bull snort and dance. Making it sweat and toss its horns and kick its hooves and gallop and turn in circles back and forth and over and over until thick froth is dripping from its jaws and it stands there, eyes dull and wondering with bewilderment and exhaustion while the butterfly, as cool and delicate as when it first landed, sits on its sweat-glossy back and basks in the sun, slowly opening and closing its wings.

She throws the crumpled cup into the bin and leaves the room, walking slowly back to make-up, wondering if he's really going to be there. If he has any sense, if he's applied any reason to what she's asked him to do, he won't be. He can't be. For a man in his position, the risk is far too great. It's not sensible, it's not rational to risk your career and your reputation for the sake of your cock. If you lay career and reputation in the left-hand scale and then cock in the right-hand scale, the left-hand scale ought to stay where it is. But, so often, it doesn't. So often it shoots up towards the ceiling. The way to a man's heart isn't through his stomach or even through his chest: it's through his zip.

She reaches the make-up room and sees that the door is open at the same angle as before. So is he there? Maybe not. But as she puts her hand out to push it fully open she smiles, because the flutterfly has just fluttered its wings inside her stomach again and she knows it knows he's there. She pushes the door fully open, walks inside, closes it, locks it and turns around, allowing the smile to slide off her face and be replaced by a look of cold contempt.

'Kneel,' she says. 'Kneel. On your knees to me, now.' She walks down the room.

'Do you know what I'm going to do, *Bill* –' she sniffs as she says it '– Bill, *dearest* –' she sniffs again '– just as soon as I've finished with you? Do you know what I'm going to do even before I've had a shower to get the stink of you out of my nostrils? I am going to ring the *Sun*. Or maybe the *Daily Express*. Or the *Mirror*. Or even *The* fucking *Times*. And I'm going to tell them everything. And produce the pictures to prove it. That's what I'm going to do.'

She slowly circles him as she speaks. Now she stops, standing behind him, staring at his neck and the back of his head. From the way he's stiffened and started to tremble, he believes her. Just the thought of it is enough to frighten him. She puts her hand over his shoulder from behind and starts to loosen his tie, putting her mouth down to his ear to whisper there.

'That's what I'm going to do, Billy boy. Go to the old *Currant Bun*. Or the *Express*. Or the *Mirror*. Or *The Times*.'

She pulls his tie loose and drops it on the floor, then unbuttons his shirt and puts her hand inside it, down over his chest. A mat of thick hair meets her hand and

68

she surfs through it with her fingertips as she whispers again.

'But I can only do it if I can produce the pictures. And I can only produce the pictures if you stay and let me take them.'

She pauses and lets her fingers find one of his nipples. She rubs it for a moment, feeling sweat slide under her fingers, then begins to squeeze as she starts whispering again.

'So, if you don't want it to happen, all you have to do is get up and leave now.'

She slips her other hand inside his shirt and finds his other nipple, beginning to squeeze that too.

'That's all you have to do, Billy boy. Get up and leave. I can't stop you. Not a big boy like you. Not a big brave boy like you who doesn't take orders from a pathetic little female like me.'

He's trembling all over and she can hear a groan beginning to gather in his throat. He believes her all right. He really believes her. She stops squeezing his nipples and starts to stroke and pluck them instead. They're stiff and he shudders.

'Time's passing, Billy. Your chance is slipping away. Get up and leave if you don't want me to do it. Get up now. Now, Billy.'

She pulls her hands out of his shirt and leans back away from him. He isn't just trembling now, he's shaking. She turns away from him, wiping her fingers on her skirt, and walks over to the make-up desk. She tugs open one of the drawers noisily and pretends to take something out, then turns and faces his back again.

'I've got my camera out now, Billy. Ready for the photos. The first one I want is you kneeling on the floor with your dick out. So get your dick out for the lady, turn around and say "Cheese".'

This is it. This is the moment. Either he pushes himself to his feet and walks out of the room, not looking back, or he reaches down in front of himself and pulls his zip down. She waits, watching his shoulders shake, then suddenly relaxes, releasing her own tension as the sound of his sob of fear and frustration is bisected by the sound of his zip going down. There's a rustle of cloth as he pulls his cock out, then he shuffles clumsily in a circle, turning himself on his knees to face her and the camera he thinks she is holding ready for him. She puts her hands up in front of her face, framing him with a square made from her thumbs and forefingers, and feels the flutterfly again as his stiff cock swings into view. It's enormous, truncheon-like, possibly the biggest she has ever seen, and she knows this is going to be some of the best fun she's had in a long time. And the look on his face when he's finally facing her and sees that she's not holding a camera is priceless.

'Say "Dickcheese", Billy,' she says, and makes a clicking noise with her tongue.

Five

When she got back home afterwards, she did what she always did after a successful session: she walked across the room to her framed flutterfly and planted a broad red kiss on the glass, right over its thorax. The neat label pasted below it said *Danaus chrysippus (Linn.)*. She hadn't known what its scientific name meant when she first bought it or what its common name was or what '*(Linn.)*' stood for or where it lived or what it lived on. Now she did. It lived on milkweeds as far north as Syria, as far east as Japan, as far south as Australia and as far west as the Canary Islands. So she didn't think one of its common names was very appropriate: the Lesser Wanderer. Plain Tiger was nearly as bad, African Monarch better, African Queen better still, and Golden Danaid best of all. The '*(Linn.)*' after its scientific name stood for Linnaeus, the Swedish naturalist who had first named it in 1758. And *Danaus chrysippus* meant something that made her smile every time she thought of it. 'Chrysippus' meant 'golden horse'. In Greek. And 'Danaus' was the name of a king with fifty daughters called the Danaids. Of whom forty-nine, on their father's orders, had murdered their husbands on their conjoint wedding night, presenting their father in proof with forty-nine severed heads. One of the daughters, she discovered, had been called Chrysippë and had been married to Chrysippos, and all of them, save for the one

71

who had refrained, had been punished in the Underworld by being set to draw water eternally from a well with sieves.

She had passed the story on to her regional Secretary and learned later that the Domina had laughed and clapped Her hands when She heard of it, and that She had named a squad of Her supervisors at the Heart of Darkness after the Danaids. The make-up artist was delighted to hear of it, knowing that it might mean a pay rise and speedier promotion, but she wanted to keep just a little of the story to herself. So she had invented a special sex game called the 'golden horse'. She had played it with the Rt. Rev. Richardson that evening and now, as she lifted her mouth from the flutterfly, admiring the outline of her lips on the glass for a moment, then turn to walk to the bathroom for her shower, she started to turn over her memories of it in her mind. It had been half an hour into their session and he had already come twice, copiously, against her express orders, each time leaving a pool of sperm soaking into the carpet on the floor. She had made him go down on his face each time to suck it up and swallow it, then lick the patch clean.

The second time, she decided she was ready. The sight of him stretched naked on the floor, broad-backed, narrow-hipped, four or five stones heavier than she was, and licking up his own sperm at her orders, was exciting her in the old way. She went over to his clothes, hung carefully over the back of one of the make-up chairs, hooked them loose one after another and dropped them on the floor. Then she turned back to him.

'Finished, Billy boy?'

His flushed, sweating face lifted to hers.

'Yes, Mistress,' he said.

'You're pathetic, Billy boy. Roll over and let me see.'

He rolled over, his erect cock bouncing as it came loose from the floor, pointing at the ceiling like a derrick. She strolled over and examined the patch of carpet he had spilled sperm on, kneeling to rub her fingers over it, lifting them to her nose and sniffing.

'OK,' she said. 'Now, something new. Follow me over here.'

He rolled to his stomach again, pushed himself up on his hands and knees, and crawled after her to where his clothes lay scattered on the floor.

'This is an excellent suit, Billy boy. How much did you pay for it?'

'Fifteen hundred guineas, Mistress.'

'Billy boy,' she said, slowly spacing her words, her pussy tingling as she watched him start to shiver, already well trained to the nuances of threat and discipline in her voice. 'I've already warned you about pretension and arrogance. You are not to use a word like "guinea" in my presence. Do you understand?'

'Yes, Mistress.'

'Then let's begin again. How much did you pay for it?'

'A little over fifteen hundred pounds, Mistress.'

'Good boy. But you have no objection, of course, to my making use of it as I see fit.'

He paused, then said, 'No, Mistress.'

She smiled, pleased by his hesitation.

'Good. Very good. Then spread it for me. Spread it out on the floor for me. Now!'

She barked the word, feeling her pussy squirm between her thighs and liquefy at the way he jerked when she did so. Then she said, speaking more quietly, 'No. Not like that. Do it with your mouth. Tug them into place with your mouth while I get my skirt and knickers off. And if I see you peek, Billy boy, let me promise you that your balls will suffer for it most severely. Do you understand?'

'Yes, Mistress.'

'Good boy. Get on with it, then.'

She watched him put his face down to the scattering of clothing on the ground and begin to spread it out the way she had ordered, closing his mouth over a sleeve or leg, tugging it back, then releasing it to close his mouth over another sleeve or leg or another garment. She walked a yard or two to the left, so that she would be clearly in his line of vision should he decide to be disobedient, and stooped left and right to tug off her shoes. She tossed them aside, watching his reaction to the soft thuds as they hit the floor, and began to unbutton her skirt. He had jerked when her shoes hit the floor; now he shivered as the soft sound of the unbuttoning began. She could see that he was trying to watch her out of the corner of his eye, but he wasn't being too obvious about it and, anyway, the poor thing had been waiting for this for a long time. She had stayed fully dressed until now, adding to the humiliation of his near-complete nakedness – ordering him to keep his socks on, knowing how ridiculous he would feel – and to her increasing dominance over him. But, now they had established their proper relations, she felt that it was time for a treat. A treat for both of them.

There. The last button. She wriggled her hips and her skirt slid off her with a whisper of cloth. She stepped out of the crumpled ring of cloth around her feet, still watching him.

'Knickers next, Billy boy.'

She could see that his cock was nearly brushing the black fur of his belly, it was so stiff. Was he hoping that he would get to use it, to penetrate her? Ah, if he was hoping that, how much he still had to learn. The true Mistress penetrates, She is never penetrated Herself, and certainly not by any of Her slaves. Though it would, she admitted to herself, hooking her thumbs into either side of her knickers and tugging downwards, be nice. She seriously doubted that she had ever had one that size before. He shivered again at the sound of her knickers coming down, and she almost thought she saw his cock brushing the black fur of his belly. She stepped out of her knickers, hooked them up on one foot, then flicked them towards him.

'They're off, Billy boy,' she said.

They hit his flank and fell to the ground, and his cock really did jerk up against his belly that time. Goddess, what a size it was. It really was a whopper. Was that where his confidence and his arrogance came from? The knowledge that he was so well endowed? That he was literally a big swinging dick? She thought it was, but she also thought that it was a two-edged sword. The big dick must always fear the bigger dick, and the ageing dick must always fear the younger dick. His big dick gave him the desire for two kinds of domination. He longed to dominate, and to be dominated. As he was now. But he still had a long way to go and a lot to learn.

She smiled again and started to walk towards him, rubbing her fingers through her pubic hair, watching him shiver at the silken rustle of it, walking around him till she stood just in front of and above his bent head.

'That's enough,' she said. 'Look up, Billy boy. Look at the treat I have in store for you.'

He raised his head and was staring straight into her pussy. It was open and oozing, she knew. She could feel pussy-juice beginning to trickle down her thighs.

'You've been a very naughty boy, Billy. You've made me stain my knickers, and they were clean on at the beginning of the month.'

Another shiver ran through him at that, and she snorted silently with laughter. So he was a knicker-sniffer too. He fetishised dirty knickers, worn for days by some lusted-for woman, soaked and soiled by her most intimate secretions.

'Sniff, Billy. Take a good sniff. Draw the scent of it into your lungs.'

He sniffed.

'Again, Billy.'

He sniffed again.

'Does that excite you, Billy boy? Does the scent of my pussy excite you?'

He nodded.

'Then say it, Billy. Tell your Mistress how the scent of her pussy excites you.'

She could hear him swallow, trying to clear the constriction in his throat. When he spoke, his voice was strangled.

'Mistress ... The scent of your pussy, Mistress. It excites me.'

'Does it make you stiff, Billy?'

He nodded again.

'Yes, Mistress. Very stiff, Mistress.'

She paused, then said, 'Would you like to lick my pussy, Billy?'

He nodded, trying to disguise his eagerness.

'Well?' she said.

'Yes, Mistress.'

'Yes what, Billy?'

'Yes, I would like to ... to lick your pussy, Mistress.'

'Then you shall, Billy. You shall. But you must pass a little test first. You must make up a poem about your Mistress's pussy. If it pleases your Mistress, she will let you lick her pussy. Very well?'

He nodded, swallowing again.

'Very well, Mistress.'

She moved closer to him, almost pushing her oozing pussy into his face.

'Then, for inspiration, take another sniff, Billy.'

He took another long, shuddering sniff, his back and buttocks quivering.

'Does that inspire you, Billy?'

He nodded and she felt a drop of something wet hit her bare feet. His mouth was watering at the smell of her pussy.

'Yes, Mistress.'

76

'Then recite a poem in honour of your Mistress's pussy. Come on, a poem, little Billy. Recite a poem in honour of her pussy and your Mistress will reward you by letting you lick it.'

'I . . . I'm trying, Mistress. I'm thinking.'

'Then think harder, Billy. Your Mistress is growing impatient. She may decide that you are not to lick her pussy after all, if you don't get a move on. But perhaps I have a way to summon your Muse.'

She stepped back from him, hearing him groan softly as her pussy left his face, and walked around him to stand behind him.

'Well, Billy? Do you have anything yet?'

'Yes, Mistress. The first . . . the first two lines.'

'I want at least six lines, Billy. Two are not enough. But let us hear them anyway.'

He swallowed, then began to recite:

My . . . my Mistress's pussy is oozingly sweet,
To lick it for Billy would . . . would be such a treat.

She put her head back and laughed.

'Pathetic, Billy. Pathetic. You'll have to do much better than that in the next four lines if you want any chance at all of licking it. So let me help you. Open your legs a little for me.'

She watched him shuffle his legs apart, opening his thighs for her, then waited a few moments, allowing him to grow apprehensive. Then she put her hand on his lower back and began to slide it down towards his buttocks, running her fingers through the black hair that clustered around his cleft, then down his cleft, between his buttocks, running her fingers through the thickening line of hair, till she reached a positive glade of the stuff around his bumhole. She lingered there a moment, tweaking at it, plucking at it, then ran her fingers on, over the sweaty warmth of his perineum, till she reached the leathery skin of his scrotum. It was drawn up against the fork of his thighs, as though he was near orgasm, and, as she closed her hand on it, tickling it, joggling its warm, moist weight on her palm, he groaned and quivered.

'Quiet,' she said.

It was too big for her to grip it one-handed and she had to kneel and put her other hand between his thighs, hold his scrotum in both, cupping it, ready to begin squeezing and torturing his big balls.

'Ball-torture, Billy. I often find it inspires men to poetic heights of which they never thought themselves capable. Of which *I* never thought them capable. So let us see how it works for you. You will give the command.'

She waited.

'Well, Billy? Give the command.'

'Mistress? I . . . I don't understand.'

'You will tell me when to begin squeezing. I wouldn't want to surprise you.'

'Wh– what do I say, Mistress?'

'Oh, Billy, Billy. What an unimaginative fellow you are. First you produce two of the tritest lines of pussy-worshipping poetry it has ever been my misfortune to endure, and now you can't find the words for the simplest task on earth. Just say, "Please, Mistress, I am ready to have you torture my balls. Please be cruel with them, Mistress. It is all they deserve. It is all *I* deserve." Then say, "Go!" '

'Yes, Mistress.'

'Well. Go on then.'

She could hear him swallowing, then he said, 'Please, Mistress, I am ready to have you torture my balls. Please be cruel with them, Mistress. It is all they deserve. It is all *I* deserve.'

He paused, swallowing again, then said, 'Go.'

She did nothing.

78

'Not loud enough, Billy. I might almost think you didn't want me to do it. Try again.'

Another pause, then: 'Go!'

'Better, but not good enough. Try again.'

She heard him draw in breath, then shout, 'Go!'

She jerked her hands shut on his balls, digging her nails into his scrotum, tugging downwards, twisting it from side to side. She heard him groan and felt his body shudder with pain. Then she stopped, feeling pussy-juice trickling freely down her thighs. Her heart was beating faster and she was a little out of breath.

'Well, Billy, has that helped? Have you come up with some more lines yet?'

He sobbed, panting with pain. 'No, Mistress.'

'Then I shall have to do it again, shan't I?'

He sobbed again. 'Yes, Mistress.'

'Then as before, Billy. Let's have the formula, then tell me to go.'

'Yes, Mistress. Please, Mistress, I am ready to have you torture my balls. Please be cruel with them, Mistress. It is all they deserve. It is all *I* deserve.'

She waited.

'Go!'

And she jerked her hands shut on his balls again, tugging at them, twisting them, squeezing them, hearing him groan with pain. His back and the hairy cleft of his buttocks were glistening with sweat now, and it was trickling down over her hands. She stopped the ball-torture, and she was panting now too.

'Has inspiration come, Billy?'

She felt him shake his head, then say almost in a whisper, 'No, Mistress.'

'Then command me to the ball-torture once again, Billy, and let's hope, for your sake, that it is third time lucky.'

'Yes, Mistress. Please, Mistress, I am ready to have you torture my balls. Please be cruel with them, Mistress. It's . . . it is all they deserve. It is all *I* deserve.'

She waited.

'Go!'

She jerked, tugged, twisted, squeezed, torturing his balls to inspire him with four new lines. Her hands almost slid off, his balls were so moist with sweat, and she could taste the stink of him in her mouth as she gasped her own pleasure at what she was doing. She stopped the ball-torture, panting, feeling her heart trip-hammer in her chest and pussy juice sliding down the inner surfaces of both thighs. She drew in a deep breath, controlling her voice.

'Well, Billy? Have I inspired you?'

Again she felt the movement of his head transmitted to her clutching hands on his balls, but what had it been? A nod or a shake? She didn't know till he spoke.

'Yes, Mistress. You have inspired me, Mistress.'

She let go of his balls, slid back on her knees and stood, rubbing her sweat-wet hands against each other, then wiped them on her bare thighs. She walked back around his crouched body and stood in front of his head. It was bowed and he was groaning faintly, still in pain from the ball-torture.

'Are your balls aching, Billy?'

'Yes, Mistress.'

'I am glad, Billy. You must suffer for your art. Head up. Gaze upon your Mistress's pussy once more.'

He lifted his head and she moved nearer to him.

'Sniff again, Billy. Reassure yourself that it is worthy of your worship, then recite your poem.'

He sniffed, seeming to forget the pain in his balls for a moment, then asked, 'All of my poem, Mistress?'

'All of it, Billy. From the beginning. I would like to hear how the quality improves.'

'Yes, Mistress.'

She waited.

'Go on, then. Recite your poem.'

'Yes, Mistress. Th– this is my poem.'

80

He swallowed, then began:

My Mistress's pussy is oozingly sweet,
To lick it for Billy would be such a treat.
Its lips are the doors to a heaven on earth,
For Billy to kiss them is more than he's worth;
But seeing the way that poor Billy does drool
His Mistress won't stop him – she isn't so cruel.

She threw back her head and laughed again, genuinely amused, knowing that her hips moved slightly forwards at the movement, so that her pussy almost touched his face. The scent and sight of it must be maddening him. She wiped tears of laughter from her eyes and looked down, putting her right hand on his head and ruffling his hair. She could feel the sweat in it, and heat in his scalp.

'Poor Billy,' she said. 'Are you really drooling? Look at me when you answer.'

He raised his head and looked up at her, having to bend his neck almost at right angles to see up the vertical shelf of her body, past her naked belly and her clothed torso. She dropped her right hand from his scalp and took hold of his left ear with it as her left hand took hold of his right ear. His face was flushed and sweating, his eyes red and damp with tears, and, yes, there was a trickle of spittle at one corner of his lip. He licked at it as he replied to her, and his voice was moist, as though his mouth really was full of drool.

'Yes, Mistress. I am drooling for you.'

'Open your mouth,' she said.

He opened it. She tugged at his ears, adjusting his head so that she could see properly inside.

'You're right,' she said. 'You really are drooling for me. Would you like me to spit into it?'

As he nodded she felt his ears tug against her fingers. She bent her head down to him, gathering spittle in her own mouth, then opened her lips and allowed a string of it to slide out, hanging, stretching over the few inches between them, then breaking and falling inside his mouth without a sound. She closed her mouth, smiling at him.

'There, Billy. Now, I think you had better get on with it, hadn't you? Head forwards.'

He dropped his head to face her pussy again and she tightened her grip on his ears as she shuffled forward, pushing her pussy hard up against him.

'Lick me, Billy. Lick me clean.'

She couldn't restrain a shudder of pleasure as his tongue emerged and began to obey her command. It was so large, so moist, so warm and so eager. A puppy's tongue, she thought. Sliding and slurping, chasing its own tail over the oozing flesh-folds of her delighted pussy. Puppy-tongue on her pussy. She sighed and tugged harder on his ears, pulling his mouth even harder to her pussy as she put her head back and closed her eyes, savouring the sound and sensation of his cunnilingus. He was very good. Expert, she would even say. Highly practised at pleasuring a pussy. A practised practitioner of pussy-pleasuring. Knowledgeable in nooks, cunning in crannies. Thorough on her thighs, loving on her labia. She moaned softly, almost involuntarily, and felt his pleased start of surprise and the sudden even greater eagerness with which he set to work. But she wasn't having that. She would decide when she orgasmed, not him.

She let go of his ears and stepped back, hearing him groan with frustration as his tongue suddenly worked against nothing but air. She pursed her lips, looking at him as she fingered herself, testing her state of arousal with her fingertips. His face was glistening thickly with pussy juice and saliva. He suddenly snorted and shook his head, a bubble of pussy juice winking open in one of his nostrils for a moment, then bursting with a minute silver glitter. She lifted her hand away from her pussy and raised it to her mouth, licking the fingertip, then sucking it. She stared at him, waiting for him to read the anger in her face. Yes, he was beginning to read it. Beginning to look apprehensive. She waited a few moments more, then her finger pulled out of her mouth with a small pop. He jerked at the sound and she smiled cruelly.

'You got a little carried away there, Billy. You forgot something rather important. Didn't you, Billy?'

He blinked.

'I said: "Didn't you, Billy?" '

He licked his lips and snorted again, another bubble of pussy juice winking open and bursting in one of his nostrils.

'Yes, Mistress.'

'Then what did you forget, Billy?'

'I . . . I don't know, Mistress.'

'You don't know? Then why did you agree with me when I said you had? Eh, Billy?'

He swallowed, then said, 'Because if my Mistress says I have forgotten something, then I must have forgotten something.'

She smiled.

'Billy, you're a natural. You really are. Shall I tell you what you forgot?'

'Yes, Mistress.'

'Yes *please*, Mistress.'

'Yes please, Mistress.'

'Then I'll tell you, Billy. What is the golden rule of orgasm, Billy? You must remember that I instructed you in it carefully at the beginning of our little session.'

'Yes, Mistress.'

'Then repeat it to me, Billy.'

'Yes, Mistress. The golden rule of orgasm is that nobody comes until the Mistress says so.'

'That's right, Billy. Nobody comes – not the slave, not the Mistress, not *anybody* – until the Mistress says so. But you were trying to make your Mistress come, weren't you, Billy? Weren't you?'

He paused, then nodded.

'And had your Mistress instructed you to make her come, Billy?'

Another pause. He shook his head.

'So you've been a very naughty little boy, haven't you, Billy?'

He paused, nodded.

'I said: "Haven't you, Billy?" '

He swallowed and said, almost croaking: 'Yes, Mistress.'

'Then I must punish you, Billy. Mustn't I?'

'Yes, Mistress.'

'Then what you do suggest, Billy?'

His eyes lifted to hers for a moment, then blinked and dropped to fix on her pussy again. His lips trembled, opened, closed, then he said, almost whispering: 'Ball-torture, Mistress.'

She tilted her head slightly, lifting her hand to one ear and pushing it forwards with a finger as though she had not heard him properly.

'What was that, Billy?'

He licked his lips, blinked, swallowed.

'Ball-torture, Mistress. I would like to be punished with ball-torture, Mistress.'

'Ah. I see. Ball-torture. You would like ball-torture, would you, Billy?'

'Yes, Mistress.'

'But, if you would like it, it wouldn't be punishment. Would it?'

A pause.

'No, Mistress.'

'You're a silly Billy, aren't you, Billy?'

'Yes, Mistress.'

'So let's have another poem from you, Billy. But not one of yours. Let's have "Ride a cock-horse". Do you know it?'

84

'Yes, Mistress.'

'Then recite it to me. Sing it to me.'

He licked his lips again, cleared his throat, opened his mouth uncertainly. She slipped out of her jacket, walking over to hang it on one of the chairs at the make-up table. She turned back, starting to unbutton her shirt.

'Come on, Billy. Sing it to me. Like this.'

She cleared her throat and sang in a light voice: ' "Ride a cock-horse to Banbury cross!" That's how it goes, Billy. Sing it to me.'

Her shirt was unbuttoned. She pulled it open, sliding her arms out of it left and right. He released a deep and apparently unconscious sigh as her black bra was exposed. She reached behind herself to unclip it, then stopped, her breasts pushed forwards towards him, straining in the bra-cups that held them.

'I'm waiting, Billy. Sing it. Now.'

She released the clip of her bra and as though it had been a signal he began singing, uncertainly at first, then more confidently, his deep voice filling the room. She listened, smiling, holding the straps of her bra in place, waiting for him to finish.

Ride a cock-horse to Banbury cross,
To see a fine lady on a white horse.
With rings on her fingers and bells on her toes,
She shall have music wherever she goes.

She put her head back and laughed, still holding her bra in place.

'Very good, Billy! Very good. Now, I want you to tell me something.'

She peeled the bra from her breasts with a sigh and started to walk towards him, letting the bra swing in one hand, knowing his eyes were lifting to follow her breasts as she got nearer. She stopped in front of him, pussy

85

almost in his face, so that when his eyes dropped he would be staring straight into it. She looked down at him down the bare cliff of her body, his face half-obscured by the swell of her breasts.

'Tell me, Billy,' she said. 'Am I a fine lady?'

She slipped a finger of her free hand into her pussy-hair, rubbing at it with a faint, silky rustle. His eyes dropped from hers, watching her finger. She started to twist a lock of her pubic hair around it. He released another long sigh, apparently unaware that he was doing it, then said: 'Yes, Mistress.'

'Then I ought to ride a white horse, oughtn't I?'

'Yes, Mistress.'

'Will you be my white horse, Billy?'

'Yes, Mistress.'

'And can I ride you as hard as I like?'

'Yes, Mistress.'

'Good Billy.'

She slipped her finger from her pubic hair, leaving a twisted lock sticking from it like a little horn.

'Kiss your Mistress's pussy, Billy.'

His head came forwards and he kissed her pussy.

'Again, Billy. Higher. Kiss my love-locks.'

He raised his head and kissed her pubic hair.

'Good Billy.'

She turned away from his head, walking halfway down his flank, then pausing.

'Flat to the floor, Billy. Your Mistress wishes to mount you.'

He flattened himself to the floor, his cock pressed hard underneath him. She swung a leg over his body and sat down on his lower back, bouncing her buttocks a little, sliding them up and down, feeling hot sweat slide under them.

'Yuck. How hot and sweaty you are, Billy. Does my bottom feel cool against your skin?'

'Yes, Mistress.'

'I thought it might. Now, where is your belt?'

'To your right, Mistress.'

'Where? Ah, I see it. Thank you, Billy.'

She transferred her bra to her left hand and leaned over, picking up his belt, laying it over his back, ready for later. Now she worked on her bra, twisting the straps around her left hand, leaving the cups free.

'Head up, Billy. Mouth open.'

He lifted his head and she leaned forwards and slipped the bra over his head, letting it slide down his face until it was over his mouth. She tugged backwards sharply on the straps, trying to fit the bra securely into his mouth.

'Wider, Billy. Let some slide inside.'

She tugged again. There. It was in.

'Those are your bra-reins, Billy.'

She took a firmer hold of the straps in her left hand, then picked up the belt in her right, folding it in half and taking firm hold of it by both ends. Now she twisted her upper body and looked back down his body, examining the swell of his buttocks, lifting the doubled belt above them.

'Up you get, Billy.'

She brought the belt down on his buttocks with a fleshy crack. He grunted with pain into his improvised bra-reins, then began pushing himself back onto his hands and knees.

'Faster!'

She brought the belt down again, not having to watch this time. His back rocked and she slid her knees forwards, tightening them on his flanks as he began to rise beneath her, keeping her feet well clear of the floor so that he was lifting, then carrying, her full weight. Now he was up and she was two feet above the floor, ready to ride him.

'Forwards, Billy.'

She brought the belt down with a crack and he began to crawl forwards.

'Faster!'

She brought the belt down again, tightening her knees again as he lurched beneath her and began to crawl faster, making her breasts bounce. She tugged sideways on the bra-reins.

'Left, Billy. Let's trot around the room a couple of times, then see how much of a gallop you can get up from end to end.'

She brought the belt down again to encourage him, feeling her pussy beginning to re-moisten as her buttocks bounced and jolted on his working back. She adjusted herself, loosening her knees a little so that her pussy could work directly against him, knowing how the sticky slide of its lips and the silky rasp of her pubic hair would excite him. What a hard-on he must have by now! She tugged on the bra-reins again, guiding him left, bringing the belt down with another crack on his buttocks. He was gasping through the cloth filling his mouth, snorting with the exertion of carrying her, and she could feel sweat sliding down his back to meet her bouncing pussy.

'Faster!' she said. Another crack of the belt, and her pussy bounced harder, her breasts shuddering and swaying with complex, never-repeating rhythms. She took him around the room twice, then paused him at the door, facing him across the room to the make-up table. His back was streaming with sweat and she could feel his flanks working between her knees as he laboured for breath through his nose and half-choked mouth. Still holding the doubled belt in her right hand, she patted his back between his shoulder blades.

'Good Billy,' she said. 'But I'm sure you haven't shown me everything you're capable of yet, have you? You can crawl much faster than that. Eh?'

She tugged at the bra-reins and he nodded, saying something indistinct into the bra-reins.

'Good boy. Then are you ready?'

She patted him again, then lifted the belt back behind her, poised it high, then brought it down with a crack.

'Go! Gallop!'

He lurched underneath her and set off again, crawling hard. Her head jerked back and she let out a whoop, bringing the belt down again, then again, breasts shuddering, pussy bouncing against his hot, streaming skin.

'Faster! Faster, Billy!'

Her pussy bounced again on his streaming back, her pubic hair already soaked with his sweat and her own. They were already almost on the far side of the room, moving fast towards the make-up table.

'Whoa!' she said, bringing the belt down, laughing, tugging him left, turning him to face back down the room towards the door. He lurched beneath her and she felt her buttocks begin to slide off him. She had to tug hard at his bra-reins and bounce herself back on, getting herself ready for the return gallop. Sweat was positively dripping off him now, falling in large drops from his flanks to the carpet, left and right, and through his tortured gasps and snorts for breath she could hear them landing with soft, unconcerned clicks. Ah, it was delightful, so delightful to sit secure above such effort, to direct it and exploit it! Her pussy was seething, answering the sweat pouring from his back with a thicker, stickier flow of its own, and she thought the bouncing it received on the return gallop might finally bring her to orgasm. She brought the belt down, crack, crack.

'I want to come this time, Billy,' she said. 'Make me come or you will suffer for it.'

She lifted the belt high, held it poised, then brought it down.

'Go! Gallop!'

And he was off again, crawling hard, his back bouncing beneath her pussy, kissing its stickiness with hot skin swimming with sweat. She bounced back at it, flattening herself to him, sliding at him, grinding at him, bouncing, laughing, bringing the belt down again and again, feeling orgasm bud between her thighs, blossom in her belly and bloom through her body in a couple of heart-hammering seconds. When she dragged drunkenly back on the bra-straps and halted his gallop at the door, she was gasping almost as hard as he was. His back felt almost cool now, her pussy was so hot, and when she rubbed herself luxuriously at him, kissing him with her oozing lips, smearing him with her juice, she wondered whether he could feel it burning against his skin.

'Good Billy,' she said, still gasping for breath. She drew air into her lungs, released it, trying to control her breathing. 'Come on, let's get over to your suit. But take your time, Billy. No need to rush.'

She brought the belt down almost gently now, just flicking, setting him on his way, back over to the suit that lay spread on the floor. His back was steady this time, not bouncing beneath her, and she could pleasure herself on it properly, hauling on the bra-straps to pull herself forwards, then leaning back, letting her buttocks slide on his slick sweat, rubbing her pussy hard at him, bouncing herself a little so that her pussy-thorn was titillated on him. But then they were there.

'Whoa, Billy!' she said, tugging at the bra-straps for him to stop. He obeyed, positioned on hands and knees over his spread-out suit. She relaxed her grip on the bra-reins and glanced down left and right, making sure he was positioned just right, right over the top of the suit, so that it would catch everything.

'Left a bit, Billy,' she said. 'Good boy. And perhaps . . . yes, back up a little. Little more. Good. Very good. Now, Billy, you've been such a good horse that I've decided that it's time for another little treat for you. Can you guess what it is? Whinny once for yes, twice for no.'

She waited. Nothing. She lifted the belt carefully, not wanting him to feel the tremors in her buttocks and thighs that would warn him of what she was about to do. She held it poised high above his buttocks.

'Oh, Billy,' she said in a sorrowful voice, and brought the belt down with a crack.

Caught by surprise, he jerked, grunting with pain.

'I asked you a simple question, Billy. You did not answer it. Can you guess what little treat I have ready for you? Whinny once for *yes*, and twice for *no*. That's simple enough, isn't it? Well, isn't it?'

She felt the bra-straps jerk in her hand as he lifted his head and produced a strangled noise through the bra-cloth half-filling his mouth.

'I'll take that as a "yes", Billy. So here is the question again. Can you guess what little treat I have ready for you?'

Two strangled noises this time.

'I'll take that as a "no", Billy. So I'll tell. No, on second thoughts, I'll *show* you. Actions speak louder than words.'

Was she ready? For a moment she thought she wasn't, her pussy still quivering with the after-seethe of her orgasm, but in the next moment she knew it would obey her. There: it had. She looked down and saw a clear yellow tail of piss lifting from beneath her sweat-darkened pubic-hair, falling on his back a moment later, pooling there, spreading up the cleft of his spine, little arms of it reaching left and right, climbing over his ribs to pour over his flanks and splatter downwards onto the suit that lay spread to receive them.

'Do you know what I call this, Billy?' she said quietly, conversationally, almost to herself, grunting a little as she forced more of her piss out, watching it jerk in time with her efforts. He didn't whinny in reply but she didn't mind, answering her own question anyway, still in the same quiet, conversational tone.

'I call it the "golden horse". Do you like it?'

Still no reply. She released the bra-straps in her left hand, letting the reins fall loose in his mouth, and suddenly became aware of a pulse of squirting fluid sounding underneath her through the thinner splatter of her falling piss, as though someone was discharging a thicker fluid against his suit. She realised what it was. When she ordered him to get dressed and sent him from the room, one of the Domina's telephone-strips would be tucked inside a pocket of a suit that was soiled not just with female urine but also with male sperm.

Six

And now the draw has been made and the instructions have been despatched. The Domina thinks of the postal service as a vast network of blood vessels in which letters are like blood cells. They stream in their millions along the vast arteries that connect city to city; then in their thousands along the broad veins that radiate out into the districts of a city; then in their hundreds down the narrower veins that snake through the streets of a district; then finally in dozens down the capillaries that end in the letter-boxes of a single street. Most of these blood-cell letters are white, some are brown. Hers, for the final stage, are black. She can picture them moving through the blood-vessels of the British postal network, black cells in a sea of white, carrying their promises of pain and pleasure along the vast arteries, the broad veins, the narrower veins, then finally the capillaries, to spill through the letter-boxes of five lucky, lucky men. How their hands will tremble as they pick them up, maybe raise them to their nostrils, sniff them, eyes closing with pleasure, the groins of their dressing-gowns or trousers bulging with sudden, irresistible arousal.

Then they open them with hands that are not simply trembling, but shaking, fingers sliding on the smooth, silky, expensive paper that the Domina uses for all Her most important correspondence. These five letters, despatched every three months, are among the most important correspondence of all. It is not true, as some among Her employees whisper, that there is no element of chance in the selection of the five, but it is certainly true that the Domina does not allow Herself to be guided entirely by the electronic caprice of Medusa (Masochists' Electronic Domination and abUsage Selection Apparatus), Her lottery computer. How far She intervenes is not known, and it may even be true that one or two of each trimester's lucky five are not chosen at random at all. It may even be true that for the final lucky five the Domina does not, in the end, rely on the computer at all, but on some older, more traditional means of random choice. Dice or cards or even tea-leaves. Perhaps She has a list before Her of suitable candidates, fifty or a hundred of them, and sits rolling or shuffling or swirling in Her scented, black-walled, black-floored, black-ceilinged underground chamber until the fifty have become twenty-five, and then the twenty-five ten, and then the ten five. Five lucky, lucky men.

The instructions they are sent cover no more than a single side of a single sheet of black paper. As before, the sheet is blank when it is first pulled from the envelope, but the cloud of perfume that comes with it is more than enough to remind the winners of the technique whereby the secrets of the sheet are revealed. A few are spilling their sperm atop it within less than a minute, kneeling before the slot of the letter-box and dragging their stiff cocks out in the slanting morning sunlight that glows through the frosted glass above the door, pumping themselves to orgasm in a few brutal strokes. Others, no less aroused but considerably less impulsive, choose to linger over the task, carrying the blank sheet around with them in an inner pocket for the rest of the day, delighting in the perfume that leaks from it and in the secret knowledge of what awaits them when they have finished work for the day. For them, for these lucky, lucky men, these privileged perverts, spilling sperm on to the scented sheet of a letter from the Domina is more pleasurable by far than vanilla sex with an ordinary woman, or S&M sex with an ordinary Mistress. Though they have not yet met Her, not yet, in some cases, even guessed that they are waiting to meet Her, Her power is too great to be confined by the conventions of space and time, and they feel Her presence even in Her letters and envelopes. She is the Domina, and Her slaves worship Her from afar, spilling their sperm with agonised bliss and gasps of unconscious prayer.

The instructions that are revealed as the chemicals of their sperm soak into the sheet are concise, unambiguous and non-negotiable. Each of the five is first to write or redraft his will, leaving all that he owns to the Domina, either on his certified death or after he has been missing for more than a year. The will is to be witnessed at some lawyer's in the same or a nearby city and whose phone number will be included on the sheet. The firm will be always female run, often entirely female staffed, and always, of course, in the employ of the Domina. The firm will despatch a copy of the will to the Domina for final approval, and then prepare the tickets for the winner's final journey to the Heart of Darkness. The first stage will take him to London, the second onto the underground, where he is to board the final, deserted carriage of a train pulling out of a station on the Bakerloo Line sometime between one and two o'clock on a weekday afternoon. There is no third stage of the journey: somewhere deep beneath the capital's streets, as they bask in summer sunshine or are pelted with autumn rain, are sprinkled with spring blossom or veiled in winter snow, the train will make a brief, unscheduled stop. A single door of the final carriage will slide open and the winner will step forth onto the platform of a deserted station lit only by the dim lights of the carriage itself. He will have arrived, and his heart will pound or his stomach roll with fear as the train hums back into life and slides off down the tunnel.

When the sound of its engine and the glow of its lights have finally dwindled to nothing, he will be standing in perfect silence and darkness and he may jump with fright and surprise when, with shocking suddenness, the floodlights of the station snap on and powerful speakers crash into life.

'Vurm!' they will scream in a crisp, cruel, Middle European accent. The station will be echt 1930s, gleaming with art deco tiles, benches and cigarette dispensers, its walls hung with bright, vivid posters advertising drinking chocolate and holidays in the Western Isles, and directly in front of him will be a single vast copy of Harry Beck's newly designed map of the Underground.

'Vurm!' the speakers will scream again, then: 'On your knees, vurm!'

Boots will begin to crash along some distant corridor as the echoes of the speakers go grumbling down the tunnel on left and right, and the trembling winner will go down on his knees, sweat beginning to trickle under his clothing and the tie he has been ordered to wear. The boots will crash nearer, nearer, and the Domina's hand-picked *Empfangkommando* or Reception Squad will be on the platform itself, dressed in one of Her seasonal uniforms: white leather with black collars, caps and hems for spring; yellow leather with red collars, caps and hems for summer; purple leather with orange collars, caps and hems for autumn; and black leather with white collars, caps and hems for winter, which begins much earlier and finishes much later in the Domina's subterranean realm than in the world above. The women will advance on him, boots thudding in unison on the bare, swept platform, and it has been known for some exceptionally susceptible winner, overcome with the glory and majesty of the six-foot, broad-shouldered, full-breasted *Walküre* of the Reception

Squad, to come in his trousers as the weight of their heavy boots and bodies shudders in the platform beneath his knees.

But whether the new arrival has come in his trousers or not – and his cock is always erect, straining upwards in worship of the Squad – when they reach him the questioning will begin. The thirteen members of the Squad – the *Kommandantin* herself, her two chief lieutenants, her three sub-lieutenants, her six sub-sub-lieutenants, and her batwoman – will circle the kneeling figure on the platform, the *Kommandantin* standing directly in front of him, her two lieutenants directly behind. However tall he is, however important and well known in the world above, however strong and broad-shouldered, he will seem to shrink within that circle of sturdy female flesh, so tall and imposing and strong are the members of the Reception Squad themselves. Seen at kneeling height their gleaming black boots will seem to cage him in like the polished ebony posts of a prison stockade. The *Kommandantin*, her cold eyes all-seeing beneath the peak of her cap, will gaze down upon him. Sometimes he will return her gaze, looking upwards almost eagerly at her frigid blonde beauty; more often he will be staring straight ahead, his gaze directed at her thighs, or his head will be bowed and he will be shivering with fright. In these cases she will order him to look up, her voice harshly, shiveringly, ball-tighteningly flavoured with Middle European braying vowels and crisp consonants.

'Look up at me, vurm,' she will say. Or: 'Vurm, raice your eyes!'

A shudder will run through him and he will obey, raising the lust-and-fear-heated brown or green or grey of his eyes to the glacial blue of hers. A sneer will cross her pale, strong, perfectly sculpted face, and she'll bend forwards, lowering her face to his, and, at a range of a foot or less, demand: 'Paperss.'

Her narrow lips will form the 'P's of the word so vigorously, so energetically, that he will feel puffs of her cool, cigarette-spiced breath against his face, and perhaps even specks of her spittle. His own mouth will fall open uncertainly, and he may frown or begin to shake his head, but before he has the chance to speak she will bark, 'Your papers! Vhere are your papers?'

She will allow him to stutter, 'I . . .' or 'But . . .', then will interrupt as he tries to carry on, snarling into his face at even closer range, specks of her spittle hitting his skin and eyes, making him blink.

'I do not vant vords, I vant papers! Of vords zere is no reqvirement! Only of papers!'

He has no papers, of course: the orders on the instructions he received a week or fortnight before and revealed by his filthy sperm-spilling will have been quite explicit. He is to make the second stage of his journey to the Heart of Darkness without any form of identification. Even his clothing, which must be brand new and anonymous, is to be stripped bare of labels. He is to arrive only as a male, a representative of his sex bearing no individuality, no history, with no credentials but the cock and balls between his legs, the unsightly hair upon his body and face, and the androgenic chemicals circulating in his bloodstream.

'Your papers! Vhere are your papers?'

By now the chemicals in his bloodstream will have been joined by the adrenaline of fear and excitement and the hormones of sexual arousal. If he has chosen, in his extremity, to produce whatever he can to meet her demands, his hand will shake as he reaches inside his jacket, but he will stiffen into immobility as the *Kommandantin* orders, 'Shtop. For vhat are you reaching?'

'M– my wallet,' he will quaver.

Her eyes will widen with anger on his and he will hear a murmur of outrage run around the circle of pale, perfectly sculpted faces that look down on him.

'Disrespect,' the *Kommandantin* will hiss. 'You vill address me by my title or zuffer zevere conseqvences. Repeat. For vhat are you reaching?'

'M– my . . . my wallet, Mistress.'

'No!' the *Kommandantin* will bark, making him jerk with surprise. 'Zat is not my correct title. I am –' and the pride and arrogance with which she announces her name sometimes make the interrogatee groan involuntarily with worship '– I am ze *Kommandantin*.'

She will pause, then say, 'Zo. Answer. For vhat are you reaching?'

'My wallet, *Kommandantin*.'

She will straighten from him and her leather-gloved hand will swing out, palm upwards.

'Giff.'

His hand will move again, reaching inside his jacket, reappearing with his wallet. He will place it on her palm, then watch, licking his lips nervously, as she raises her hand and stares at the wallet, the sneer returning to her face.

'Examine,' she will demand, holding her hand out to one of her lieutenants.

The lieutenant will take the wallet from her palm and fold it open, riffling through its contents, before tugging out and retaining the notes of the two or three hundred pounds that he has been ordered to bring with him, then holding the wallet upside down and shaking it. Then she will let it drop to the floor, perhaps striking the interrogatee's face as it falls.

'Giff,' the *Kommandantin* will order.

The lieutenant will hand her the sheaf of banknotes taken from the wallet.

'Vhat,' she will ask, shuffling through them, 'is zis?'

'M– money,' the interrogatee will answer.

'Zen it is not papers,' the *Kommandantin* will say.

It will be a statement, not a question, but the interrogatee may nod and quaver, 'Yes.'

'Zen it is not reqvired.'

Again it will be a statement, not a question, but the interrogatee may again nod and quaver, 'Yes.'

'Zen it is useless,' the *Kommandantin* will say, and before the interrogatee can nod or reply she will have pushed the notes back into a wad, lifted them and, as she repeats the word 'Useless', torn them in half with a single flick of her wrists. The power, the strength evident in the action will make some of the interrogatees whimper again with worship; and they whimper yet again as she places the two halves of the torn wad over each other, making a thicker wad, and tears this in half too with a single flick of her wrists, repeating, 'Useless.'

She will then release the torn notes, allowing them to fall from her fingers, to flutter downwards, veil the face of the interrogatee, land across it, before sliding off to the floor of the platform. Sometimes one or two pieces – the face of the Queen or Elgar or Sir John Houblon – will still be clinging to his face as she looks down and passes judgement on him.

'You haff no papers. You are under arrest.'

Some of the interrogatees will wet themselves at this point, and it is a sorry day for them as the trickle of their piss, having worked its way down their inner thighs to their knees, soaks through the cloth of their trousers and emerges to begin trickling across the platform towards the track. The ominous silence of the remaining members of the Squad will suddenly deepen in tone and begin to vibrate sonorously with outrage, and the gaze of the *Kommandantin* will blaze ferociously. Her narrow lips will compress a strong arm will swing up and a leather-gloved hand point steadily at the trickle of piss. Then she will ask quietly: 'Vhat is zis? Vhat haff you done?'

When some of these men are asked to account for their filthy behaviour, some can no more than squeak and a few will even faint, falling forwards across the boots of the *Kommandantin* herself. She will glance around the circle of grim faces, meeting eyes that have already, so perfect is the training and interpersonal sympathy of the Squad, raised to meet hers, and then snarl a single, long-anticipated order. The Squad will slide their pre-lubricated truncheons from the long leather holsters on their hips and, when the *Kommandantin*'s two lieutenants have de-trousered the fainted man and poised him, arse up, on the cold platform floor, they will have formed themselves into an orderly queue, ready for the gang truncheon-rape that now commences.

But if the interrogatee does not wet himself when the *Kommandantin* announces his arrest, and most do not, the rape must be justified more elaborately. If the *Kommandantin* sees from his eyes that his joy–fear has not overwhelmed him, her eyes will lift from his, and she will nod curtly, as though responding to a raised hand or signalling for a hand to be raised.

'Ja?'

'*Frau Kommandantin*,' one of her *Sturmtruppine* or female storm-troopers will begin. 'You will remember that *She* has expressed concerns about smuggling.'

The *Kommandantin* will blink at the mention of 'She', then nod when the *Sturmtruppin* has finished speaking.

'Ja. It is so. Shtrip him.'

Six strong hands will fasten inexorably on the kneeling interrogatee, lifting him bodily to his feet, beginning to strip him with brutal efficiency. Cloth will tear as they grow impatient with the buttons of his trousers and they will slap stingingly at his hands as he tries to conceal the unmistakable evidence of his arousal: the stiff cock revealed when they wrench his trousers and his underpants down.

'Shtop,' the *Kommandantin* will say.

The strong hands will let go of him and the members of the Squad will step back, leaving him bare below the waist, his trousers and underpants pooled around his ankles, his tie half undone and collar awry, his jacket tugged half off so that his arms are pinioned.

'Vhat,' the *Kommandantin* will ask, pointing at his stiff cock with a blunt, gloved forefinger, 'is zat?'

He will moisten his lips, perhaps, start to open his mouth, but the voice of one of the *Sturmtruppine* will cut across his.

'It is a cock, *Kommandantin*.'

The *Kommandantin* will turn her head to the speaker, raising a thin blonde eyebrow.

'A . . . cock? *Verstehe nicht*.'

'*Ein Hahn, Kommandantin. Das ist für "ein Schwanz".*'

'*Ach, so*. So we haff here,' the *Kommandantin* will say, turning her head back to stare at the interrogatee's cock, 'zis semi-mystical creature, "ze cock".'

'Yes, *Kommandantin*.'

'Very goot. A cock. But more zan zat. A *shtiff* cock. It is evidently classifiable as a concealed offensive weapon. Ja?'

Murmurs of 'Yes, *Kommandantin*' will run around the circle of *Sturmtruppine*.

'Very goot. Zo we haff now two charges. He does not possess papers, and yet he does possess a concealed offensive weapon. Recommence ze shtripping.'

The three *Sturmtruppine* assigned that watch to stripping newly arrived contestants will step forwards again and complete the stripping, dragging his jacket off, then tearing his shirt off so roughly that buttons fly off it ahead of him, one or two of them hitting the *Kommandantin*'s uniform and bouncing away to join the others on the floor. Finally, mockingly, one of them will march in front of him and gently unknot his tie, then slide it from around his neck, drop it to the floor, then take her place with her two companions back in the watching circle of *Sturmtruppine*. He will stand naked, the focus of twenty-six cold blue eyes, his clothes scattered on the platform around his feet, buttons of his torn and discarded shirt lying on the platform for feet ahead of him.

'Hands down!' the *Kommandantin* will sometimes bark, if he tries to inch his hands forwards over his stiff cock. 'Ve are unconcerned wiz your modesty, und shcarcely see vhy you should take zis trouble at concealment. Now, turn yourself. Goot. Now, open your legs. Lift your balls. Turn again. No, you must hold your balls up. Yes. Und shtop. Now, hands on head. Clasp zem. Turn again. Goot. Now, lift your foot. Left foot. Turn on ze shpot. Left foot down. Right foot up. Turn on the shpot. Right foot down. Goot.'

Then she will turn to her *Sturmtruppine*.

'*Fräuleinen*,' she will say. 'Do you consider he iss clean?'

There will be nods and crisp '*Ja*'s or 'He is clean's, but one of the *Kommandantin*'s chief lieutenants will raise her gloved hand.

'*Leutnant*?' the *Kommandantin* will say.

'On the outside, *Kommandantin*,' the lieutenant will begin, 'I consider he is clean. We have seen nothing in his armpits, under his balls, on the soles of his feet. But we have not yet checked between his toes or in his ears and mouth.'

The *Kommandantin* will nod, a cold smile lighting her face for a moment.

'Zat is correct, *Leutnant*. Ve haff sinned by omission. You vill please to repair it.'

The chief lieutenant will stamp her boots together, saluting crisply, then step forwards out of the circle, nodding two sub-lieutenants with her.

'You,' the *Kommandantin* will say, staring coldly at the interrogatee. 'Raise your left foot again.'

As he raises it one of the sub-lieutenants will seize it, dragging it higher, almost throwing him off-balance, and strong fingers will tug his toes apart, searching between them for contraband. Then the hand will release the foot and the interrogatee will put it gratefully back to the floor of the platform.

'Nothing, *Fräulein Leutnant*,' the sub-lieutenant will say in a clear, steady voice, a tone above that of the lieutenant, who will nod and say, 'Nothing, *Frau Kommandantin*,' in a clear steady voice, a tone below that of the sub-lieutenant, a tone above that of the *Kommandantin*, who will nod and say, 'Right foot,' in her clear, steady voice, a tone below that of her lieutenant, two tones below that of her sub-lieutenant.

The interrogatee will lift his right foot and it will be seized and examined in the same way, before 'Nothing, *Fräulein Leutnant*,' from the sub-lieutenant and 'Nothing, *Frau Kommandantin*,' from the lieutenant and 'Ze ears,' from the *Kommandantin*.

From each side strong gloved fingers will seize and examine his ears, pushing them forwards, then back, then folding back the tragus and anti-tragus from his earholes. A gloved fingertip will probe but be too large to enter. It will be withdrawn and he will hear gloves being tugged off; then the fingertip will return, ungloved, but still be too large.

'Vhat is ze problem?' the *Kommandantin* will ask.

'My finger is too large to probe his ear, *Frau Kommandantin*,' the lieutenant will reply.

'Who hass ze *Ohrensonde*?' the *Kommandantin* will ask.

'I, *Frau Kommandantin*,' one of the sub-lieutenants will say.

'Examine zem,' the *Kommandantin* will say, and the ungloved hands will withdraw from his ears as the boots of the lieutenant rap closer to him.

'Hold his head,' the lieutenant will order, and the ungloved hands will return, locking his head between their cool palms. After a moment, one of his ears will be seized and something hard, cold and narrow will slide into his earhole, probing brutally, making his eyes water with pain, then slide out.

'Left ear: nothing, *Frau Kommandantin*,' the lieutenant will announce.

Her boots will circle him, returning on his right, where the ear there will be seized and brutally probed.

'Right ear: nothing, *Frau Kommandantin*,' the lieutenant will announce.

'Very vell. Now ze mous,' the *Kommandantin* will say.

The interrogatee will start to open his mouth, but he will be too slow and strong ungloved hands will seize his jaws from both sides, dragging it up and down, tugging his lips wider as blunt bare fingers slide along his gums and palate and lift his tongue. Then, wiping her fingers on a handkerchief before dropping it to the floor of the platform, the sub-lieutenant who examined the interior of his mouth will turn to the *Kommandantin* and report, 'Nothing, *Frau Kommandantin*.'

'Goot,' the *Kommandantin* will say. 'Ve haff finished. Ve vill –' but another hand will evidently have been raised in the circle surrounding the interrogatee, for she will pause and ask, 'Ja, vhat is it?'

A sub-lieutenant will cough deprecatingly and say, '*Frau Kommandantin*, if you please, we have not examined all his orifices.'

'But vhat remains? Ve haff examined mous und ears. Nipples are too small, also eyes. Vhat remains?'

'There's his urethra, *Frau Kommandantin*. And his rectum.'

'Ureesra? Rec-tum? Vhat are zese?'

'His urethra is his piss-tube, *Frau Kommandantin*. And his rectum is his arsehole. Or rather his arse-chamber.'

'Piss-tube? Arse-chamber? *Ach, ich verstehe. Seine Harnröhre. Und sein Mastdarm. Seine Arschkammer. Nicht wahr?*'

'Yes, *Frau Kommandantin*.'

'Very vell. I sank you for your diligence and devotion to duty. I vas mistaken: ve haff not yet finished. There remain his ureesra und his rectum. His piss-tube and his arse-chamber. *Leutnant* Anna, if you please to examine them.'

There will be a soft grunt as the lieutenant squats to examine his cock. The ungloved hands will fasten on it, one of them holding his shaft steady as the other tugs his foreskin fully back and probes at his urethra, pushing at it hard with the tip of her little finger, but barely entering it.

'Try ze *Ohrensonde*,' the *Kommandantin* will advise.

After a moment's pause, the interrogatee will feel the probe used on his ears suddenly pushing at his urethra, sliding painfully down it, scraping and searing the delicate lining. But the probe will not be long enough to reach the full length and will jerk and stab inches short, then slide forth, leaving his urethra burning with pain and his cock stiffer than ever.

'It is no good, *Frau Kommandantin*,' the lieutenant will announce, letting go of his cock. 'I cannot plumb the full depth.'

'Very vell,' the *Kommandantin* will say. 'Ve vill leave it for *Frau Doktorin*. Now, please to commence wiz his rec–' But she will pause again. Another hand will have been raised in the watching circle. 'Ja?'

'If you please, *Frau Kommandantin*, we do not need to leave it to the *Doktorin*.'

'No?'

'No, *Frau Kommandantin*. If he has concealed anything in his urethra, it will be forced out when he comes.'

'Comes?'

'Yes, *Frau Kommandantin*. If we make him come, that will force anything in his urethra out too.'

'Come? Come und go? Vhat is zis you are trying to say? He hass already come. Zat is vhy he is here.'

'I mean semen, *Frau Kommandantin*. Sperm. He may refuse to urinate, but he cannot refuse to ejaculate.'

'Oh, ja. *Ich verstehe*. Eja-cu-late. *Ausstoßen*. But you say he cannot refuse? Vhy is zis? Is zis ejaculate not of the same kind as urinate?'

'No, *Frau Kommandantin*. Ejaculation is not under voluntary control. If we stimulate him sufficiently, he will come.'

'Very vell. Zen ve vill shtimulate him und ve vill see vhat he hass concealed in his ureesra, if anysing. *Leutnant*, if you please to make ze prisoner ejaculate.'

'At once, *Frau Kommandantin*.'

The lieutenant will squat again with a grunt, seize hold of his cock halfway down the shaft, and start waggling it up and down. There will be silence for a few moments, then the *Kommandantin* will say, as though someone has raised her hand again, 'Ja?'

'If you please, *Frau Kommandantin*.' It will be the sub-lieutenant who recommended making him come. 'Not like that.'

'Not like that? Vhy not like zat? She is shtimulating him. Very soon he vill come.'

'Perhaps, *Frau Kommandantin*, but not soon. It is better to work directly on the glans.'

'Ze glans?'

The lieutenant will still be working futilely on the shaft of the interrogatee's cock.

'The glans, *Frau Kommandantin*. The head of his cock.'

'The head of h– ah, *ich verstehe*. The head of his cock. *Der Schwanzkopf*. Zis is better, for making a man ... come?'

'Yes, *Frau Kommandantin*.'

'Very vell. *Leutnant*, if you please to work on ze head.'

The hand working on his cock will pause, move higher, before settling around the head and taking a firm hold of it, then beginning to pump. The inter-rogatee will gasp and the *Kommandantin* will nod, and look towards the sub-lieutenant who recommended the change of position.

'You vere right, my dear. He vill evidently come wiz much greater ease in zis fashion. *Leutnant*, if you please, a little faster, a little more brutally. Ve are already behind schedule.'

The hand working on the interrogatee's cock will speed up, gripping more tightly, and the interrogatee will groan again, feeling orgasm start to gather in his balls.

'Ja?' the *Kommandantin* will say.

The sub-lieutenant, emboldened by her success, apparently has another suggestion to make.

'And please, *Frau Kommandantin*, if the lieutenant tickles his balls now, it will ensure a more copious ejaculation.'

'Ja?' the *Kommandantin* will say, a little coldly. 'Zis expertise of yours, Kaserine, wiz ze male sexual organs und wiz male ejaculation. Ve shall go into it more fully at a later time. Neverzeless, it hass been useful on this occasion. *Leutnant*, please to tickle his balls. Goot. He iss evidently on ze point –'

Here the *Kommandantin* frequently breaks off, for the pumping hand on the head of his cock and the cool fingertips tickling at the hot, taut skin of his scrotum have often by now had their inevitable effect, and the interrogatee is coming like a horse, spurting creamy sperm in long jets. When the final jet has sprayed forth and splattered into silence, the lieutenant's hand will close around the base of his cock and then slide upwards, forcing the sperm remaining in his urethra up and out. The lieutenant will watch it pour forth, before dripping to the floor, then she will raise her head.

'Nothing in his urethra, *Frau Kommandantin*.'

'Goot,' the *Kommandantin* will say. 'But ze same is not true, I am afraid to say, of my boots.'

The interrogatee, still recovering from his orgasm, will struggle to focus pleasure-blurred eyes, then shiver suddenly back to sobriety. The *Kommandantin*'s glistening black boots will glisten with something other than polish and spittle: they will have been splashed by leaping jets of his sperm.

'Und look,' the *Kommandantin* will continue, 'at ze platform. It is soiled wiz zis brute's foul emissions. Ve cannot leave it in such a state, can ve, *meine Mädchen*?'

The circle of watching *Sturmtruppine* will chorus: 'No, *Frau Kommandantin*.'

'Ve cannot, und must not, zerefore ve vill not. Before ve take him for medical inspection, he shall repair his fault wiz his tongue.'

Then she will break off again, as though another hand has been raised. It has: but it is the same hand as before.

'Kaserine,' the *Kommandantin* will say. 'Since you bear a partial responsibility for ze state of meine boots und of ze platform, I am no longer interested in your suggestions. *Leutnant*, force ze vurm down on his knees. He shall crawl to me und lick my boots clean, zen lick ze platform clean also. Und, of course, vhile he does ze two, ve shall be investigating ze final orifice in vhich somesing may be concealed. Ja, Kaserine: zat vas your suggestion, no doubt? You suspected your *Kommandantin* of overlooking zis most important matter. I forgive your zeal, und grant you ze right of first insertion. *Leutnant*, please to force ze vurm down to his knees, und arse lifted. *Meine Mädchen*, prepare your truncheons.'

The lieutenant who wanked the interrogatee will have put her gloves back on now, and the hand that closes around his neck and forces him roughly down will be encased in leather. Other gloved hands will be unbuttoning the long holsters that sit on the right hips of the Squad, seizing the loops on the handles of the truncheons that sit within, then drawing them forth, glistening with the lubricant with which the lining of the holsters is coated. The interrogatee, now on his knees, the lieutenant forcing him forwards and lifting his arse, will hear the sound of the truncheons sliding forth and look up to see them being lifted in the hands of the *Sturmtruppine*. His half-softened cock will, of course, instantly twitch and begin to re-stiffen.

'You vill all haff a chance to penetrate him, *meine Mädchen*, but first shall Kaserine penetrate him. *Leutnant*, please to raise his arse a leedle higher. Kaserine, shtep forwards und insert your truncheon.'

The sound of Katherine's boots advancing on him from behind will swing the interrogatee's cock fully re-erect in two heartbeats. The lieutenant will be tugging his arse-cheeks apart by now, exposing his hairy arsehole to the blunt head of the truncheon Katherine is already beginning to lower into place. A look of disgust will now evidently pass over her face, because the *Kommandantin* tuts and says, 'Ja, Kaserine. It is disgustingly *haarig*, *nicht wahr*? But he shall be shaved shortly. Please to insert your truncheon wizout furzer delay.'

The interrogatee will suddenly grunt with pain: the truncheon-head has been placed on his arsehole and rotated briskly for a moment, coating his arsehole with lubricant. Then Katherine's strong wrists will force it into him as he grunts again, more loudly. The *Kommandantin* will laugh cruelly.

'Relax, vurm, und let ze leedle truncheon in or else it vill burst your arsehole und be in regardless.'

The interrogatee will grunt again, then groan with pain. Despite the lubricant, the truncheon isn't going to enter him easily.

'A firm srust,' the *Kommandantin* will advise. 'On ze count of sree, *meine Mädchen*. Ready? *Ein!*'

The circle of watching *Sturmtruppine* will take up the count.

'*Zwei!* . . . *Drei!*'

And Katherine's strong wrists will thrust the truncheon with sudden brutal and irresistible force at his cringing arsehole, shouldering it aside and sending the truncheon sliding deep into his bowels. The interrogatee will almost expect to hear a crack of parting flesh as though his sphincter has broken, and will howl with pain and humiliation, his cock jerking ceilingward, his balls tightening to the fork of his thighs. But in almost every case it is too soon after his previous ejaculation for him to come again. Even the delighted laughter of the circle of women around him, chiming through the echoes of his howl, will be insufficient to start his sperm spraying.

'Goot girl, Kaserine,' the *Kommandantin* will say. 'You haff your *kandierter Apfel* vell skewered. Your toffee-apple, *nicht wahr*? Is zere anysing in ze interior of ze apple?'

Katherine will smack her lips meditatively and start to work the truncheon in the interrogatee's arse, jerking it up, down, left, right, rotating it, pushing it forwards, tugging it back. The interrogatee will bite his lip, trying to keep back grunts and groans of pain, feeling his balls ache as his cock strains to release a tribute to the torture his arse is enduring.

'No, *Frau Kommandantin*,' Katherine will conclude. 'I believe nothing is concealed within.'

'Very vell,' the *Kommandantin* will reply silkily. 'But you vill not object, of course, to your *Kommandantin*'s seeking a second, und a sird, und a fors und fifs opinion?'

'As the *Kommandantin* pleases.'

'Sank you. But your *Kommandantin* vill do so later. For now, bring ze toffee-apple to me for ze boot-licking.'

The pain of the truncheon in the interrogatee's arse will suddenly flare as Katherine jerks at the truncheon-

111

handle, signalling him forwards. Whimpering, he will crawl towards the *Kommandantin*'s boots, arse raised behind him, skewered by the cruel truncheon. Katherine will jerk at the handle of the truncheon again and he will groan, feeling his cock bouncing against the taut muscles of his belly.

'Here it is, *Frau Kommandantin*,' Katherine will say as she manoeuvres the interrogatee into position in front of her commander. His arse will be raised high, skewered by the truncheon, his face forced down in compensation, almost scraping the floor of the platform.

'I see it,' the *Kommandantin* will murmur throatily. '*Ein lecker kandierter Apfel*. A delicious toffee-apple. Make it lick my boots, Kaserine.'

'At once, *Frau Kommandantin*.'

The interrogatee will suddenly groan or gasp as Katherine's strong wrist jerks the truncheon in his arse, directing his head up and forwards against the *Kommandantin*'s boots.

'Lick them,' she will order.

Whimpering again, he obeys, beginning to lick the sperm-splattered leather of the *Kommandantin*'s right boot, his mouth filled with the sharp taste of polish. It almost overpowers the briny tang of the sperm that he has to lick and suck off and swallow. At intervals he groans as Katherine, watching closely, jerks the truncheon up or down, left or right, directing his mouth to fresh patches of sperm. When he has finished the right boot, she swings him across to the left. For a moment he is unable to begin, his throat and stomach revolting against the prospect of more polish and sperm; then a threatening jerk of the truncheon in his arse makes him cry out and he opens his mouth and begins licking. Sometimes he will be able to lick for only a moment: the fresh taste of polish and sperm is too much: the stomach of the interrogatee will not merely protest but rebel, and a stream of vomit will rise irresistibly up his throat and into his mouth, filling it. For a moment more he manages to lock it back behind clenched teeth and compressed lips; then it overwhelms him: he's choking, and he has to release it, spewing copiously over the *Kommandantin*'s left boot.

Gasps will sound around the watching circle, but none of them will be louder or more fear-provoking than the cold silence that beats down on him from the *Kommandantin* herself. He will positively feel the rays of her anger beating against his bare back and head and on the buttocks he holds raised to the momentarily forgotten pain of the inserted truncheon. Holding the silence for an expert three seconds, then four, five, six, the *Kommandantin* will break it with a hiss of outraged disbelief, allow it to settle again briefly, then speak: 'Vhat . . . vhat is zis he hass done? Kaserine, vhat hass he done?'

Katherine will stammer when she starts to speak, as though her outrage and astonishment match that of the *Kommandantin*.

'He . . . he . . . he has thrown up, *Frau Kommandantin*. Thrown up on one of your boots.'

'Srown up. On von of *meine* boots? I cannot beliefe it. A second opinion. You, Leonie: vhat hass he done?'

'Thrown up, *Frau Kommandantin*. On one of your boots.'

'You, Amanda. Do you agree?'

'Yes, *Frau Kommandantin*. He has thrown up on one of your boots.'

'Anyvone else? Does anyvone disagree wiz zis? No? Zen it is true. He hass srown up on von of my boots.'

Her voice will grow softer, almost wondering, as though she is still struggling to master her disbelief. Then, as though she has shaken her head and brought herself back to reality, her voice will harshen again, and she will say, almost spitting, '*Ach*, if only zat ve had sufficient time to punish him as he deserves for zis, at ze scene of his crime. But an hour vould not suffice for it und ve must hurry. Kaserine, I vill now seek ze furzer opinions of vhich before I shpoke. Please to wizdraw your truncheon und let *deine Kameradine* probe ze interior of ze delinqvent wiz zeirs. *Sturmtruppine*, please to form a queue wiz truncheons at ze ready. Kaserine, you und Leonie vill supervise ze investigation. Hold him down wiz his arse ready.'

'At once, *Frau Kommandantin*.'

The interrogatee, his face still hovering near the *Kommandantin*'s vomit-splattered left boot, will groan again as the truncheon in his arse quivers and suddenly slides out. Strong hands fasten on his bare flesh, dragging him back, pushing his bare chest against the cold floor of the platform, lifting his arse and tugging his buttock-cheeks apart, preparing him for the gang truncheon-rape that is about to commence. Boots will sound on the floor behind him as the *Sturmtruppine* form an orderly queue, truncheons ready in their strong right hands. When the interrogatee is prepared the *Kommandantin* will clap her hands for attention.

'You vill haff a minute apiece, *meine Sturmtruppine*, und anyvone who discovers anysing suspicious in ze toffee-apple shall haff a veek's leave wiz immediate effect. Very vell? You are prepared? Zen commence at my vord of command. Und please to remember: do not be gentle wiz him.'

The interrogatee will hear boots shift on the floor behind him as the first of the truncheon-wielding *Sturmtruppine* steps forwards, poises the head of her truncheon at his already-gaping arsehole and waits for the *Kommandantin* to order her to slide the truncheon in.

'*Los.*'

The screams of the interrogatee will echo along the corridors and stairs of the station for minutes, and might echo for many minutes more, but the whisper of an approaching train will warn the *Kommandantin* that they have already lingered for too long, and she will snarl another brief order. The truncheon being rammed between the man's buttocks by a thick-wristed *Sturmtruppin* will be withdrawn as brutally as it has been inserted, and he will be lifted from the ground and hung over the broad shoulder of one of the *Kommandantin*'s lieutenants as the Squad forms into marching order once again and then, the *Kommandantin* at their head, marches swiftly off the platform. The floodlights will snap off behind them and the dwindling tramp of their boots will be swallowed in the howl of the train that flashes by the platform thirty or forty seconds later. The Domina values before almost all else the absolute privacy of Her subterranean domain, where She can enact tortures undreamed of, unheard of, unwritten, unknown in the sun-gilded or moon-silvered world above, and Her deputies all know that nothing must be done to threaten that privacy.

The truncheon-buggered man may come again as he bounces over the shoulder of the *Kommandantin*'s lieutenant, the sperm-shiny head of his still-stiff cock irritated over and over against the white or yellow or purple or black leather of her uniform, but the two *Sturmtruppine* marching directly behind the lieutenant will not call her or the *Kommandantin*'s attention to his further delinquency. It will be noted in good time, when they have reached the reception rooms where all new arrivals undergo the medical inspection that is for some the highlight of the first day of their stay, surpassing even the boots and uniforms – and truncheons – of the Reception Squad itself.

Seven

When the lottery winner is brought to the entrance of the Heart of Darkness by the Reception Squad, hanging over the shoulder of one of the *Kommandantin*'s lieutenants, he is often unconscious or semi-conscious, either from the pain in his violated arsehole or from the erotic delirium of his reception, or from both. The entrance to the Heart of Darkness is a broad flight of marble steps leading downwards to the great bronze doors beyond which lies the entrance hall. The doors are decorated with scenes from the matriarchal myths of many nations: Hekate, Kali, Persephone, Lilith, The Fates, The Furies, Morgana, Hel, Medusa, Medea, Circe, The Sirens, Cerrwiden, Isis; and above the doors stand the sculpted metal heads of great women of history, resting with closed eyelids as though in sleep: Tomyris Queen of the Massagetae, Artemisia of Halicarnassus, Boudicca Queen of the Iceni, Pentheseleia Queen of the Amazons, Camilla Queen of the Volscians, Cleopatra Queen of Egypt, Zenobia of Palmyra, Theodora Empress of Byzantium, Wu Zetian Empress of China, Eleanor of Aquitaine, Catherine the Great of Russia, Christina Queen of Sweden, the artist Artemisia Gentileschi, the anthropologist Margaret Mead, the FBI chief Janet Reno, the tennis-champion Martina Navratilova, and the politicians Eleanor Roosevelt and Hillary Clinton.

The Reception Squad will march down the steps and form up a phalanx in front of the doors; after this the *Kommandantin* will stride forwards, her single pair of boots sounding oddly louder than the synchronised crash of the entire Squad's, which will have been ringing in the winner's ears for minutes now as the Squad has marched up from the secret underground station on which he had his reception. If he has been unconscious, he may begin to struggle to semi-consciousness now; if semi-conscious, to struggle back to full consciousness, becoming aware of the strong female shoulder over which he is draped naked, of his hot cock erect and pressed to sticky sperm-soiled leather, his truncheon-raped anus stinging between his buttock-cheeks. As the *Kommandantin* picks up the hammer waiting in an alcove by the doors and strides back to stand for a moment gathering herself before she knocks, he may try to lift his head and look ahead of him, may even see the *Kommandantin* lifting and swinging back the hammer, to bring it forwards with a head-filling crash on the resonant hollow marked by the cauldron of husband-vengeful Medea. The *Kommandantin*'s boots will sound into the echoes of the crash as she returns the hammer to its alcove, then motions the phalanx of the Squad forwards, positioning herself at its apex as it comes. Above the door the sculpted metal eyelids of one of the great female heads will suddenly slide up over gleaming crystalline lenses, and the head will crane forwards and look down, its sculpted metal eyebrows lifting in enquiry.

'Hello? Did somebody knock?' it will ask in an appropriate, electronically filtered accent.

The *Kommandantin* will look up at it, her sharp-peaked cap seeming to defy gravity as the top of her head tilts almost vertical.

'*Der Empfangkommando,*' she will announce. 'Ve bring a criminal for processing.'

At this point another of the heads will occasionally come to life, its eyes blinking open, its neck craning forwards, peering downwards, then turning to call along the row to the first-awakened head.

'Who is it?' it will ask; and the first head will reply, 'The Reception Squad.'

'Well, let 'em in,' the second head will say, and the mechanism of the doors will begin to grind and whirr before the two great valves swing slowly open.

If two heads have awakened the *Kommandantin* will sigh heavily and theatrically before she leads the Squad in with its prisoner, knowing the sigh will be picked up on the microphones the door-guards use, perhaps composing a new memo to the Domina about the harm done by frivolity to the awe-inspiring effect of the Tube-Station Reception. As the Squad marches through the open valves of the entrance door, the sub-lieutenant directly behind the dangling prisoner will be licking her lips, ready to report that he has come across the lieutenant's uniform. When the Squad has stopped in the middle of the entrance hall and the lieutenant has shrugged the prisoner off her shoulder, letting him slither heavily to the cool marble floor and land with a thump, the sub-lieutenant will speak: '*Frau Kommandantin*, if you please!'

The *Kommandantin*, who will have been preparing to meet the *Doktorin* and her medical Squad, will turn, blonde eyebrows lifting.

'Ja?'

'The prisoner, *Frau Kommandantin*. He has come against the lieutenant's shoulder.'

'Vhat is zis?'

The lieutenant will turn to see the sub-lieutenant who has spoken, and her back will swing to face the *Kommandantin*, whose eyes will widen suddenly with anger.

'Ach, it is so. *Leutnant* Patricia: your shoulder is soiled wiz sperm.'

The lieutenant will continue turning, trying to see over her shoulder and look down her back, reaching for the spot with a gloved hand.

'*Nein!*' the *Kommandantin* will bark. 'Do not touch it!'

And now the stiletto heels of the *Doktorin* and the dozen nurses of her medical Squad, having ascended the heavily carpeted stairs that lead to the lower levels of the Heart of Darkness, will begin clattering over the marble of the entrance hall, two of them at the rear pushing a wheeled stretcher that they and two others have just carried up the stairs. But for her large breasts, the *Doktorin* might almost be the *Kommandantin*'s antithesis: petite, slender, elegant; and where the *Kommandantin* is blonde, she is dark, her glossy hair flowing over her shoulders where the *Kommandantin*'s is tucked under her sharp-peaked cap; where the *Kommandantin*'s uniform is leather and cut with severe masculinity over black boots, the *Doktorin*'s is silk and cotton, flowing in feminine curves and ruffles over stockinged calves and stiletto heels; where the *Kommandantin*'s make-up is minimal, almost invisible, and in the palest of shades, the *Doktorin*'s is thick, almost whorish, and bright, almost garish, like the make-up of the Squad of petite, slender, big-breasted, stiletto-heeled, silk-and-cotton-uniformed nurses who come with her.

As the *Kommandantin* hears the sound of their approaching stilettos she will gesture dismissively, leaving the sperm-soiled shoulder of her lieutenant for later, and turn to face the advance of the *Doktorin* and her Squad, bowing her head and clicking her heels together as she throws up a stiff-armed salute.

'*Kommandantin*,' the *Doktorin* will purr. 'Back so soon. Have you lost the prisoner?'

She too will have a German accent, but a fainter one, less brutally obtrusive, merely caressing the vowels and consonants of the English she speaks, not gripping and throttling them as the *Kommandantin*'s accent does. The

Kommandantin's eyes will glitter with pale fire for a moment.

'No. Here he is.'

She will turn, stepping aside a little to reveal the prisoner sprawling naked on his face where he has been dropped by the lieutenant. The *Doktorin*'s eyes will widen with shock and horror.

'But the poor dear!' she will say. 'What have you done to him?'

'He vas wizout papers. He hass srown up over my boot. He hass come on ze uniform of von of my *Leutnants*. How iss you expect zat he be delivered?'

Now the *Doktorin*'s eyes too will glitter with fire, but with dark fire where the *Kommandantin*'s was pale.

'This is no excuse,' she will say, signalling her nurses forwards. 'You have brutalised him most severely.'

'*Ja,*' the *Kommandantin* will reply with satisfaction as the *Doktorin*'s nurses clatter forwards on their stilettos, deserting the wheeled stretcher, pushing past the *Kommandantin* into the ranks of the Reception Squad to where the prisoner lies sprawled on the floor of the entrance hall.

'And you are proud of it,' the *Doktorin* will say accusingly.

'*Ja.*'

One of the nurses is carrying a rectangular medical briefcase emblazoned with a red cross; now she sets it on the floor, ready for use as the others set to work examining the prisoner. Their soft hands will run over his naked body, checking him for bruises, for broken bones and hernias. His cock, which may have softened after he came on the lieutenant's back, will begin to stiffen again, thickening and lengthening against the cool marble floor in tribute to the gentle pressure and stroking of their soft female fingers. Then one of the nurses, who is examining the prisoner's lower back and buttocks, will gasp loudly. The *Doktorin*, who has opened her mouth to throw another angry accusation at the faintly smiling *Kommandantin*, will stop and stare at the nurse who gasped.

'Josephine, what have you found?'

The nurse, her warm brown eyes wide with horror and disgust, will look up.

'*Frau Doktorin*, he has been . . . has been . . . *violated*.'

'Violated?'

'Yes, *Frau Doktorin*. Anally.'

'Anally? *Die Gottin im* . . . Let me see!'

The *Doktorin* will push through the ranks of the Reception Squad too, reaching the prisoner and kneeling with a rustle of soft cloth and a waft of French perfume over him.

'Here, *Frau Doktorin*,' the nurse will say, gently fingering apart the prisoner's buttocks, exposing his gaping and swollen arsehole.

The *Doktorin* will gasp too as she sees it, reaching out to gently slide a fingertip around the rim of the arsehole, provoking a long moan from the prisoner. She will raise the finger to her face and twist it to catch the light, confirming that it is sheened with lubricant. Then she will turn her head to glare at the *Kommandantin*.

'*Du Barbarin*!' she will snarl. 'You . . . you barbarian! You have buggered him.'

The *Kommandantin* is not discomfited.

'Ass I say, he vas wizout papers. He hass srown up on my boot. He hass come on ze –'

'I do not want to hear your excuses! You will be reported for this and I promise you – I *swear* to you – that you will face a court martial.'

'Ass you please,' the *Kommandantin* will say.

'And if he is seriously injured . . .' the *Doktorin* will continue menacingly. 'I will check now. Nurse, a glove if you please.'

'He iss not,' the *Kommandantin* will say. 'He had no more zan sree or four truncheons up him, for no more zan five minutes. Perhaps five truncheons, for six minutes, at most.'

One of the *Doktorin*'s nurses will produce a plastic glove and the *Doktorin*, still glaring at the *Kommandantin*, will hold her hand up, holding her fingers and thumb together as the nurse tugs the glove over it, then splaying them as the nurse tugs it further down, letting it fall into place around the *Doktorin*'s wrist with a crisp little snap.

'You are lying,' the *Doktorin* will say. 'From the look of his poor bottom, I judge that he has been violated by considerably more than five truncheons, and for considerably more than six minutes. I should not in the slightest be surprised if you inserted two or even three truncheons at once. But we will see.'

She turns her face away from the *Kommandantin*, who purses her lips moodily now that the *Doktorin*'s hot, accusing glare has left her face. The *Kommandantin* watches as the *Doktorin* begins to examine the prisoner's arsehole, sliding a plastic-sheathed finger through his gaping sphincter, probing gently at the rectum beyond. The prisoner will shudder and moan, and perhaps try to pull away from the probing finger. The *Doktorin* will order two of her nurses to hold him down if he does, lifting her ungloved hand to pat his naked shoulder, her gloved forefinger still inserted into his anus.

'*Du Armchen*,' she will say. 'You poor little thing. But this is for your own good. I must –' she will continue, sliding her forefinger out so that she can re-insert forefinger and middle finger instead '– I must gather evidence for the trial.'

As she says this, she will turn her head and glare at the *Kommandantin* again for a moment, then turn back to the prisoner, who shudders and moans as she begins to probe deeper with her two fingers, inserting them beyond the second knuckle, gently rotating them, passing her fingertips slowly and conscientiously over the curving wall of his rectum. The *Kommandantin* clicks her heels again and salutes the *Doktorin* as she kneels behind the prisoner conducting her rectal examination.

'I vill leafe you to it, my dear *Doktorin*,' she will announce.

The *Doktorin* will not answer, and the *Kommandantin*'s lips will be touched with a cold smile for a moment. She will turn to address the Reception Squad, walking backwards a few steps to stand well in front of them.

'*Meine Mädchen*! Ve vill salute ze *Doktorin* as she gazers ze evidence for our trial, und zen ve must be on our vay!'

She will then nod and her *Sturmtruppine*, knowing what is in her mind, moving in perfect synchrony with their beloved commander, will raise their left boots and bring them crashing down on the marble floor of the entrance hall, throwing up a stiff-armed salute and shouting, '*Frau Doktorin*!'

The *Kommandantin* will then turn on her heel without another word and lead her Squad away at the goose-step. They will pour away from the kneeling group of nurses around the prisoner like a departing wave that leaves in its wake a cluster of beautiful but predatory seashells ready to begin consuming a crippled fish. The *Doktorin* will listen to the departing crash of their boots, pushing her fingers deeper into the prisoner's rectum, then sniff disdainfully, withdrawing her hand with a soft pop and patting the prisoner's bare shoulder with it, leaving a shining little patch of lubricant.

'Do not worry, my dear. I have found nothing conclusive in your poor bottom yet, but I will try a deeper examination. Nurses, if you please, prepare him. Josephine, I think a little more lubrication will be in order.'

And, as the nurses firmly but gently prepare the prisoner for the full rectal examination, the *Doktorin* will hold up her gloved hand and Chief Nurse Josephine will snap open the rectangular medical briefcase prominently emblazoned with a red cross and remove one of the tubes of lubricant that are all that it seems to contain. She will coat the *Doktorin*'s gloved hand with it, squeezing a white worm of lubricant in spirals around each of the *Doktorin*'s splayed fingers, then crisscrossing her palm and the back of her hand with it before beginning to rub it in thoroughly. The nurses will have made the prisoner lean forwards on his face with his arse in the air, balls dangling beneath his gaping, red-rimmed anus, and four of them will be squatting beside him, two to each flank, holding him firmly in place. When Josephine has finished lubricating the *Doktorin*'s hand, the *Doktorin* will nod with satisfaction and say, 'And a little on his bottom too, if you please.'

She will watch as Josephine squirts some of the lubricant around and into the prisoner's rectum, then come forwards on her knees to him, flexing her gloved hand.

'Do you have a firm grip, girls?' she will ask.

'Yes, *Doktorin*.'

'Good.'

She will position herself behind the prisoner, then say, 'Flora, Bella, if you please.'

Two nurses will come forwards, each kneeling on either side of her and taking hold of a buttock each.

'Open,' the *Doktorin* will say, and they will tug hard.

The prisoner will groan, finally aware of what is about to happen to him, maybe starting to protest. If he does protest, the *Doktorin* will motion to another nurse, who will produce an elasticated bandage and swiftly gag him with it, looping it expertly around his mouth and the back of his head. He will now be ready for the full rectal examination: gagged by one nurse; held down by four more; buttocks held apart by yet two more; anus fully exposed and thoroughly lubricated in preparation for the insertion of the *Doktorin*'s gloved hand. The remaining two nurses, with the nurse who gagged him, will be crowding behind the *Doktorin*, peering over her shoulder to watch the rectal examination.

'Watch his balls, girls,' the *Doktorin* will tell them as she puts her bunched fingers and thumb to the prisoner's arsehole, then slowly starts to push them inside, gradually separating them as she does so, stretching his sphincter, preparing it to accommodate her hand.

The watching nurses hold their breath, then giggle delightedly as they hear the prisoner groan into his gag and see his balls stir and tighten to the fork of his thighs. The prisoner will struggle, trying to break free of the soft hands that are holding him down, but the nurses are well practised and very strong, and only their gently shaking breasts and a slight quickening of their breathing reveal the effort they are having to put into keeping him immobile as the *Doktorin*, the pink tip of her moist tongue poking from one corner of her red-lipsticked mouth, pushes her gloved hand deeper and deeper into his bottom. Perhaps she will pause for a moment, allowing the prisoner's sphincter to adjust to the severe stretching it is forced to endure; but she is too conscientious to stop the examination, despite his muffled moans and the quivers of protest that run through his firmly held body.

'There, there, dear,' the *Doktorin* may say as she prepares for the final push, reaching between his thighs with her free hand and tickling soothingly at the tight, sweating, reddened sack of his balls, 'it will be over in a minute.'

And then, rotating her wrist as she pushes, still tickling and soothing his balls, she will slide her hand firmly and fully into his bottom. Young prisoners, despite the two or three powerful orgasms they have already had in the past half-hour, may come again at this moment, tormented to the brink by the cool tickling fingertips on their balls, then shoved firmly over it as the hand slides into their arses, their cocks squirting hot jets of sperm against the cool marble of the floor. Older prisoners may be unable to respond so liquidly to the sensation of a lubricated, rubber-gloved hand invading their already aching bowels, though they will plainly be powerfully moved by it. If the *Doktorin* hears sperm squirting against marble she will pause and drop her free hand from the prisoner's balls, reaching forwards beneath him, dropping a fingertip into the little sperm-pool now lying beneath his raised belly, lifting it back to hold it up in front of her face and examine it.

'He *is* an excitable boy,' she will say, then wipe her finger on one of his buttocks and resume her examination, pushing her hand deeper into his bottom, rotating it clockwise and anticlockwise, humming a little to herself, maybe glancing up at Josephine and asking, 'Jo, how deep did I get yesterday?' or 'How deep did I get this morning?'

'Beyond the wrist, *Frau Doktorin*,' Josephine will answer, or 'A good part of your forearm, *Frau Doktorin.*'

And the *Doktorin* will nod, pouting a little as she tests the flexibility and size of the arse into which she has inserted her hand, before making her choice. 'Maybe I can do as well with this one, or even a little better,' or 'I don't think I can beat that with this one ... but there's no harm trying. Is there, girls?'

The nurses holding the prisoner, the nurses holding the prisoner's buttocks apart, the nurses peering over the *Doktorin*'s shoulder, all of them will chorus happily, 'No, *Doktorin*!'

The *Doktorin* will nod, and begin trying to beat her record, starting to pull her lubricated hand out of the prisoner's arse, then pushing it forwards again, trying to get a little deeper each time, beginning to fist him thoroughly. As his balls respond to her efforts, she will raise her free hand again and tickle at them, stroking them, nudging them from side to side, and even, as she begins to fist him harder, cupping them in her palm and squeezing them. The faces of the nurses holding the prisoner now are too thickly covered with make-up to show very much sweat, but it will be obvious by now that they are having to work hard to keep him still and submissive for the thorough fisting he is receiving from the *Doktorin*. At last, when the *Doktorin* is satisfied either that she has beaten her previous record or cannot do so, she will pull her hand a little back and begin to massage the prisoner's prostate with her knuckles, preparing him for his fourth or fifth orgasm of the day.

'Come on, dear,' she will say, cupping and squeezing his balls, the tip of her tongue wiggling in one corner of her ripe, red mouth. 'Come for Mummy. There's plenty in these big balls of yours still, I know there is, so let's make a clean breast of it, shall we?'

But even the youngest prisoners will find it hard to perform on demand so quickly, despite the expertise with which the *Doktorin* massages their prostates and manipulates their balls. She will sigh, and continue, 'Oh, we're not going to be stubborn, are we? Mummy doesn't want to get rough with her little boy. Really she doesn't. But if she must . . .'

And she will massage his prostate more firmly, more brutally, beginning not simply to squeeze his balls but to torment them. Some prisoners will respond now, their quivering bodies suddenly stiffening as their protesting balls give up sperm yet again, firing it from their quivering cocks to splash into the little pool of sperm that is already there. The remaining prisoners, those who have come too hard or too often to respond even to a brutal prostate-massage and full ball-torture, will have to be persuaded finally to orgasm by other means. The *Doktorin* will pause in her arse-fisting and ball-tormenting, and look along the double line of nurses holding the prisoner down, then glance over her shoulder at the nurses watching from behind her.

'Mary, dear,' she will say, or 'Tania, dear.'

When the nurse asks, 'Yes, *Frau Doktorin*?' she will say, 'Take Phoebe's place, will you?'

And one of the nurses watching from behind her will move around the prisoner's naked body to take the place of one of the nurses holding him down.

'Thank you, Mary,' the *Doktorin* will say, or 'Thank you, Tania.'

Phoebe, who is easily the biggest-breasted of the nurses, will have stood up, gratefully arching her back, the firm globes of her breasts bouncing beneath her tight nurse's uniform as she relieves the strains of holding the prisoner down.

Now the *Doktorin* will say, 'Phoebe, he's being a little bit stubborn and not making a clean breast of everything for his mummy, so I want you to help him. I think just a little mammary asphyxiation will do the trick. If you could?'

A smile will touch Phoebe's face for a moment, but she is too much of a professional to allow her satisfaction at the *Doktorin*'s words to become too evident, and she walks towards the wheeled stretcher, unbuttoning her tunic as she goes, stilettos clicking on cool marble. When she reaches the stretcher, the last button is undone and she can slip the tunic off and put it neatly over the foot of the stretcher. Now she reaches behind herself for the strap of her tight pink silk bra, her breasts straining forwards. The *Doktorin* watches her patiently, her hand still inserted into the prisoner's bottom. There will be a click as the bra-strap opens, and Phoebe will peel the bra from her breasts.

She will glance down at them for a moment with professional pride, then drape the bra over her tunic and walk back to the group of her colleagues clustered around the prisoner, her stilettos clicking on cool marble. She will stand above and in front of the prisoner's head, lifting first her left foot, then her right, slipping her stilettos off before holding them in her hands as she lowers herself to the floor. Now she puts the stilettos carefully to one side and slides forwards on her knees, taking hold of the prisoner's head and lifting it as she pushes her knees and thighs under his chest. She will glance up the prisoner's body to the *Doktorin*, waiting for final confirmation that she may proceed. The *Doktorin* will nod, and she will push herself forwards a little more, lifting the prisoner's head, fitting his face between her large, soft breasts, planting his nose and mouth firmly in her tit-cleft. She may sigh a little, looking down at the prisoner as she grips the back of his head with her forearms and hugs him to her, sealing his face in breast-flesh.

'Can he breathe, dear?' the *Doktorin* will ask.

Phoebe will shake her head, a smile quirking her red lips.

'Then we'll give him a minute before I recommence fisting and ball-squeezing. Just to get those lungs nicely straining, eh, boysy? On your cue, if you please, Josephine.'

'Yes, *Frau Doktorin*.'

Josephine will slip her nurse's watch from its breast-pocket and watch the second hand make its circuit. The prisoner may already have begun to quiver, his body protesting at the entombment of his face between Phoebe's large, soft breasts, but his cock will have stiffened even further, and the *Doktorin* will feel pre-orgasmic tension begin to gather in the muscles of his buttocks and rectum.

'It's working already, Phoebe,' she may announce, and Phoebe will smile again, feeling the heat of the prisoner's frantic struggles for breath compressing moistly in her tit-cleft. If the prisoner is specially susceptible to this form of torture – a breast or asphyx fetishist or both – he may come of his own accord

130

before the minute is up, simply from the joy of having his face buried between such large, such soft, such cool, cruel breasts; and those who do not come of their own accord often come very, very soon after Josephine has said, 'The minute is up, *Frau Doktorin*,' and the *Doktorin* has begun fisting him again and working at his dangling, supremely vulnerable balls with her strong, skilful fingers. Sperm will squirt again into the deepening pool beneath the prisoner's belly, and the *Doktorin* will smile with satisfaction.

'Good boy,' she will say. 'Good boy. Mummy knew you had it in you.'

Then, timing the withdrawal so expertly that she often prolongs his orgasm by another two or even three spurts, still manipulating his balls, she pulls her gloved hand from his bottom, stretching and tormenting his sphincter for the final time. Then she releases his balls and squats back on her haunches, holding her fisting hand out over the prisoner's back.

'Thank you, dear,' she will say as one of her nurses, without prompting, takes hold of the unsoiled hem of the glove and begins to peel it off, turning it inside out as she does so. 'That's enough, Phoebe. Let him breathe again.'

Phoebe will relax her grip on the back of the prisoner's head, sitting back a little and allowing her tit-cleft to swing open, releasing the imprisoned face. A gush of hot, moist air will hit her own face, rising in an instant, and she will hear the prisoner gasping greedily for air, still overwhelmed with the sensation of orgasm. The glove will come off the *Doktorin*'s hand, turned neatly inside out, and the *Doktorin* will reach again for the prisoner's balls, gently tickling them.

'That was nice, wasn't it, dear? But we'd better get you to the clinic to give you a thorough examination, hadn't we? Let's have him on the stretcher, girls. Face up. I think the poor thing's going to have some difficulty sitting on that poor bottom of his for some time to come.'

Two of the nurses who have been watching the prisoner fisted over the *Doktorin*'s shoulder will rise to their feet now and trot to fetch the wheeled stretcher as Phoebe slides her thighs and knees from under the prisoner's chest, pushes herself back a few inches, then stands up. The nurses who have been holding the prisoner down will alter their grip, taking hold of him under his armpits and hips before half dragging him, half carrying him towards the stretcher. The prisoner will be hoisted into the air and swung over the stretcher, then gently lowered onto it face down as one of the nurses tucks a pillow under his hips, elevating his abused bottom. The *Doktorin* will walk over to him and run her hand down his back, gently stroking his buttocks, pursing her lips as she looks sorrowfully at his gaping arsehole, reaching beneath it to tickle at his balls again, then lifting her hand away and pointing to a set of lifts along the far wall of the entrance hall.

'Well, girls, let's get him to the clinic for a proper examination.'

Two nurses will start pushing the stretcher forwards, the naked body that lies atop it flanked by the other nurses, the *Doktorin* at the prisoner's thigh, occasionally reaching her hand beneath his arsehole to tickle his balls.

'You'll soon be there, dear.'

One of the nurses will trot ahead as the Squad approaches the lifts, pressing one of the lift buttons, and the Squad will not even have to pause, for one set of doors will open immediately, revealing a spacious lift into which the *Doktorin*, her dozen nurses, the wheeled stretcher and the helpless, whimpering, stiff-cocked prisoner fit very easily. Then the doors of the lift will close and lights will begin to wink on and off in sequence above them as it descends to the clinic where the next stage of the prisoner's medical examination awaits him.

Eight

When the doors close the prisoner will feel the centre of his body invaded by the acceleration of the lift as it descends swiftly even deeper into the earth; and a few seconds after he is wheeled into the lift, face down on the soft mattress of the stretcher, the doors will open a hundred feet below and he will be pushed out into the reception area of the clinic. Disturbing hospital smells will meet his nostrils, redolent of doctors' authority and dominance and patients' submission and pain: floor polish, antiseptic, a whiff of chloroform; and a sudden shriek of agony in a male voice, cut short by the slamming of a door, will sound far away down long corridors. The prisoner will struggle to lift his head and look around him, but nurses' hands will be instantly on his neck and shoulders, holding him down as a voice murmurs: 'Keep still, little man.'

The stretcher will rumble across a tiled floor to the reception desk, where a medical secretary waits.

'Good morning, *Frau Doktorin*,' she will say, and the prisoner will be able to hear the broad smile in her voice. 'Are we welcoming a new patient?'

'Good morning, Gwen, dear,' the *Doktorin* will reply. 'Yes, a new patient. Please take his details.'

'Righty-o. Ready when you are.'

The prisoner will moan suddenly, his back stiffening as something cold and metal slips between his thighs, settling under his balls, lifting them.

133

'Testicles two-hundred-and-eighty-three grams, inclusive of scrotum,' one of the *Doktorin*'s nurses may say.

'Testicles two-hundred-and-eighty-three, inclusive of scrotum,' the secretary will repeat, and her fingers will rattle on a keyboard.

The cold something will slip away from the prisoner's balls. His left ball will be gripped gently between cool fingertips, tugged away from his scrotum, and something else cold and metal will touch it at both ends, as though it's being held between gentle pincers.

'Left testicle, longitudinal axis, seventy-eight millimetres,' the nurse may say.

'Left testicle, longitudinal axis, seventy-eight millimetres,' the secretary will repeat, her fingers rattling again on the keyboard.

The fingers gripping the prisoner's left ball will adjust their grip, and the cold metal something will touch the ball from side to side.

'Left testicle, horizontal axis, thirty-one millimetres,' the nurse may say.

'Left testicle, horizontal axis, thirty-one millimetres,' the secretary will repeat, fingers rattling again on the keyboard.

'Left testicle, antero-posterior axis, thirty-four millimetres,' the nurse may say.

'Left testicle, antero-posterior axis, thirty-four millimetres,' the nurse will repeat, fingers rattling.

The cool fingers will then release the prisoner's left ball and take hold of his right, and each measurement will again be echoed by the secretary.

'Right testicle, longitudinal axis, sixty-nine millimetres . . . Right testicle, horizontal axis, twenty-eight millimetres . . . Right testicle, antero-posterior axis, thirty-one millimetres.'

The cold metal something will be withdrawn, the cool fingers will release his right ball, and the nurse's voice will say, 'Lift him, please.'

Cool hands will slip under his hips and thighs and his hips will be hoisted off the stretcher, allowing his stiff cock to swing free beneath him. It will be gripped in cool fingers again, adjusted, held steady as a long metal edge is laid against it. The soft voices and rattle of the keyboard will begin again.

'Penis, erect, longitudinal axis, twenty-two point eight-six centimetres.'

'Penis, erect, longitudinal axis, twenty-two point eight-six centimetres.'

The long metal edge will leave his cock, replaced by the cold pincers that measured his balls.

'Penis, erect, horizontal axis, three point oh seven centimetres.'

'Penis, erect, horizontal axis, three point oh seven centimetres.'

'Penis, erect, antero-posterior axis, two point five-nine centimetres.'

'Penis, erect, antero-posterior axis, two point five-nine centimetres.'

The pincers will leave his cock, replaced by something smooth, flat and plastic that loops around his cock and tightens on it, then slips away.

'Penis, erect, circumference, nine point three-seven centimetres.'

'Penis, erect, circumference, nine point three-seven centimetres.'

The cool fingers will leave his cock again but his hips will still be held clear of the stretcher. He will hear murmurs, the rattle of a metal dish, pouring water, splashes and drips, then suddenly gasp as something wet and freezing is slapped atop his dangling balls and scrotum, rubbed vigorously into them, then passed up and over his cock, wrapping around it, sliding up and down it. It's a sponge, a sponge soaked in ice-cold water. It will mop at his cock, then be withdrawn, leaving his cock dripping ice-cold water, then return soaked with more ice-cold water, mop at his balls again, return to his cock, sliding up and down it, thoroughly soaking it in ice-cold water. Sometimes his cock responds as the nurse wishes it to, by softening, beginning to droop and flag, but more often it remains fully erect, perhaps even stiffening a little more from the icy attention it is receiving. If his cock does go down, the nurse will repeat her measurements and the soft voices and rattle of the keyboard will begin again: 'Penis, flaccid, longitudinal axis, nine point three-two centimetres.'

'Penis, flaccid, longitudinal axis, nine point three-two centimetres.'

'Penis, flaccid, horizontal axis, two point four-seven centimetres.'

'Penis, flaccid, horizontal axis, two point four-seven centimetres.'

'Penis, flaccid, antero-posterior axis, one point eight-three centimetres.'

'Penis, flaccid, antero-posterior axis, one point eight-three centimetres.'

'Penis, flaccid, circumference, seven point four-seven centimetres.'

'Penis, flaccid, circumference, seven point four-seven centimetres.'

But if his cock does not soften, even when sponged with ice-cold water, the nurse will lift the sponge away from it and say, '*Frau Doktorin*, his penis is not softening.'

'No?'

'No, *Frau Doktorin*. Not even a little.'

'Bring him to orgasm again and see whether that helps.'

'Yes, *Frau Doktorin*.'

The prisoner, his hips still lifted clear of the stretcher, will hear soft squeaks and pops as the nurse puts on a pair of plastic gloves, then there will be a few seconds of silence explained when the nurse takes hold of his cock again: one of the gloves, the one that grips the head of his cock when the other has gripped the neck, has been coated with lubricant, ready to work directly on his naked cockhead. It will rub the lubricant in, then grip his cock-crown, beginning to twist at it, almost as though the nurse is trying to unscrew the head of his cock, the smooth plastic of the glove sliding round and back, over and over, slowly rotating him to orgasm as the other hand holds his cock steady. Then the gloved hand will start to pump at his cock-crown, as though it's trying to tug the head of his cock off ... then it will twist at it again ... then pump ... then twist ... pump ... twist ... pump ... twist ... and then the other hand will let go of his cock and drop to grip and squeeze his balls.

He will groan, utterly helpless as these two firm, strong, skilful hands have their way with him, the lower hand squeezing his balls to the rhythm set by the upper hand pumping and twisting at the head of his cock. It will be too much: even the pain in his arse, shafting through him as the muscles of his sphincter tighten with the pleasure the hands are forcing on him, will be seized by his greedy cock to heighten its joy, and he will suddenly start spurting sperm, spraying it, splashing it, on the stretcher beneath his hips. The hands will now release his cock and he will hear the gloves being briskly peeled from them and dropped with hollow thuds into a bin. He will hear water splash and drip again, and then the sponge will be mopping at his cock and balls again. This time, so soon after orgasm, he will almost certainly soften, almost certainly grow flaccid, almost certainly droop and dangle, and the hands can lift the sponge away and return to take the delayed measurements:

'Penis, flaccid, longitudinal axis, nine point three-two centimetres ...'

And when this is finished the hands that have held his hips up will suddenly release him and he will fall back to the stretcher, landing in the cold patch of water from the sponge and still-warm patch of sperm from his own cock.

'Right girls,' the *Doktorin*'s voice will say. 'I think it's time for his bath.'

Stiletto heels will begin clicking and he will feel the stretcher gliding forwards, then hear the creak of a door pushed open ahead of him, then feel the air suddenly moister and cooler on his naked back and buttocks. The door will creak again as it closes, and the *Doktorin* will say, 'Up you get, then, dear.'

But he's still too weak, barely able to turn his head as he lies face down on the pillow, not even flinching as there's a sudden crash of plumbing beside him and water begins to rush into what sounds like a bath, flooding against bare porcelain for the first few seconds, then beginning to churn into rapidly rising water instead. Tiny splashes of it hit his back and buttocks, warm for a moment on his skin.

'Let's get him up, girls.'

Soft hands will grip him. He's tugged, lifted, swung into the air, carried like a child, able to look around him now and see the bathroom into which he's been rolled: tiled green walls and floor, white ceiling and, in the middle of the floor, a large bath into which steaming water is pouring from a large steel tap. But the bath is glass, not porcelain, resting on four gilded lion's feet and with a row of six bronze frogs croaking towards it from the floor on each side. Through the glass and the water he can see, faintly distorted, the lower bodies of four nurses kneeling on the far side between the frogs, watching and waiting for him. Four more nurses are carrying him to the bath; and the *Doktorin* stands supervising.

'And in he goes,' the *Doktorin* says.

As the nurses lower him into the bath he sees a row of brand-new scrubbing brushes propped along the end of it above the tap, then forgets them in the pain of his buttocks and balls meeting the hot water. The hands lower him till his buttocks touch the bottom of the bath, then release him and he's sitting waist-deep in the bath, feeling his drained balls and exhausted cock loosen and float in the hot water.

'Soap him,' the *Doktorin* will say.

The soft hands that have left his body will now return with cakes of scented soap, rubbing him all over, covering him in lather: back and arms and armpits and chest and stomach and flanks and face and scalp. He will have closed his eyes when they started to soap his face, and beneath the water he will feel his cock twitch and slowly, like an exhausted hound responding to the distant cry of the hunting-horn, begin to lengthen and stiffen. The hands splash into the water, lathering his legs and buttocks too, passing between his thighs, rubbing the soap over his cock and balls. One of them pauses, gropes, fingering his cock, testing it for turgidity, and he hears a nurse giggle.

'What is it?' the *Doktorin* asks.

'He's stiffening again, *Frau Doktorin*.'

'Dear me. So soon? What an excitable little boy he is. Well, we'll put a stop to that. Time for scrubbing, girls.'

The hands leave his body again and he sits in the hot water, eyes closed, the upper half of his body covered completely with soap-foam. The tap is turned off and now that the water is no longer rushing and churning ceases he can hear the stiletto heels of the nurses clicking on the tiled bathroom floor as they walk to pick up the scrubbing brushes propped up on one end of the bath. The heels click back and he hears the rustle of soft cloth as the nurses kneel again along both sides of the bath.

'Scrub him,' says the *Doktorin*, and the hands return, armed with the scrubbing brushes, beginning to scrub at his well-soaped skin. He will yelp and feebly begin to struggle, for the brushes are stiff-bristled and wielded energetically, seeking out and scrubbing every patch of his body, particularly, it seems to him, the most sensitive: his armpits, his ears, his eyes, his nipples and navel, his elbows and the backs of his hands.

'Balls and bottom too, girls,' the *Doktorin* says, and the brushes descend beneath the water, splashing vigorously, seeking out the most sensitive spots in the lower half of his body: his buttock cleft, the hollows behind his knees, the soles of his feet, his inner thighs, and his cock and balls.

He's struggling harder now, trying to fend off the brushes, trying to close his legs and protect himself from their relentless bristles, but it's no good: the *Doktorin* orders: 'Stop him'; and some of the nurses drop their scrubbing brushes into the water and grab him, holding him steady and helpless for the still-scrubbing nurses to work on, hoisting him half out of the water so that his bottom and balls are fully accessible. He groans and swears, for all the remaining brushes seem to be working between his legs now, scrubbing the delicate skin of his inner thighs, working hard at his cock, mercilessly at his balls, in long strokes at his perineum, even working into his aching arsehole, sending shafts of pain up into his body. He can open his eyes now and sees as well as feels that his cock has responded to the torture by flowering into full erection. One of the nurses has seized it by the shaft and is working at the bare head with her brush.

'OK, enough, girls,' the *Doktorin* says, and the shock of the sudden departure of the brushes from his body is almost as painful, for a moment, as their continued presence.

The clutching hands release him and his buttocks splash back into the water, hitting the glass bottom of the bath with a gentle shock that sends another shaft of pain up inside him. He sits in the hot water feeling the afterglow of the scrubbing everywhere in his skin and, around his upper waist, the soft nudge-nudge of the scrubbing brushes dropped into the bath by the nurses who held him down. His stiff cock juts up through the soap-clouded water, its swollen head covered and uncovered by the lapping surface.

'Plug out,' says the *Doktorin*. 'Then hose him down with cold.'

A slim tanned arm darts into the water ahead of him where the steel chain of the plug disappears into the water, and tugs, pulling the large black plug out of the water.

'But please, *Frau Doktorin*, what about the special treatment?'

'Do we have time?'

'Yes, *Frau Doktorin*. Plenty of time. Look.'

The water is draining quickly, sliding away from his cock and balls, beginning its first faint gargle as the tip of his swollen cockhead rises free of the surface. For the first time he notices glints of steel beneath the water on both sides of the bath, as though something is protruding from the walls.

'Oh, very well. Did you all drink two pints of water at lunch today?'

'Yes, *Frau Doktorin*,' the nurses will chorus from each side of the bath, one of them adding, 'I had three, *Frau Doktorin*.'

'Did you indeed, Rachel?' says the *Doktorin*. 'Well, you can have first go then, after he's been hosed clean. Get him chained down, girls.'

The water is gurgling loudly away now, barely covering his thighs, and his cock is almost fully exposed, jutting into the air, its glistening shaft scrubbed angry pink. The glints of steel are almost above the surface now too, and as soft hands seize him again, pulling him back and flat to the bottom of the bath, he realises that they are eyelets. Eyelets for the hooks at each end of the cold lengths of steel chain that are now dropped over him, looping across his neck, chest and belly, his thighs, knees and shins, chaining him flat to the bottom of the bath, tightening hard as the hooks are slipped into the eyelets. The back of his head is resting against the warm glass of the bath just where it begins to slope upwards, the last two or three inches of water lapping around his ears as it slides groaning down the plughole. The nurses are kneeling around the bath again, lips oddly pursed, and after a moment he realises that they're suppressing smiles, as though they have some secret they're trying to conceal from him.

'OK, girls, ready to hose him.'

And now the secret is revealed: six hands come forwards over the edge of the bath holding the ends of transparent plastic hoses, pointing them along his body, three to each side.

'Hose, girls.'

The hands suddenly tighten hard on the hoses, but he won't have time to deduce what this means. He will hear distinct puffs of air leave the hoses in the moment before the water bursts against his body, so fast does it rush to meet him, and he may even feel the puffs of air against his skin. But, if he does, he will doubt that he has done so in the next moment, for the shock as the freezing water first lances against him will seem to drive memory back. Two streams of it will be directed direct against his cock and inner thighs, churning in the space between his thighs, and to the pain of impact will be added the pain of the freezing water, aching into the shaft of his cock. The nurses will all be openly smiling now as they direct the streams against his body, hosing him down, and, when he manages to gasp breath back into his startled lungs and start to protest at his treatment, the *Doktorin* will murmur another order and one of the nurses directing water against his face and chest will reach with her free hand for his mouth, folding a soft palm over it and silencing him.

By now he will have started to shiver violently, making the steel chains jerk and rattle, and the warmth

142

preserved beneath his back in the glass will heighten the cold he feels in his chest and stomach and legs. But even though the plug is still out the water will be spraying from the hoses so fast and heavily that the bath will begin to fill again, and the warmth will be taken from him. But the *Doktorin* is not excessively cruel, and after thirty seconds – which will seem to the prisoner like two or three minutes – she will murmur, 'OK, he seems clean enough. But just make sure his balls are, will you, Rachel?'

And a hose will be tugged down into the bath and directed directly against his balls at a range of only a few inches, the force of the water making them shake and wobble, aching with the icy cold.

'OK, enough. Get ready for the special treatment. Rachel, you're first.'

And the six streams of icy water will suddenly be cut off, leaving him lying in the bath blue and shivering, his cock quivering to the movement of his body, his teeth chattering beneath the soft warm palm held over his mouth. Then the palm will be removed and the nurses will stand up and move back from the sides of the bath, stilettos clicking. He will watch them tugging zips down and slipping out of their skirts and knickers, then returning around the bath to look down at him again, his cock twitching as he tries to raise his head and look at neat little triangles of pubic hair each of them is revealing above her pussy. Something moves above him and he looks up and behind himself to see a nurse squatting above him on the end of the bath, knickerless but still wearing her dark stockings, opening her smooth, lightly tanned thighs to reveal the pink lips of her pussy and a triangle of the red hair that peeps from beneath her nurse's cap. His quivering cock twitches, swinging back a little as it stiffens even harder, as though straining, impossibly, to reach the pussy he can see.

'Is the water again drained yet?' the *Doktorin* will ask from where she supervises the pissing session. If the answer is 'Yes, *Frau Doktorin*', she will say, 'Then put the plug back in, will you?' If the answer is 'No, *Frau Doktorin*', she will say, 'Then let it drain and put the plug back in.'

And when the plug is back in, she will say, 'Ad lib, Rachel, dear,' and the prisoner may not even have time to blink as the nurse squatting above him sighs with relief and releases a jet of sparkling yellow piss from the pink lips of her pussy. It may fall full on his face, warm and scented and stinging the eyes he now, a second too late, closes hard. He will hear piss splattering from his face and hitting the side of the bath, then the nurse will piss harder or push her hips forwards and the jet will leave his face and land high on his chest, beginning to move slowly down his body, landing halfway down his chest, then on his solar plexus, a ray of liquid gold, then on his stomach, blessing his frozen skin with warmth, fresh and faintly spiced. Then it's suddenly coming in spurts, not in a solid stream, and he hears the nurse sigh with disappointment as she realises she is unable to piss down his body as far as the tower of his straining cock. Then it's over and, eyes still screwed shut against the trickles of piss running down his face, he will hear the nurse climbing down from the bath.

'Very good, Rachel,' the *Doktorin* will say. 'You nearly did it. You'll get the timing right in the end.'

'Yes, *Frau Doktorin*. I'll drink four pints next time, I promise.'

He hears another nurse climbing up onto the bath to squat above him. Rachel's piss has gathered on the bottom of the bath and he can feel it kissing his cold back, warm, the scent of it rising to his nostrils.

'Yes, but don't get carried away. Now, wipe the poor thing's face, girls, and don't piss directly on it, Kelly. Let him watch as well as wallow.'

The nurse squatting above him giggles.

'Yes, *Frau Doktorin*,' she says.

A damp cloth lands on his face and wipes piss from his eyes, mouth and nose. As it lifts away he opens his eyes and looks up, seeing another pair of slim legs in dark stockings, another pair of splayed and lightly tanned thighs, another pair of pussy-lips, darker pink this time, and another pubic triangle, but thicker, bushier, and black this time.

'Ad lib, Kelly.'

He blinks as the jet of piss springs from the pussy above him, but Kelly is obeying orders and it falls on his chest, not on his face, only splatters of it reaching his chin and wiped-clean lips. Rachel's piss has just covered the lower floor of the bath, sitting warm against his back and buttocks and arms; Kelly's piss will make the pool just a little deeper, a little higher on his skin, thicken the warm, moist air at the bottom of the bath a little more with the steamy spiciness of female piss. He's still shivering with cold, his cock still quivering with the rhythms of it, and the pleasure of the warmth beneath him is almost painful. One of the row of faces looking down on him disappears, leaving a gap as Kelly's piss starts to come in spurts now too, fading quickly. The last lands on his face, splattering there weakly but warmly, like an absent-minded kiss. He was ready for it this time and his eyes are still closed as he hears her climbing down and another nurse climbing up.

'Good girl, Kelly. Ad lib, Imogen.'

He opens his eyes a crack, peering up at a third pair of stockings, a third pair of splayed thighs, a third pink-lipped pussy, a third pubic triangle, honey-blonde this time. He can see drops of Kelly's piss on his eyelashes, catching the light and turning it gold, then Imogen releases her golden-tailed comet, arcing a stream of her piss onto his chest like a warm golden rainbow. Her stream is more copious, darker than

Kelly's or Rachel's, more richly endowed with the fragrant chemicals filtered from her blood by her firm kidneys, treasured in her slowly swelling bladder, and now gifted to him by her piss-hole, a tiny portal above the narrow, sugar-walled gate of her pussy. The piss in which he's lying, Rachel's and Kelly's and more and more of Imogen's, is starting to lap against his flanks, warm as water but richer against his skin. Imogen's piss-trail is starting to come in spurts now too, but as her bladder empties she pisses harder, sending a jet of piss sailing through the air to land with a warm shock directly on his damp pubic hair, splattering forwards against the erect shaft of his cock, which twitches happily, barely quivering at all now, for his shivering has almost stopped.

Then she too is done, leaving him a little deeper in piss, his stomach and chest dappled with golden patches. In one or two places, where it's started to dry, he's itching a little, but the sensation only increases the pleasure in his cock, which twitches again as another nurse climbs up to replace Imogen. He looks up to see pale gold thighs and a pale-pink-lipped pussy, its *mons* faintly pubesced with black velvet. He thinks she's Chinese.

'Ad lib, Tania.'

Out springs the piss-trail, arcing through the air above him, warm and scented and golden, landing on his chest, moving back a little, forwards a little, like a long golden finger rubbing at him, teasing him. His cock is bouncing a little now on his heartbeat, ticking away the half-seconds to his next orgasm. If only he could get one of his arms off the bottom of the bath, reach up through the chains and tug at his cock, his hand still dripping with piss. He tries it, straining against the chains, trying to draw his right arm up and back, but he can't. Tania's piss is coming in spurts, her bladder nearly emptied, and the piss he's lying in doesn't seem to be getting any deeper. It splashes against his back as

146

he struggles to free his arm, then Tania's piss splatters on his skin in a final spurt and she's finished.

'What's he doing, girls?' the *Doktorin* will ask now, and one of the row of heads watching him as he lies at the bottom of the bath will turn and say, 'He's trying to free his hand, *Frau Doktorin*.'

And one of them will add, 'For a wank, I think, *Frau Doktorin*.'

The *Doktorin* will tut and say, 'Poor thing. Well, he can't have a wank, I'm afraid, but two of you can splash some piss over it. Play with him too a little, if you like, but don't let him come. Rachel, I think you and Kelly or Imogen, seeing as you've already pissed on him. Or all three, if you like.'

'Yes, *Frau Doktorin*,' three voices will chorus, and as Tania climbs off the bath, the row of watching faces shuffles a little, as Rachel, Kelly and Imogen change places with the nurses watching above his hips. Then, as a fourth nurse climbs up to replace Tania, six slim arms reach over the edge of bath and six slender hands start splashing piss up and over his balls and cock, soaking them.

'Ad lib, Melanie,' says the *Doktorin*.

Despite the warm piss lapping along his back and legs, the prisoner will shiver, because one of the hands has started to rub piss into the shaft of his cock, working upwards towards the swollen head. Melanie releases her piss-comet, her piss-arc, her piss-bow, and as it splatters on his chest and belly two other hands lift from the piss, carrying piss in cupped palms to tip over the head of his cock as the first hand works its way up. How he will gasp when the first hand reaches its destination: the piss-moistened head of his cock, throbbing with denied orgasm as the cupped hands again tip piss on him! He looks upwards, almost glaring at Melanie's splayed thighs and pink-lipped pussy, lusting for them savagely as she tickles him with her long golden finger. But now she's spurting too, her bladder-treasury emptying, its contents raising the piss in which he's now lying another fraction of an inch.

The hand on his cockhead is rubbing piss into him, working slowly, carefully, irregularly, pleasuring him but not properly wanking him, so that he groans with frustration. The cupped hands tip piss down his cock again and Melanie releases her last spurt of piss and climbs down from the bath. There's another gap in the row of heads, a nurse sliding back on her knees, standing and walking to climb up on the bath and replace Melanie.

'Two of you at once now, girls. Join Pauline, Fiona.'

As Melanie's head fills the gap she left in the row of heads, another gap is created, Fiona sliding back to stand and walk round to the head of the bath. Red-pussied Pauline moves a little to one side as Fiona climbs up beside her, splaying her thighs, exposing her blonde pussy to him.

'Ad lib, girls.'

Two sparkling trails of piss leap out at him, crossing in mid-air, touching, breaking apart in a golden shower that lands all down his body. The hand on his cockhead is rubbing piss into his piss-hole, wood to the forest, coals to Newcastle, sand to the Arabs, and the thought of sand in his piss-hole, irritant, painful, makes his balls tighten, lifting a little from the warm piss in which they are dangling.

'Look out,' one of the watching nurses will say, 'his balls are tightening.'

The hand working at his cockhead will pause.

'No, it's OK.'

But the hand lets go of him, leaving his cockhead moist with piss. Pauline's and Fiona's piss-streams are still falling on his chest and belly, just starting to come in spurts, and he must be lying in two-and-a-half inches of piss now. The other hands on his cock let go too, and he can feel the first tickle of irritation on his cockhead as the piss there starts to dry. There. Pauline's and Fiona's piss-streams are coming in definite spurts, their bladders nearly emptied onto him, and he tenses, ready to screw his eyes shut if a final spurt or two lands on his face. None does; the two nurses start to climb down, and the *Doktorin* will order another two up. 'Good girls. Rose and Zoë, your turn.'

Which would make it a dozen nurses, a dozen pairs of gold-tanned thighs splayed above him, a dozen pink-lipped pussies peeping, a dozen piss-streams leaping. Rose and Zoë climb up onto the bath, squatting ready to piss on him, and he looks up to see a black-capped and a brown-capped pussy above pink pussy-lips.

'Ad lib, dears.'

And they release their bladders, hurling golden streams of piss at him, goddesses slaying a helpless prey with liquid spears. One of them, out of perversity or disobedience, aims directly for his face, landing her thick warm piss-stream on the bridge of his nose, shifting it forwards and back a little, up his nose to his forehead, down his nose to his mouth and chin, while the other piss-stream patrols his chest and belly, break-ing against him to slide down his flanks into the deepening pool under his back and buttocks and legs. The piss is rising around the back of his head now too, almost deep enough to begin to cover his ears, and he longs for the hands to return to his cock, to baste it again in piss, to massage the piss in, anointing his shaft and cockhead with it. His balls, half-submerged in piss, hoist themselves upwards at the thought of it, and then Rose's and Zoë's piss-streams are coming in spurts, and the perverse nurse, the one who pissed directly onto his face, is trying to direct hers down his body in the final second or two her bladder is allowing her.

Then it's done, and, eyes still screwed shut, he hears them climbing down. Then he will hear stilettos on the tiled floor of the bathroom and sense the *Doktorin* peering over the rows of heads into the bath.

'Good girls,' she will say. 'But that's not really deep enough, is it? The poor dear's not even half-submerged yet. Josephine, have reception put out a GPC, will you?'

'Yes, *Frau Doktorin.*'

More stilettos click on the tiled floor of the bathroom, but moving away this time, and he will hear the door open and close.

'While we're waiting, girls,' the *Doktorin* will then say, 'you can splash him.'

'Yes, *Frau Doktorin,*' they chorus, and then what seem like dozens of hands are brushing his skin, reaching down the walls of the bath to scoop up the piss lying beneath him and splash it over his body. Over his face too. Over his cock and balls again, and his cock twitches with frustration when no hand closes on its shaft or cockhead and rubs the piss well in. They're only splashing him, only keeping his skin moist with piss while Josephine has reception put out a GPC. Then it comes: a high tone sounds on speakers outside the bathroom, echoed a fraction of a second later by a high tone from speakers further away, and further away, and then a voice starts to speak, and starts to speak, and starts to speak: 'Attention please. Attention please. This is a general piss-call. Will all available personnel please make their way to bathroom 18P in the medical centre. Attention please. Attention please. This is a general piss-call. Will all available personnel please make their way to bathroom 18P in the medical centre. Thank you.'

Then the speakers are switched off and a couple of seconds later, through the splashing of the busily working hands, he will hear the door pushed open again and the stilettos clicking back across the floor.

'Thank you, Josephine,' the *Doktorin* will say. 'Would you like to take your turn now, before the rush begins?'

'Yes, *Frau Doktorin.*'

And through the busy splash of the hands he will hear Josephine climbing up on the bath and imagine her opening her thighs, baring her red- or blonde- or black- or brown-capped pussy to his piss-splattered face, her aching bladder aching suddenly far worse in the moment before she is allowed to release it.

'Ad lib, dear.'

He didn't think he would feel the piss-stream bursting on his body, not when the hands are splashing him so copiously, but he does: not only is it falling on him from height, it's warmer too, for even in the few minutes the piss of the other eight women has been lying at the bottom of the bath it has begun to cool. Josephine's is fresh and piping hot, pouring direct from her bladder, bursting against his chest and belly like a ray of liquid sunlight or a golden shower of tropical rain released from sun-bathed clouds. There's a noise outside the bathroom door: a confused chatter of women's voices and clatter of stiletto-heels, then the door is pushed open and the voices are suddenly much louder, the heels almost deafening on the floor as the general piss-call is answered and the first of the available personnel enter the bathroom. Josephine's piss is coming in spurts now, falling warmly against him, and in another second she'll have finished.

'OK, girls,' the *Doktorin* will say quietly, speaking to her nurses. 'You can leave that now.' Then, raising her voice as the hands stop splashing piss up and over him and the last spurt of Josephine's piss falls against his body, she turns away from the bath and addresses the chattering, giggling newcomers: 'Ladies! Please, ladies!'

Is she holding her hand up for silence? Dominating the room by sheer force of personality? Ah, he thinks she is, hopes she is, knows she is; for the room is suddenly silent and the faint sounds Josephine makes as she climbs down from the bath seem unnaturally loud.

'Thank you, ladies. Now, I'm sure most of you are familiar with the GPC, but for the benefit of any new

151

employees I'll run through it again quickly. Are there any new employees? Raise your hands, please, dears. You, dear? And what's your name?'

He hears a young woman say, 'Sandra.'

Then someone whispers something and he imagines Sandra being pinched, for she squeaks and says hurriedly, 'Sandra, *Frau Doktorin.*'

'Thank you, Sandra. Anyone else? You, dear? And your name is?'

'Alison, *Frau Doktorin.*'

'Very good. And you two, dears? Your names?'

'Chloë, *Frau Doktorin.*'

'Janet, *Frau Doktorin.*'

'And is that it? Oh, and you too, dear. Your name?'

'Naomi, *Frau Doktorin.*'

'Very good. Well, Sandra and Alison and Chloë and Janet and Naomi, you'll soon get used to all this. You've just answered a general piss-call, or GPC for short. We put one out regularly when we have a new internee, such as the one we have here. Come and have a good look. The rest of you, if you'll just let the new girls come forwards? Thank you.'

He can hear murmurs and the brisk click of stilettos on the tiled floor of the bathroom. The new girls are coming forwards to look into the bath. He opens his eyes a little, trying to blink away the piss still clinging to his lashes, and there they are, staring down on him, two on one side, three on the other, a blonde, two redheads, a brunette and a blackhair, with pretty young faces, discreetly made up, and wearing expressions of disgust and disdain. But one of them, the blackhair, has a rather cruel smile on her face instead, and her eyes widen a little as they rest on his cock. What is she thinking of?

'Do you see, girls?' the *Doktorin* asks.

The eyes of the two women on his right look up, away from him, towards the *Doktorin*, and the heads of the three women on his left turn to look behind them. The five women chorus, 'Yes, *Frau Doktorin*.'

'And what do you think of him? Chloë?'

'I think he's disgusting, *Frau Doktorin*. Lying in piss with a hard-on. He's perverted.'

Chloë is the blonde.

'Hmmm? And you, Alison?'

'Definitely perverted, *Frau Doktorin*. Lower than a Tory MP. Lower than a Tory MEP, even.'

One of the redheads.

'Very eloquent, Alison. And you, Sandra. What do you think?'

'He's sickening, *Frau Doktorin*. But I didn't notice any hard-on.'

Sandra is the blackhair.

'No?' says the *Doktorin*. 'Then look again, Sandra. It's there, I promise you.'

He sees the blackhair glance back into the bath, sees her nostrils flaring with disgust, then sees her look back at the *Doktorin*.

'It's more like a toothpick than a hard-on, *Frau Doktorin*.'

'Good, Sandra. Very good. Excellent disdain. And you, Naomi. What did you think?'

'I agree with the others, *Frau Doktorin*. He's a disgusting pervert. A normal human being shouldn't be sexually aroused by being pissed on.'

'Right-oh. And you, Janet?'

'I agree too, *Frau Doktorin*. But he isn't a normal human being, is he? He's a man. They're all disgusting perverts. But especially this one, I would say.'

'Excellent, girls. You're coming on very well. So, we have our disgusting little pervert lying in the bath in about three inches of piss, but that's not anywhere near enough, is it? So what do you think we should do? Sandra?'

'Piss on him till he drowns in it, *Frau Doktorin*. I think there are enough of us here for that.'

'I admire your enthusiasm, Sandra, but you're getting a little carried away. Drowning him in piss is taking things a little too far, at least on the first day of his internment. And you're forgetting, I think, that he'd certainly enjoy it.'

'I'm sorry, *Frau Doktorin*.'

'No need to apologise, my dear. Enthusiasm never goes amiss, as you may yourself hear a very special person tell you herself one day.'

He sees the smooth glossy bell of Sandra's black hair shake a little, as though with excitement. What did the *Doktorin* mean? Who was the very special person?

'Anyone else? Suggestions?' the *Doktorin* continues. 'Chloë?'

'I think we should all piss on him, *Frau Doktorin*, but not drown him. Not on the first day of his internment.'

'OK. What do you others think? Alison? Janet? Naomi? Do you agree with Chloë?'

He sees heads nod and hears the three others murmur agreement.

'Good. You're right, Chloë. That's the solution. That's what a general piss-call is all about. When we need a pervert covering in piss, *submerging* in it, we invite all available personnel to come and piss on him. That's why She likes everyone to keep topped up during the day, as it were, particularly around this time in the afternoon, when the piss-calls generally go out. Are you five all topped up?'

He sees them nod again and hears Alison say, 'I'm bursting, *Frau Doktorin*.'

Naomi adds, 'Me too.'

'I'm glad to hear it, girls. And so you can have first piss, after you've seen how it's done. Tansy, you and Ruth come and show the new girls how it's done. And Wendy, can you just fetch the piss-snorkel? Take the other three new girls with you, so they know where it is.'

'Yes, *Frau Doktorin*.'

'Good. And –' he can hear how she turns to address the whole room again '– the rest of you, if you'll just be getting your skirts and knickers off, ready for pissing on him. Thank you.'

The bathroom is suddenly full of noise again: the clatter of shoes on the tiled floor, as Wendy takes three of the new girls with her to fetch the piss-snorkel; giggles and whispers as the newcomers slide their skirts and knickers down and line up to piss on him as he lies chained in the bath; the familiar sound of two women climbing up on the end of the bath to squat above him, opening their thighs to reveal their pubic triangles and the lips of their pussies. But only one pussy is pink-lipped this time: one of the women, Tansy or Ruth, is black, and the lips of her pussy will be dark chocolate beneath a neat triangle of crisp black pubic curls.

'Ad lib, girls,' the *Doktorin* will say, and yellow piss will leap from the pink-lipped pussy and the chocolate-lipped one, landing warm on his chest and streaming off him to deepen the pool of piss in which he's lying.

'Do you see how it's done, girls?' the *Doktorin* says to the two new girls, Alison and Naomi.

'Yes, *Frau Doktorin*.'

'Good. Then you're up next.'

He hears the door open and stilettos click over the tiled floor towards the bath.

'Ah, Wendy,' says the *Doktorin*, 'have you got it? Good. When Tansy and Ruth have finished you can put it on him. He's going to need it very shortly, I think.'

Pink-lipped-pussied Tansy's-or-Ruth's piss is coming in spurts now, but chocolate-lipped-pussied Ruth's-or-Tansy's is still going strong, arcing into the bath, splattering onto his chest, streaming over his skin, running down his flanks to trickle busily into the piss-pool beneath his back. Tansy-or-Ruth releases a final spurt, nearly landing it on his face, and Ruth-or-Tansy's piss is coming in spurts now too. There. Hers comes in a final spurt, landing on his face as he screws his eyes shut, and then both women start to climb down from the bath.

'OK, Wendy,' the *Doktorin* says, and one pair of stilettos approaches the bath.

He risks a peek through the piss-drops soaking his eyelashes and sees a brunette leaning over the edge of the bath, reaching down for him with a diving-mask and oddly angled snorkel in her left hand. Her right hand wipes piss from his eyes then slips under his head, lifting it as she puts the mask and snorkel on him, adjusting the mask over his eyes, pushing one end of the breathing tube into his mouth. A little of the piss on his lips comes with it as she pushes it in and as he bites down on it and starts to breathe through it he can taste it, sharp and salty beneath the blunter taste of the rubber. Then the hand lowers his head to the bottom of the bath again and through the glass oval of the mask he watches as the woman leans out of the bath and walks away.

'OK, Alison and Naomi. Up you get and do your stuff. Don't worry about pissing on the end of the snorkel. It's got a little ball in it and nothing will go down, so you'll only stop him breathing for a while, and he might quite like that.'

Alison and Naomi, skirts and knickers off, are climbing onto the end of the bath.

'Yes, *Frau Doktorin*,' they say, squatting there, splaying their thighs, but the glass oval has faintly steamed over for a moment and he can't see their pussies properly. One of them, Alison, too eager, releases a sudden shaft of piss, and he sees it arc down at him and splatter on the glass in a thousand golden droplets. He breathes in through his nose and the glass clears and he can see up between their splayed thighs to the pink-lipped pussies spangled with the golden droplets on the glass. Alison is saying something.

'Sorry, *Frau Doktorin*.'

'Quite all right, dear. As I told you before, She never disapproves of enthusiasm in the right cause and She will be delighted to hear how eager you were to piss on the wretch. But now, ad lib.'

And Alison sighs with relief and pleasure as she releases her bladder for the second time, pissing down on him, landing the stream full on the mask of his piss-snorkel as Naomi pisses more conventionally onto his chest. Alison is trying to land piss on the open end of his breathing tube, which stands as erect as his cock and will allow him to breathe even when the piss inside the bath has covered his face and he lies inches deep in cooling female piss. There: even as her bladder empties and her piss starts coming in spurts, Alison has succeeded, landing a spurt of piss directly on the breathing tube, cutting off his air for a moment. Then they're climbing down, both of them, and two more women are climbing up, quickly and efficiently.

'Ad lib, girls,' the *Doktorin* says, and they start pissing.

The glass of his mask is still covered with Alison's piss and he sees their splayed thighs and pink-lipped, piss-spouting pussies through a golden haze, as though he's looking at them through a glaze of treacle. But his mouth is full of the taste of rubber, thicker on his tongue all the time, and his lungs feel full of it as he breathes in and out through the tube. The women finish, climb down and are replaced, and the *Doktorin* says, 'Ad lib, girls', and the two new women start pissing on him. The piss beneath his body is already deeper, lapping higher around his flanks, and he doesn't think it will be long before it's creeping up and over his hips, starting to rise and flow over his chest, kissing and kissing against the point of his chin as it slowly and inexorably rises to cover him, to submerge him in piss. It's still warm, but it's getting cooler now too, and each new double stream of warm, fresh piss will make less and less difference, till he's lying submerged in it staring up at the world through a two- or three-inch sheet of yellow, salty, cold female piss.

The two new women's piss is coming in spurts, then has stopped, and they climb down to be replaced. He wonders how many pints of piss it takes to fill the bath, how many bladderfuls of piss it takes to make a pint. A female urolagnic might be luckier, lying chained and piss-snorkelled at the bottom of a glass bath and pissed on by men. Ten or a dozen of them could stand around her at once, cocks out and pissing down onto her, replaced by other men from the eager queue waiting behind them as soon as their larger bladders were emptied. She would be submerged in minutes, maybe, her white body shimmering through the warm golden depths of the piss. But that would be crude, uncouth, like male sex in general. Always rushing at things, always eager for orgasm. This was better. More subtle, a prolonged piss-submergence, stretching pleasure over half an hour, maybe even an hour, as double streams of warm female piss arc down on him and he is slowly covered in it.

The only problem is that the piss is getting cold. As the two new women empty their bladders, climb down, and are replaced, he feels that this is definitely starting to become a problem. The higher the piss rises against his body, the cooler it's getting and the less exciting it seems. No longer piping-hot from a woman's bladder, squirted seconds before from a pink-or-chocolate-lipped pussy, but lukewarm, Laodicean. Just a yellow, salty fluid, not piss, not truly, dick-stiffeningly piss. Only the double streams that burst hot and fresh on his body are truly that. But as the latest double piss-streams begin to come in spurts and he waits, hoping that one of them would land atop his mask, the *Doktorin* seems to read his mind, for she says, 'Josephine, I think he might be getting a little *cold* in there, the poor thing. Take the temperature of the piss he's lying in.'

'Yes, *Frau Doktorin.*'

Stilettos click on the floor and he turns his head to watch Josephine walk towards him, her slim right hand slipping a thermometer out of pocket over her large left breast. She kneels beside the bath, her skirt sliding up her dark-stockinged legs with a silken whisper to reveal that she's not put her knickers back on, and reaches over and into the bath, slipping the thermometer into the piss in which he's lying. With her free hand she flips up the silver watch lying under her left breast and watches it with professional calm for thirty seconds. Then she withdraws the thermometer, shakes off drops of piss, examines it and looks over her shoulder towards the *Doktorin.*

'Twenty-five point three degrees, *Frau Doktorin.*'

Two other women have climbed up on the end of the bath, splaying their thighs above him, and he looks up at them now, his cock ticking a little faster as he sees two more pussies, one pink-lipped between the lightly tanned thighs of a white woman and another chocolate-lipped one between the dark brown thighs of an Indian girl. They're looking towards the *Doktorin,* waiting for permission to begin.

'That doesn't sound too good, Jo. Yes, ad lib, girls,' the *Doktorin* says, and the two women start pissing on him.

'Jo,' the *Doktorin* continues, 'take the temperature of this fresh piss. I suspect it will be much higher.'

'Yes, *Frau Doktorin.*'

Josephine turns back to the bath, shaking the thermometer hard, then slipping it under the streams of piss as they fall onto his chest. He tries to raise his head and look at it, to see the line of mercury lengthening like a stiffening cock, but he can't, not properly, and perhaps it's not mercury anyway. All he can see through the piss-gilded mask of his piss-snorkel is Josephine's slim white hand holding the thermometer steady in the streams of piss. Drops of piss are splattering up from his chest and landing on the hand, as though golden warts are sprouting on it everywhere, but she doesn't seem to mind. As the piss-streams break and start to come in spurts, she lifts the thermometer and takes the reading.

'Thirty-one point eight, *Frau Doktorin*,' she says.

'Right,' says the *Doktorin*. 'It's much as I suspected. Time to fire up the frogs, I fancy. Angie and Rukhia, can you do the honours?'

The white girl and the Indian girl are climbing down from the bath. They say, 'Yes, *Frau Doktorin*,' but he doesn't understand what the *Doktorin* has ordered them to do. Fire the frogs around the bath? What does that mean?

Josephine has shaken the thermometer again and is about to wipe it and her hand with a white handkerchief, but the *Doktorin* continues, 'Hold on, Jo. Take his temperature first.'

Josephine stops moving the handkerchief towards the thermometer and looks back over her shoulder.

'Rectal or oral, *Frau Doktorin*?'

'Both, dear.'

'OK.'

She slips the handkerchief away and turns back to the bath. As she reaches into it again, pushing the thermometer towards his mouth, the *Doktorin* says, 'What's wrong, girls?' and one of the two women who have just pissed on him says, 'We haven't got any lighters, *Frau Doktorin*.'

'Ah. Who's got one? Mandy? Good. Throw it over. What about you, Sonia? You've given up? Oh, good, you, Violet. Throw it over.'

Light flashes on something flying through the air from the patiently waiting queue of women, and the Indian girl who has just pissed on him moves forwards and catches the lighter neatly between two hands. Light flashes again as another lighter flies over, but this one is thrown too hard and too high and the white woman's jump and raised hands are too late. It hits the inner wall of the bath an inch or two from the rim and drops with a splash into the piss near his left hip. Josephine is pushing the thermometer into a corner of his mouth, sliding it between his lips, poking it past the mouthpiece of the piss-snorkel, and he can taste the piss on it as it settles on his tongue.

The white woman is leaning over the bath, reaching down into it to retrieve the lighter, her hand brushing his flank as she puts it into the piss and scrabbles for the lighter. She finds it, lifts it dripping from the piss, shaking piss off it, then tests it. He sees a flame spring from it as she flicks her thumb at the wheel. Two more women are climbing onto the bath, ready to piss on him, and Angie and Rukhia are crouching on opposite sides of the bath, pressing the head of a frog with one hand while they hold the lighter ready in front of the frog's mouth. What are they doing?

'Ad lib, girls,' says the *Doktorin*.

The twin streams of piss arc down on him before he even thinks to look up and see the splayed pussies between the smooth thighs. But as he does so, seeing two white women above him this time, the twin flames of the lighters spurt on either side of him, shining through the glass walls of the tank, and there's a sudden blue flame burning from the mouth of each frog, licking at the glass wall of the bath directly against the piss lying there. As he turns his head and looks at the frog on his left, the one lit by Angie, he sees that the flame has left an odd patch of condensation on the glass, its upper edge rising over the level of the piss, but it's disappearing fast and when he turns his head and looks on the other side, at the flame lit by Rukhia, there's no patch of condensation there. The two women have shuffled along to the next pair of frogs, each pressing the frog's head with one hand while holding the lighter out ready in front of its mouth with the other. There must be a button on its head, releasing gas, and when the gas was burning the button must stay on as they move along to the next frog.

There. The lighters have spurted flame again and two more frogs are croaking blue flame at him, leaving patches of condensation for a moment on the sides of the bath as Angie and Rukhia move down to the next pair of frogs. The piss falling on him from the two women is coming in spurts, and Josephine has let her breast-watch fall from her fingers and is leaning over the bath again, reaching for the thermometer she left in his mouth. Spurts of flame from the lighters again, and two more frogs are croaking blue flame at him. He can feel shifting patches of heat on his skin where the first four frogs are croaking flame against the glass walls of the bath: the piss is starting to get hot and convection currents are carrying the heat away from the wall. Josephine pulls the thermometer from his mouth and raises it to read his temperature.

'What is it?' the *Doktorin* asks.

'Thirty-two point seven,' Josephine says.

'Fine. Now take his rectal temperature.'

There come more spurts of flame from the lighters as the thumbs of Angie and Rukhia spin the lighter-wheels, and two more frogs are croaking blue flame at him. Only two left now. The patches of heat on his skin are starting to get bigger and hotter and where the frogs are croaking flame against the glass walls of the bath he sees faint wisps of steam beginning to rise from the piss. The two women above him have emptied their bladders and are climbing down. Josephine's reaching down his body, pushing her hand into the piss by his hip then sliding it underneath him, ready to poke it up his arse. He hears her say 'Oh!' softly, as though something has startled her. Two more spurts of flame from the lighters and the final two frogs, the ones near his feet, are croaking blue flame against the glass walls of the bath. Josephine has taken her hand out of the piss but leaves the end of the thermometer in it, watching carefully. Two more women are climbing up onto the end of the bath to piss on him. Josephine pulls the thermometer out of the piss and looks at it, then turns to address the *Doktorin*.

'*Frau Doktorin*?' Josephine asks.

'Yes, dear?'

'The piss is getting too hot. The frogs are set too high.'

'Yes? Ad lib, girls.'

And twin streams of piss start falling on him again. The piss has risen high enough to cover his shins and lower thighs now, leaving his knees like islands, and tongues of it have almost met across his belly and hips. But the patches of heat on his skin are painfully hot, and the wisps of steam rising from the surface of the piss have thickened and become steady, almost veiling him inside the bath.

'Yes, *Frau Doktorin*. It's already almost at forty degrees.'

'Right, I see what you mean. We don't want to boil him alive. Angie, Rukhia, the frogs are set too high. Adjust them, will you?'

'Yes, *Frau Doktorin*.'

And as two bladders above him empty and the piss falling on his chest starts to come in spurts again, Angie and Rukhia crawl back along the line of frogs, pausing at each, fingers working on a different part of the head for a moment, then crawling to the next, leaving the flame burning much more gently, not so much croaking out at the sides of the bath now as puffing out at it. All the piss along his flanks and down his legs and around his feet and shoulders is hot, almost painfully hot, and he can feel the contrast with the cooler piss still lying underneath him and between his legs. But as soon as the flames are trimmed back he can feel the currents in the piss weaken. He's not going to be boiled alive. He's just going to lie in lovely warm piss. Josephine reaches back into the bath, putting her hand into the piss by his hips then sliding her hand underneath his buttocks, ready to poke the thermometer into his anus, and two more women are climbing onto the bath above his head, ready to piss down on him. The piss is going to get higher. And higher. And higher. Soon, very soon, he's going to be submerged in piss. Warm piss. Lovely warm piss.

'Ad lib, girls,' says the *Doktorin*.

Nine

It will usually be the 22nd and 23rd pairs of women who submerge him completely in piss: after the contributions of piss-pair 20 and piss-pair 21 the piss will be lapping across the glass of his piss-snorkel, not quite covering it. The contributions of piss-pair 22 and piss-pair 23 will tip the balance, so that piss covers the glass completely, even when he tries to raise his head. Now he will be completely submerged – every inch of him, except for the five or six inches of his cock, jutting up from the piss that covers his hips and thighs, still stiff at the excitement of being chained in the bath and pissed on. His ears will have been covered by piss-pair fifteen or sixteen, and he will no longer be able to hear the instructions of the *Doktorin*, though he will, just barely, be able to hear the click of heels on the tiled floor of the bathroom as women walk to the bath to climb up on it and piss down on him from splayed thighs, or walk from the bath, having climbed up on it and pissed on him.

So he won't hear the *Doktorin*'s final instructions, when piss-pair 36 or 37 have pissed on him and the piss is two or three inches deep above the glass of his piss-snorkel. The *Doktorin* will come forwards and look down into the bath, seeing his body distorted beneath the golden piss that covers it, and nod with satisfaction.

'Very good, girls. Now, we can leave him to simmer. Alison and Naomi, you can stay and watch over him.

Keep the frogs trimmed properly – the gas pressure isn't quite as reliable as it should be, I'm afraid. Very well?'

'Yes, *Frau Doktorin*,' Alison and Naomi will say, and Alison's face will be touched, just for a moment, like a glitter of sunlight on ice, by a cruel smile.

No, the prisoner submerged in the bath won't hear any of this, but he will hear the mass clatter of heels as the bathroom empties, the *Doktorin* thanking the secretaries and dungeon supervisors again for the promptness with which they responded to the general piss-call and reminding her nurses when they will have to report back to the bathroom for the next stage of the prisoner's induction. And then he may hear the door close and, sensing the silence that now surrounds him, suppose that he has been left alone in the bathroom to lie in warm, gently steaming piss. But he will be wrong, and he will hear that he is wrong as stiletto heels click again on the tiled floor and Alison and Naomi come forwards to the bath to examine their charge. He will look up and see them and may be struck, even through the two or three inches of piss covering the glass of his piss-snorkel, by something in the way they stand looking down on him, one on either side of the bath.

For there will be something menacing, somehow, in the way they stand. Their piss-gilded faces will be stern and thoughtful, and, even if his slow male brain does not inform him what thoughts are working behind them, his cock may do so. It may twitch and stiffen harder, and he will suddenly realise that they are looking down on him hungrily, like spoiled rich girls with a vulgar new doll. The doll cannot be kept, but it can, while it is destroyed, be played with. And so even under the warm piss he will feel himself shiver, the head of his cock blurring with the movement. A sense of his situation will rush in on him fully for the first time. He is helpless: utterly helpless. Utterly, utterly, utterly helpless. Lying chained at the bottom of a glass bath, inches deep in female piss, breathing through a narrow rubber tube. Unable to move, unable to call out for help, unable to do anything but submit to whatever awaits him at the hands of these two cruel young women who stand on either side of the bath looking down on him with stern, thoughtful faces.

And then they will look up at each other and he will see their eyebrows rise and their mouths move. What are they saying to each other? What are they discussing? What are they deciding on? He cannot hear, but he will know, soon enough. Ah, now they are laughing, and one of them is glancing into the bath again, but not at his face, at his cock. He feels it twitch and the woman who is looking at it laughs again, and says something that makes the other woman look at his cock too. Now they walk down the bath a little, opposite his cock, and lean over, reaching down to let their cool fingertips trickle down the hot, piss-itchy skin of the shaft. They look back up the bath, straight at his face, and one of them says something, moving her lips with exaggerated care. She is asking him something. She repeats it, her piss-gilded lips pursing, relaxing, pursing, relaxing, gaping a little. He realises what she is saying. *Do. You. Like. That.*

He nods his head under the warm piss, feeling his hair tugged in the currents he sets up, and both of the women laugh. Then one of them splashes piss up onto his cock, re-moistening the shaft and the cockhead, while the other walks back up the bath and kneels beside it, leaning over it, holding her hand out over his face with a protruding index finger. He quivers under the piss. The woman who splashed piss up onto his cock has taken hold of it and begun to wank gently at it, working the piss-moistened skin of the upper shaft up and around the piss-moistened rim of his cockhead. He tries to gasp in air through the breathing tube of the piss-snorkel and discovers he can't: when the woman

167

started wanking him, the other woman dropped her index finger delicately into place over the other end of the breathing tube, cutting off his air. He can only have pleasure if he also has pain. The pleasure of the hand working slowly on his piss-moistened cockhead in exchange for the pain of airlessness. Pleasure in his cockhead for pain in his lungs. He closes his eyes and prepares to pay the price. The price of pain for the prize of pleasure.

Then he feels the wanking hand stop and opens his eyes to see the index finger slip free of the breathing-tube. For a moment he thinks it's still somehow blocked, because he's sucking hard for air and none is entering his mouth, and then, with a whistle that he hears distinctly even with his ears inches deep in piss, it enters the breathing-tube again and his aching lungs are filled. He feels his heart working hard in his chest, beating against the warm golden piss that lies above it, and watches the woman who asphyxiated him working her way down the line of frogs on her knees, turning up the flames, then rising to her feet at the foot of the bath before walking around to the opposite side, where she kneels again and works her way up the line of frogs, turning up the flames. The woman who wanked him splashes piss onto his cock again, keeping it moist in readiness for wanking him again, and now the asphyxiatrix is at his head again, turning up the flame of the final frog, then leaning forwards over the bath, dropping her hand and protruding index finger over the infinitely vulnerable inlet of his breathing-tube. He sees her glance down the bath, nodding, and the hand starts working at his cock again as the finger drops and deprives him of air again.

He closes his eyes and prepares to pay the price again, the price of pain for the prize of pleasure, but it isn't only the pain in his lungs now: there's pain in his skin where the piss is beginning to get hotter and pain in his cock too. The piss in the bath is thicker than when it left the bladders of the sixty or seventy women who have squatted above him with splayed thighs. Much of its water has steamed away, leaving it saltier, more concentrated, and it is not lubricating the skin of his cock so much as clogging it and beginning to irritate it. He is paying the price of pain for the prize of pain.

Then the moving hand stops again and the index finger lifts off the inlet of the breathing tube. He opens his eyes, sucking air back into his lungs with a whistle that sounds almost like a scream. Steam is rising thickly from the piss now and he can barely see the face of the two women. His cock feels sore, covered with half-dried piss in which he can feel little prickling crystals of salt, and the currents set up by the heightened flames from the frogs are carrying unpleasantly hot water all around his body. Then the hand splashes piss over his cock again, cupping a handful of it to dribble it over his cockhead. There's a pause, and then the ritual begins again: wanking hand, asphyxiating finger. He closes his eyes, paying the price of pain for the prize of pain, and he hears a splash in the piss further down the bath, jerking a little, then jerking harder when the woman who is wanking him takes hold of his balls with her other hand. She squeezes them slowly, massaging them, tugging at them, still working at the head of his cock.

There's no cool piss anywhere in the bath now: convection currents have sucked the last of it up and out from beneath his back and between his legs, heating it against the glass sides of the bath where the flames are fluttering, then returning it around his body. The wanking hand stops, and the finger rises from the inlet of the breathing tube, but the other hand stays on his balls, gripping them but not squeezing them. Then the whistle of air being sucked into his lungs is suddenly cut through: the finger is back on the inlet of the breathing tube, but the hand hasn't started working on the sore head of his cock again. Why not? What are they going to do to him? He strains his eyes through the piss-gilded steam rising off the surface of the bath, trying to see the face of the woman looking down on him with her index finger pushed snugly into the inlet of his breathing tube, but he can't see it. His lungs are starting to hurt, not given enough chance to recover between each asphyxiation, giving up pain more and more easily each time, and then he shudders beneath the piss, making the whole surface of it ripple, because the wanking hand has returned to the head of his cock.

But not to wank it, not just yet. No, to anoint it. To anoint it with some smooth, cool, soothing lotion, so that when the hand seizes hold of it again and begins to wank it in earnest, to wank it firmly but fairly, while the hand between in the piss begins to massage at his balls again, he's paying a price of pain in his lungs and on his skin for a prize of pleasure in his cock. Because the soothing lotion has sweetened the wanking again, removing the sting of the concentrated piss, making the skin of his cock ride easily against the rim of his cockhead, and the relief of it is almost as powerful as the pleasure of it, or rather adds to the pleasure of it, so that orgasm starts boiling up in his balls almost at once. He's lying submerged in steaming female piss, unable to breathe, unable to move, wholly at the mercy of the two women, pained and pleasured at their will, not his own, and his cock rejoices in it.

The woman wanking him notes the increased stiffness of his cock and the tightening of his balls, and her hands respond, gripping harder at his cockhead, squeezing his balls more cruelly; and then he's coming and both hands have released him, allowing his cock to flower into orgasm, firing jets of white sperm clean through the white curling piss-steam that rises from the surface of the piss, curving high and then down, to splatter against the tiled floor of the bathroom two or three yards away.

170

The index finger of the asphyxiatrix slips free of the inlet of the breathing tube and he gasps in air, his whole body shuddering with the greed of his lungs and the thunder of his heartbeat. His cock releases a final shaft of sperm and stops firing, its white shaft caressed by white tendrils of piss-steam as it juts from the surface of the piss and slowly begins to soften, drooping forwards in an arc. When the two women begin the torture again, trying to set his feet on the thorny path to a second orgasm, they will often discover that he has fainted, his body and senses overburdened by orgasm in hot piss.

If so, they will turn the frog-flames down and lean over the sides of the bath, splashing at the piss to cool it, then stopping to test the response of his cock to further manipulation, waiting for a shudder of returned consciousness to run through his body. And then they will begin again, perhaps exchanging roles, so that the woman who wanked is now the woman who asphyxiates, and the woman who asphyxiated is now the woman who wanks. If he is young and heavy balled, they may coax two more orgasms out of him before the *Doktorin* returns with her nurses and discovers what they have been up to. Even with his ears submerged in piss the prisoner may hear the storm of her wrath breaking over them, and his cock may begin to stiffen again as, through the sides of the glass bath, he watches the punishment that is imposed on them: their stripping and stretching over the *Doktorin*'s knee for a thorough spanking of their firm tanned bottoms. The piss through which he watches will gild and elevate the scene, so that he seems to watch nymphs punished by a goddess. When the *Doktorin* has finished and comes over to him, leaving the two disobedient girls behind her to tug their knickers back up over burning bum-cheeks, tears glistening on their cheeks, she will stroll around the bath, examining this body, before stopping and stooping to trail a finger through the crust of piss-crystals that has begun to form on the glass just above the surface of the gently steaming piss.

Then she will order him removed from the bath. He has been under too long; his skin is starting to suffer. The nurses who stripped Alison and Naomi will trot briskly over. Six of them will begin unchaining him, unhooking and lifting away the chains from his neck to his feet, beginning to lift him from the warm, steaming piss. As his head comes forwards and his ears emerge from the piss he will hear the voices of the *Doktorin* and the nurses, the clink of the steel chains as they are hung over the sides of the bath, the wheels of the stretcher being brought up alongside the bath, and the clank of two large steel buckets being carried in from reception. As the last chain comes loose, bare forearms will slip underneath his body from each side, smooth and cool against his piss-irritated skin, and he will be hoisted expertly and carried over the end of the bath, till all six nurses can turn simultaneously and carry him to the stretcher. As he is laid to it, face up, he will hear behind him the frog-flames being turned fully on, roaring their blue breath against the glass sides of the piss-filled bath.

Once he is settled on the stretcher the *Doktorin* will order him sponged down with cold water, and the nurses will eagerly obey, setting to work on him with large, soft sponges soaked in the icy water that fills the two steel buckets, wiping away the sting of hot, concentrated piss that lingers in his skin. His cock may respond yet again to the sponges, even before the nurses start working between his legs, and when he is flipped onto his chest so they can sponge his back, a hand will quickly and expertly fold his cock up against his stomach. The *Doktorin* will watch, noting his arousal, and she may sigh when the sponging is completed and she strolls over him to inspect her nurses' work. Her warm hand will pass down his sponge-chilled back, or rather her warm fingertip, sliding in the groove of his

172

spine from the nape of his neck to the cleft between his buttocks.

'Little man,' she will say. 'You've had a busy day. Time to ride the wooden horse to Bedfordshire and let those hard-worked balls of yours top up again. Josephine, if you would.'

The fingertip will lift from his buttock cleft and three or four seconds later he will feel a prick in his buttock, sharp and painful for a moment, then fading to nothing as sleep overtakes him.

When he wakes up, not knowing how much time has passed or even, for a moment, where he is, he will find himself belly-down on another bed, face pressed to a large, fluffy pillow smelling of fresh laundry. He won't know what has wakened him for a moment, then he will hear it: a soft, repeated stropping, as of a knife or razor being sharpened. His balls, dangling bare between his splayed, pillow-propped thighs, will stir nervously at the sound, and he will feel another twinge in his arsehole as the muscles of his buttocks and sphincter tighten with fear.

'Soap him,' the *Doktorin*'s voice will say, and something wet and bristly will descend on his arsehole: a shaving-brush, lathering his arsehole with foam.

The stropping stops and a moment later the brush leaves his arsehole. He pushes at his arsehole, trying to read how sore it still is, trying to use it to estimate how long he has been unconscious, but he can't tell. Maybe the cool foam coating is distorting the reading.

'OK,' the *Doktorin*'s voice will say. 'Shave him.'

Soft hands will grasp his buttocks and tug his arse-hollow apart, exposing his lathered arsehole fully to the air, stretching it painfully, and the cutthroat razor he has just heard being stropped will descend on him, shaving away the first patch of hair around his arsehole. He may whimper, may even try to drag himself away from the contact of the cold, sharp metal, but if he does so he will now discover that he has been strapped to the bed: broad leather straps are looped over his shoulders, the small of his back, his upper thighs, his knees and his ankles. He is held down helpless, and must submit as his arsehole is shaved bare, the razor darting into his arse-hollow, shaving hair from his arsehole, then carrying it away to be splashed and wiped off in a bowl of hot water, returning to dart and shave, departing to splash and wipe, the cold metal gradually becoming cool, then warm, then hot. Swiftly his arsehole is razed, denuded of its proud ring of crisp hair and bristles. The razor leaves his arsehole and does not return, and he feels the bed shake faintly as someone else leans over him, peering between his buttocks.

'Looks good,' the *Doktorin* will say. 'Wipe him, then shave his balls.'

A hot, damp towel will slide vigorously around his arsehole, wiping away the last traces of foam, then his thighs will be tugged further apart and his balls hoisted in soft hands, the scrotum tugged flat and held ready as the shaving brush descends again, covering one side of it thoroughly with lather. He will struggle futilely in the straps, his balls feeling supremely vulnerable, unprotected, at the mercy of whatever women are clustered around his bed. He will jerk, then stiffen. The razor has touched his scrotum and begun to slide down, shaving him. But then a voice swears softly, and the razor lifts away. The *Doktorin* asks, 'What's wrong?'

'It's too wrinkled, *Frau Doktorin*.'

'Try again.'

The razor returns, slowly sliding down his stretched, lathered scrotum, then lifts away again.

'No good, *Frau Doktorin*. Look: I'm leaving too many behind.'

'Yes. Hmmm. So what to do? He must be depilated: every inch of him, balls too. Suggestions, girls. Let me have some suggestions. Fiona?'

'Tweezers, *Frau Doktorin*?'

'Hmmm. Possibly. Possibly.'

He feels a finger – the *Doktorin*'s? – poke at his dangling balls, pressing them first to one side, then the other, taking hold of one of the hairs sprinkled over his balls, tweaking at it, musing over the suggestion.

'They would certainly be satisfactorily . . . *painful*. But . . . but I think a little *slow*. Another suggestion. Zoë?'

'Pumice-stone, *Frau Doktorin*?'

'Grind it off, you mean?'

'Yes, *Frau Doktorin*.'

'Hmmm.'

He feels her plucking at the ball-hair, plucking hard, almost tugging it out. His cock, softened by too many recent orgasms, too much pleasure, quivers a little and begins to re-stiffen. The *Doktorin* plucks again at his ball-hair, then delivers her verdict on Zoë's suggestion.

'Again, that would be satisfactorily painful for him, but too slow. And perhaps imperfectly complete. These are tough hairs. Look at them, girls.'

He stifles a cry against the pillow, his cock stiffening faster, rising to half-erection. Her fingers have suddenly jerked on the ball-hair, plucking it free with a spurt of pain that heightens and is gone almost in the same instant.

'See, girls?'

She must be holding the ball-hair up, exhibiting it for the circle of watching nurses. A strange odour touches his nostrils for a moment, gone before he can analyse it.

'Yes, *Frau Doktorin*,' comes the chorus of soft, eager-to-please young women's voices, and his cock stiffens to full erection, ready for whatever new torture they have planned for him.

The strange odour is back for a moment, and he suddenly thinks it's piss. Hot and liquid.

'The hair on his balls,' says the *Doktorin* musingly, 'is very thick, very wiry. Pumice-stone might not grind all of it away fully, so let's think again. Imogen?'

'Perhaps . . . waxing, *Frau Doktorin*?'

There is silence for a moment, then the *Doktorin*'s fingers are stroking at his balls again, running through the hairs sprinkled over them, gently tweaking at them, searching through them for another to pluck at, then pluck loose. The odour's back again, stronger, lasting a moment or two longer. No, it's not piss.

'Waxing?' the *Doktorin* says. Then: 'Waxing. Waxing. Hmmm. Waxing.'

She's found a new hair now, is tweaking at it, beginning to pluck and tug.

'Yes, waxing. I do believe it could work. I do believe it would work. And it would combine the maximum of pain with the minimum of delay. Imogen, I believe you've got it. Girls, what do you think? A good idea? Yes?'

'Yes, *Frau Doktorin*.'

'We'll have a show of hands, then. All in favour of depilating his balls by waxing, raise your right hands and say, "Aye".'

'Aye,' comes the chorus.

'Nem con,' says the *Doktorin*, and, as her fingers pluck the second ball-hair free from his balls, he realises through the spurt of pain what the odour is. Wax. Wax being melted to spread over his balls. They've been heating it since before Imogen suggested it, ready for the unanimous vote in its favour.

'And look, girls, the gods are with us. There, look. Wax. Molten wax, all ready to spread generously on those hairy balls of his. Like sugary dumplings being smothered in molten chocolate. Melanie and Rose, if you'll do the honours.'

'Yes, *Frau Doktorin*.'

'Pauline and Fiona, you prepare his balls. Best wear gloves, I think, in case you get wax on your fingers when Melanie and Rose are painting it on. It might hurt. Might even scald you.'

'Yes, *Frau Doktorin*.'

He hears plastic gloves being pulled on and then light cool plastic-sheathed fingers take hold of his balls, spreading them, preparing them to be painted with molten wax. The smell of it is suddenly much stronger in his nostrils, even with his head buried in the pillow, and he imagines a steaming pot of wax being lifted between his legs, its rim thickly splattered. Molten red wax, gleaming sullenly in its pot as Melanie and Rose dip their brushes into it. Or molten purple wax. Or yellow. And then he jerks, stifling another cry against the pillow, a throb of pain–pleasure running through his cock. Hot air has touched his balls for a moment and then the head of the first waxing-brush is on his skin, painting him in swift, assured strokes with molten wax that sears into his skin for a moment before it begins to harden and set. Another waxing-brush joins it, wielded by Melanie-or-Rose, painting his balls with molten wax, and then the first, wielded by Rose-or-Melanie, returns to the pot to be charged with wax again before returning to his balls, painting him in swift, assured strokes before the second brush returns to the pot to be charged with wax again. It happens over and over, and each stroke of the brushes adds another track of wax to his balls, overlapping, building up and up, armouring his balls with wax, cocooning them in it, like sugary dumplings being coated with chocolate.

Pauline and Fiona turn his balls expertly to allow the brushes access to every crevice and cranny, lifting them, pushing them to one side, careful not to disturb the wax that has already been laid down, until finally his balls are encased in a stiff jacket of wax and the brushes lift from him and do not return.

'How long, *Frau Doktorin*?' one of the nurses will ask.

'Give him five minutes. Then we will strip it off him. Slowly. Very slowly. We want to get every last hair off. And you can all have a turn. All right?'

'Yes, *Frau Doktorin*.'

'Good girls. But in the meantime what shall we do? Tania?'

'Play noughts-and-crosses on his arse, *Frau Doktorin*. With the wax.'

The *Doktorin*'s cool fingers are back on his skin, running over his arsecheeks, ruffling through the hair that covers them.

'Noughts-and-crosses?'

'Yes, *Frau Doktorin*.'

A finger strokes slowly down his arsecleft, pausing here and there to tug gently at the hair that lines it.

'On his arse?'

'Yes, *Frau Doktorin*.'

The finger reaches his shaved arsehole, circling it, rubbing at it.

'With wax?'

'Yes, *Frau Doktorin*. First on the left cheek, then on the right. Then we strip the wax and we're ready to begin on his balls.'

The *Doktorin*'s finger lifts from his arse.

'Very well. It's a good idea. An *excellent* idea. Noughts-and-crosses on his arse, with wax. Fiona and Kelly, you can play first, on his left buttock. Heat the wax again. We want it nice and hot for him.'

He hears murmurs behind him as the wax is re-heated, and his balls try to stir in their jacket of hardened wax. But they can't: they're held rigid. Then there's a giggle, and the *Doktorin* says, 'Right, Fiona. Paint the board.'

A shiver runs through his hairy buttocks, and he flinches as a drop of hot liquid lands on his right buttock. The waxing brush must be laden with wax. A moment later the brush touches his buttock skin, sliding across it, leaving a hot trail of wax, drawing the first line for the game. The brush lifts, then returns after a couple of seconds to draw another line parallel with the first, then lifts again, returns to draw a line at right angles to the first two, lifts again, returns to draw a fourth line parallel to the third.

'There,' says a voice that must be Fiona's. 'Done, *Frau Doktorin*.'

'Good girl.'

As the wax hardens it tugs up at the hairs in his buttock-skin.

'Now,' the *Doktorin* continues, 'which of you wants noughts and which crosses?'

'Me noughts, please, *Frau Doktorin*,' says a slightly deeper, slightly rougher voice.

It must be Kelly's. He thinks she smokes and imagines her with a cigarette in her mouth, ash dropping off onto her nurse's uniform as she supervises the ball-torture of some helpless male patient.

'Are you bigger today?' the *Doktorin* asks.

He doesn't understand. Bigger? Does she mean him? His cock? It's responded to the image of smoking Kelly, straining against the bed beneath him.

'I think so, *Frau Doktorin*.'

'Fiona? What do you think? Is Kelly bigger today?'

'Um. I'm not sure, *Frau Doktorin*. I didn't look very closely this morning. She might be.'

'Well, it won't take thirty seconds to check. Unbutton, the two of you and we'll weigh your tits.'

'Yes, *Frau Doktorin*,' say the two voices at once, the higher, smoother one laid over the lower, rougher one, and his cock throbs against the bed, held down by the weight of his body.

It quivers as he strains to hear the soft sounds of the unbuttoning. What are they doing? Unbuttoning their jackets, to let their breasts out? The unbuttoning stops, then he hears a click and a sigh, a whisper of cloth and the murmurs of women's voices. The click of a bra being unclipped; the sigh a woman releases when she unclips a tight bra; the whisper of the bra being peeled away, setting her large breasts free into the hands of other women who lift them gently through the open flap of her unbuttoned nurse's jacket. There's another click, another sigh, another whisper of cloth, another cock-stiffening set of murmurs. His cock is solid against the bed beneath him as he imagines the two pairs of large breasts on display behind him, three or four nurses clustering to each pair, helping them up and out through the unbuttoned jackets.

'Weigh them, girls,' says the *Doktorin*'s voice. 'Left, then right.'

He pushes his hips down hard, wanting to start bouncing his cock against the bed with frustrated delight, trying to provoke an orgasm. His balls are straining upwards inside their jacket of hardened wax, beginning to ache with frustration. More murmurs from behind him and another sigh. No, more a gasp. A shivery little gasp, the gasp released by a woman when one of her large warm breasts is lifted and laid on the cold metal pan of a breast-scale held up by another woman. Then he hears a little metallic clink ... then another ... then another. Weights are being laid on the opposite pan of the scale, slowly filling it until the scale trembles and lifts and both pans are balanced. He counts them, his cock straining harder against the bed as he realises how large the breast being weighed must be. Three ... four ... five ... six ... seven ... eight ... nine ... ten ... eleven ... twelve ... thirteen ... four ...

There's a sudden clapping of hands behind him, and the *Doktorin* murmurs: 'Excellent, Kelly. Fourteen. I believe you may be bigger today. Clear the scales and weight her right breast now, girls.'

The weights are swept off the pan and he hears Kelly gasp again as her right breast is laid to the breast-pan. But the gasp is softer, less shivery, for the pan has been warmed by her left breast. The slow, soft, careful

metallic clinks begin again. One ... two ... three ...
four ... five ... six ... seven ... eight ... nine ... ten
... eleven ... twelve ... thirteen ...

The clapping breaks out again and he imagines
Kelly's pleased, proud, slightly yellowed grin.

'Excellent, Kelly. An average of thirteen-and-a-half.
Fiona is going to have to do well to beat that.'

'Yes, *Frau Doktorin*.'

He hears the weights being swept off the scales again
and waits for the gasp as Fiona's left breast is laid to
them. But it doesn't come: either the breast-pan has
been warmed by Kelly's breasts or Fiona is more stoical,
less demonstrative, watching with a set and serious
expression as her left breast is laid to the breast-pan and
the weights are slowly and carefully laid to the surface
of the anti-breast-pan. Clink, clink, clink. One ... two
... three ... four ... five ... six ... seven ... eight ...
nine ... ten ... eleven ... twel ...

No clapping this time and he imagines Fiona's pout
of disappointment as the anti-breast-pan trembles and
sinks, balanced against the warm fleshy weight of her
left breast.

'Right breast now, girls,' says the *Doktorin*. 'But I'm
afraid I don't think, Fi–'

She allows her voice to trail off sympathetically, and
he imagines Fiona nodding sadly, accepting that today
her breasts are surpassed by Kelly's. The slow, soft,
careful metallic clinks begin again. One ... two ...
three ... four ... five ... six ... seven ... eight ... nine
... ten ... eleven ... twelve ... thirteen ...

'No,' says the *Doktorin*. 'Not today, Fi. Kelly's are
bigger and she gets choice of symbols. Noughts, wasn't
it you wanted, Kel?'

'Yes, *Frau Doktorin*.'

'How's the wax doing? Heat it up again, will you,
Zoë? Till it's boiling, I think. We want some nice hot
wax for his arse.'

181

'Yes, *Frau Doktorin*.'

He listens to the soft sounds coming from behind him, smelling the odour of the hot wax get stronger.

'OK,' says the *Doktorin*. 'First game, on his left cheek. Insert a nought, Kelly.'

He feels the heat of the wax on the brush before it even touches his skin: it's much hotter, almost scalding him as Kelly draws a neat circle on his buttock in the middle square of the board, and even when the wax has cooled and hardened he can feel the pain still singing into his skin.

'Now you, Fiona.'

The heat of the wax again touches him a moment before the brush coated in the wax itself, and when the two strokes in the top left-hand corner of the board have cooled and begun to harden the pain of it is still singing into his skin.

'Hmmm,' says the *Doktorin*. 'I think I see what you are trying to do, Kelly.'

Another neat circle, this time in the top right-hand square of the board.

'Your turn, Fiona,' says the *Doktorin*.

Another cross, this time in the bottom left-hand corner. His skin feels branded with heat, the pain of the first nought and first cross still singing into it, multiplied as each new nought and new cross is painted onto him.

'Kelly.'

Another nought, now in the middle left-hand square.

'Fiona.'

Another cross, mirroring the nought in the middle right-hand square.

'Kelly.'

The fourth nought, in the upper central square.

'Fiona.'

The third cross, in the lower central square. The *Doktorin* clicks her tongue with frustration.

'Oh, it's hopeless. But complete the game, Kelly.'

182

The fifth nought, in the lower right-hand square, and the game is over without a winner, each square occupied, his buttock singing with wax-pain.

'We'll have to try again, girls, once you've played on his right cheek. Paint the board, Kel.'

He tenses, waiting for the brush to land on his right buttock and sweep downwards twice, then across twice, but the pain isn't so bad this time, as though his buttocks are a set of scales, each cheek a pan, and the left cheek is already heavy with weights, so that pain in the right is only making up the balance. There. Two strokes down the cheek, the hot wax lifting buttock-hairs as it cools and hardens; then two strokes across the cheek, creating a square for noughts-and-crosses.

'You first, Fi,' says the *Doktorin*.

'Am I playing noughts, *Frau Doktorin*?'

'Yes. This time you are. Swap again when you play on his left cheek again.'

The brush touches his skin, turns in a neat circle in the upper right-hand square.

'Kelly.'

The other brush touches his skin, sweeping down from left to right, then down from right to left, leaving a neat cross in the lower left-hand square.

'Fiona.'

But he's already read her strategy in the cooling wax and stretched buttock-hairs of his cheek and knows where she will place the next nought. Yes. The brush touches his skin, turns and lifts away leaving a cooling circle of wax in the upper left-hand square. He hears a murmur of admiration as the other nurses realise the trap she has laid.

'Very good, Fiona,' the *Doktorin* says. 'She's outwitted you, Kel. Your turn.'

'Yes, *Frau Doktorin*.'

But Kelly's voice does not seem abashed, and the cross she paints into the middle central square of the board is unwavering.

'Fiona.'

Fiona paints a neat circle of wax in the bottom right-hand square.

'Kel.'

Another cross, in the central square.

'And Fiona.'

Fiona paints a neat circle of wax in the middle right-hand square, lifts her brush away, and then returns to draw a neat stroke through the three winning noughts. There is the soft patter of clapping and the *Doktorin* says, 'Excellent, Fiona. An excellent win. So you won't begrudge Kelly the privilege of dewaxing his left cheek so you can play again?'

'Not at all, *Frau Doktorin*.'

'Good girl. Kelly, do you have the dewaxing knife?'

'Yes, *Frau Doktorin*.'

'Then dewax him, dear. If you do it well, you can dewax one of his balls, too.'

'Thank you, *Frau Doktorin*. I'll do my best.'

A shiver has run through him at the mention of the dewaxing knife. What kind of knife? Sharp and cold, liable to slip in a careless hand and nick his vulnerable buttock-flesh? Or blunt and painful in a more prolonged way, not with the sear of cut flesh but the burn of scraped flesh, as it clumsily removes the wax from his skin? There. It's touched his skin, cold and metallic, and his buttock shivers again. Then it moves, expertly lifting an edge of wax and then, in a single sweep, peeling the first strip up and off his skin. Buttock-hairs come agonisingly with it, tearing loose from his skin with faint pops, as though the explosion of pain in each emptied follicle is enough to burst symbolically into sound. The knife flicks the strip of wax away, lifts another edge, peels another strip with more faint pops of buttock-hairs dragged free by their roots, expertly cleaning away the useless board, preparing his buttock for the painting of the next. In less than a minute it's working the final patches of wax free and his buttock is ready.

'Excellent, Kelly,' says the *Doktorin*. 'You can certainly dewax one of his balls. Fiona, if you could paint the board again.'

This time the pain is greater, because his buttock has been partly depilated and the wax is being painted onto truly bare skin rich with sensitised nerves. One vertical stroke, searing into his skin ... another ... then a horizontal stroke, searing oddly at right-angles ... then another ... and then they're ready to play again.

'Noughts for you, Kelly,' says the *Doktorin*.

'Yes, *Frau Doktorin*.'

Heat touches his skin again before the wax-laden brush touches down, then Kelly is painting a neat circle in the lower left-hand square of the buttock-board.

'Fiona,' says the *Doktorin*.

Fiona paints a neat cross in the central square.

'Kelly.'

A neat circle in the upper left-hand square.

'Fiona.'

A neat cross in the middle left-hand square.

'Kelly.'

A neat circle in the bottom right-hand square, and clapping breaks out again.

'Ah,' says the *Doktorin*. 'Fiona.'

Fiona puts a neat cross in the bottom central square.

'Kelly.'

Kelly puts a neat circle in the middle right-hand square, lifts her brush, then returns to paint a slow stroke through the line of noughts she has created.

'Good girl,' says the *Doktorin*. 'One game all, and I think it's time to dewax his balls. You can both do half of his ball-sac, I think, girls. One ball each. Very well?'

'Yes, *Frau Doktorin*,' they say together.

'Good. Fiona, you can hold his balls steady while Kelly works on her side of his sac, then you can hold his balls steady while Fiona works on her side, Kelly. Very well?'

'Yes, *Frau Doktorin*.'

'Right. Then you can both get the wax off his buttocks. Away you go. Who's got the dewaxing knife?'

A hand takes hold of his wax-jacketed scrotum, tugging it up and away from the root of his turgid cock, holding it ready for Kelly to begin work.

'Hand the knife to Kelly, then,' the *Doktorin* says. 'Ready, Fiona?'

'Yes, *Frau Doktorin*.'

Then the dewaxing of his balls begins. Kelly grips his left ball and begins work, moving the knife slowly, carefully, prolonging the slow peeling of each strip of wax, making his buttocks shudder and clench at the pain of each ball-hair coming up and out by the roots with a faint pop. A hand pats his left buttock over the noughts-and-crosses board and the *Doktorin* says, 'There, there. You'll feel so much better when your balls are stripped, believe me. Hairy balls are so uncouth, so uncivilised. So bestial, dear.'

He bites his lip, pressing his face harder into the pillow as Kelly's slim fingers tighten on his left ball, twisting it so she can work at the wax underneath his ball-sac, peeling it away in long, slow strips, tearing his ball-hairs up and out by the roots. He can feel himself leaking above and below in tribute to the pain and humiliation: above, hot tears are leaking from his eyes; below, salty pre-come is leaking from the slit in the swollen head of his cock, pressed hard to the bed.

'There,' coos the *Doktorin*, as the last strip of wax peels away and Kelly's fingers release his left ball. 'All done on the left side. Now your turn, Fiona, while Kelly holds his ball-sac steady for you.'

The hand holding his ball-sac releases it, letting it swing back into place, and then another hand takes hold, tugging it out and away from the root of his cock. Then fingers close on his right ball and he tenses, ready for the knife to begin work. But no: 'Hold on, Fi,' says the *Doktorin*. 'You know you haven't had much practice with the dewaxing knife yet. Have you?'

'No, *Frau Doktorin*.'

'Then you'll be gentle with him, won't you?'

'Of course, *Frau Doktorin*.'

'Good. Then you can begin.'

She begins, and he jerks and stiffens, because she's not peeling the wax loose with the knife, she's scraping it loose, clumsily, inexpertly, having to tighten her fingers hard on his right ball, crushing and cracking the wax that still jackets it, guaranteeing that the dewaxing will be much longer and much more painful than it needs to be. He shudders again, releasing a cry into his pillow, feeling more tears leak from his eyes and more pre-come from his cock.

'Oh, Fiona,' says the *Doktorin*. 'What are you trying to do? Castrate the poor dear? It's not as though he has much to write home about down there already, but by the time you've finished he could have lost even that.'

'Sorry, *Frau Doktorin*.'

'I think you'll have to use your fingernails, dear. It will be slower, and more painful, I'm afraid, but much less risky. You can practise on his buttocks with the knife. It's a smoother surface, and I'm sure Kelly won't mind giving up her buttock to help you improve your technique, will you, Kel?'

'No, *Frau Doktorin*.'

'Good. Right, fingernails from now on, Fi.'

'Yes, *Frau Doktorin*.'

He hears a rattle, as though the knife has been dropped into a metal dish, and then tenses in preparation for the fingernails. Fiona's fingernails. Scraping the wax off his ball-sac slowly and painfully. There. She's begun. Slowly working an edge of wax up and then beginning to peel the strip off, tearing his ball-hairs up and out by the roots. The head of his cock is lying in a patch of moisture now, so freely has pre-come leaked from it, and his abused balls are aching for orgasm. If he can just . . .

'Hey!' the *Doktorin* says. 'What's he up to?'

The fingernails stop scraping at his ball-sac and he hears Fiona say, 'I think he's . . . he's wanking himself against the bed, *Frau Doktorin*.'

'Well, he can cut that out. No patient comes until the *Doktorin* says so. Rose and Melanie, tighten the straps.'

'Yes, *Frau Doktorin*.'

He's been trying to rub the head of his cock surreptitiously against the bed, working it up and back, trying to steal an orgasm under the watchful gaze of his warders, but he's been detected. Rose and Melanie tighten the broad leather straps viciously on him, almost crushing the air out of his lungs as they tighten the straps over his shoulders and the small of his back, then over his upper thighs, his knees, his ankles. He's held down, quite unable to move, and the dewaxing of his balls can continue.

'Fingernails again, Fi,' says the *Doktorin*.

Ten

He will wake the day after the shaving and waxing in a strange bed. For a moment or two, perhaps, or three or four, the lingering pain in his arsehole and balls will overwhelm the prickling of a rough blanket and the rasp of an overstarched sheet against his skin, but he will notice the blanket and sheet when he moves and the head of his stiff cock slides against the blanket (if he is lying on his back) or sheet (if he is lying on his stomach). He will open his eyes wonderingly to find himself the sole occupant of a long, dark, cold school dormitory.

He will usually sit up in the bed, rolling over first if he has awakened on his stomach, sitting up and looking left and right down the twin rows of empty beds, each of them, like his own, with four corroded bedknobs, then up at the shadowed text over the door, slowly piecing together the words in the two lines that arc over a gruesomely realistic crucifix:

In Labiis Sapientis Invenietur Sapientia;
Et Virga In Natibus Ejus Qui Indiget Corde.

He will almost certainly find his cock stiffening harder at the way the tail of the 'j' of 'Ejus' is elongated, curling over itself like the tail of a whip, and if he is feeling even slightly nervous or guilty – and so many of the

Domina's contestants are of a highly nervous and guilty disposition – he will gasp as the nuns glide into the dormitory through the door below the text and crucifix. Five of them, gliding in perfect silence in their black robes, four of them with faces hidden beneath veils (green, pink, yellow and blue), the fifth, at the head of the file, with a pale oval face of severe and unsettling beauty.

He will strain his ears to hear their feet on the floor but will hear nothing and may think that he is dreaming or that they are ghosts, until, as two nuns file down each side of his bed and the fifth, their unveiled leader, stands at the foot of his bed, he smells, wafted forth somehow from beneath their robes, hot menstrual blood. The leader will gaze at him unblinkingly and he will become belatedly aware of the bulge halfway down his body. Then the leader's lips will part and she will speak.

'Top o' the mornin' to ye, me child. Are ye rested after your busy day, an' ready for anudder? 'Tis your examination today, as ye know.'

Her accent will be richly and creamily Irish, almost satirically so, perhaps certainly satirically so, but most of the contestants are never able to make up their minds about that. The contestant lying in the bed will lick his lips and stammer a reply, and the nun will nod her head once slowly.

'An' it's right glad I am to hear that. Aye, an' the good sisters too, arrun't ye, Sisters?'

The four nuns standing beside his bed will nod and he will wonder where their eyes are beneath their veils. Fixed on the bulge of his stiff cock?

'But no doubt, me child, ye'll be wonderin' who it is we are, an' what business we have wit' ye this fine sunny mornin'?'

He will nod or stammer out 'Yes' and she will nod and say, 'Den I will tell ye, me child. We –' and she will look left and right '– are de Sisters of Perpetual PMT.

Ye may call me Mudder Superior. Dis here –' nodding to the nearer, pink-veiled nun on her left '– is Sister Tormenta, an' dis –' nodding to the farther, blue-veiled nun on her left '– Sister Perpetua. Dis here –' nodding to the nearer, green-veiled nun on her right '– Sister Sanguinulenta an' dis –' nodding to the farther, yellow-veiled sister on her right '– Sister Flagellatio. Ye'll be knowing de Latin, is it, me child?'

Most contestants will shake their heads and a smile will touch Mother Superior's lips for a moment.

'An' dat's a fine joke ye'll be havin' wit' me, me child, an' ye larnin' God's own language dese five years past.'

She will look hard at the contestant as he lies in the bed, apparently unaware of his cock hillocking the thin, rough blanket beneath which he lies. When she sees no response in his face to her question, her dark eyebrows will go up and she will purr, threateningly, 'Well? Is it nut so?'

Some contestants, sweating with fear, will now try to lie their way out and nod, stammering, 'Yes', then feel their hearts leap into their throats as Mother Superior raises an arm and points at the text above the door, the firm mound of her left breast shifting to the movement beneath her black robes.

'Den ye'll translate, me girl.'

And now, if he is lying, he will have to shake his head and stammer that he cannot, and Mother Superior's eyes will flash with anger.

'Ye cannot? Den de Divvil must have got into ye, for ye could do it wit' ease yesterday. But at least,' she will continue, beginning to roll up her sleeves, 'dat makes the cure an easy one. We shall beat de Divvil out of ye, shall we nut, Sisters? Sthrip her, if ye please.'

And two of the sisters will seize the blanket and begin to wrench it from him as he struggles to keep beneath it. As his body is exposed Mother Superior will cry out with horror.

'Jesus, Mary an' Joseph! What is dis? Naked in de bed ye are! An' where . . . Saints preserve us! . . . where are your bubbies, girl?'

His chest will have been uncovered, shining a little with sweat, and she will point with a shaking hand at it, tears of horror beginning to glisten in her dark Irish eyes.

'Where are your sweet innocent bubbies, girl? What has happened to ye? What horror has struck ye down owin' to your sins? Well, is it nut a tongue ye'll be havin' in your head, me girl? Explain de loss of your fine bubbies. At once, girl. Ah, I see ye cannot. But I can. 'Tis the Divvil, de Divvil has possessed ye, but de cure, as I said, is easy to find, t'ough not, I'll assure ye, easy to endure. Sisters, sthrip her an' turn her over.'

Startled by Mother Superior's cry of horror, confused at the accusations she is levelling at him, the contestant will usually react too slowly when the sisters wrench at the blanket again, and it will be dragged half off his body before he resists. Now Mother Superior will cry out again even louder.

'Sweet Mary Mudder o' Jesus! An' what . . . what . . . *what* is *dis*?'

She will point with a shaking hand at the stiff cock that springs in and out of view as he and the sisters struggle with each other, he to pull the blanket back over his body, they to drag it finally off him.

'Ah, 'tis worse dan I feared, far worse. Sisters, tear it from her.'

Startled again by Mother Superior's cry, filled with shame and foreboding by her words, he will not resist now as the blanket is dragged from him and he lies naked on the bed beneath five pairs of eyes, four pairs hidden beneath veils, one pair hot and glowing with anger as it rests on his stiff cock. He will try to cover his cock with his hands but Mother Superior will hiss a single word and from both sides of the bed the sisters will seize his forearms and drag them loose, leaving his cock on open display, stiffer than ever with fear and humiliation.

'What is dis?' Mother Superior will ask. 'What is dis *t'ing* dat has sprouted overnight between your tighs? Ah, what's dat? Speak up, girl. What is dis ye say? 'Tis your cuck? An' what is a cuck? I've nivver heard o' such a t'ing – an' I'll warrant nor de Sisters have, nider. 'Tis it nut so, Sisters?'

Four veiled heads will shake silently and in unison and Mother Superior will nod grimly with satisfaction, looking left, then right as her righteous ignorance is confirmed, then looking back at the stiff, purple-capped poker of his cock. Her lip will curl with disgust.

'Ah, but 'tis surely de Divvil's work agin. Sister Sanguinulenta, will ye not run an' tie down her feet an' hands an' den run an' fetch Sister Phallocratora for me now? Sisters, if ye'll hand over your rosaries.'

One of the silent nuns holding down his left forearm will release it and glide down the bed to his feet, tugging a rosary from a pocket of her robes. The other nuns are tugging their rosaries free too, holding his forearms down with one hand. Sister Sanguinulenta seizes one of his feet and tugs it out to the bedknob at the foot of the bed, looping her rosary expertly around his ankle, tying him firmly to the bedknob. Then she crosses to his other foot, catching a rosary thrown to her by one of the other nuns, tying the foot to the other bedknob, then gliding up the bed to his head as the nuns hoist his arms up his body, holding his hands to the bedknobs waiting at the head of the bed. Sister Sanguinulenta ties him by his wrists with the two remaining rosaries, still working in perfect silence, and then turns and glides down the bed and from the dormitory.

'T'ank you, Sister,' Mother Superior will murmur as she passes her; and then she surveys him with satisfaction as he lies spread-eagled on the bed, ankles and wrists tied by rosaries to the bedknobs, his cock quivering at the centre of his body as he struggles in vain to loosen himself.

'Whativver it is your sins have brought upon ye, me girl, ye can rest assured dat Sister Phallocratora will know an' be able to recommend de cure, dough I'll be bettin' already dat 'tis your arse will pay de price of it. Aye, 'twill pay a heavy price before ye're restored de way de good Lord made ye. I still cannot believe what it is I'm seein' here before me. Dis ... *cuck* an' your poor fine bubbies shrunken away to nuttin'. 'Tis a sin cryin' out to Heaven for vengeance, so 'tis. Cryin' out, 'tis.'

She sniffs, then fumbles in her robes for a second, producing a flattened pack of cigarettes, flipping the lid open with a click.

'Sisters?' she will say, holding it out.

The remaining three sisters will shake their heads.

'Aye, I agree wid ye dere, but 'tis de pressures o' responsibility, ye'll all be understandin' dat.'

She pulls a cigarette out, slips it between her lips, pushes the packet back into her robes, fumbles again for a second, then draws out a cheap lighter. She puts it to the end of the cigarette and sucks in air as she triggers the flame, her eyes looking coldly past the flame at his cock. As she jets smoke from her nostrils and returns the lighter to her robes, she will nod slowly, her eyes narrowing with satisfaction.

'Aye, Sister Phallocratora will know what to do wit' ye, me girl.'

Then he will see Sister Sanguinulenta gliding silently back into the dormitory, followed by another sister. She, like Mother Superior, is unveiled, with coppery eyebrows arching above sparkling eyes and a warm smile.

'Ah!' Mother Superior will say. 'Speak o' de Divvil an' she appears. Top o' de mornin' to ye, Sister.'

'An' to ye, Mudder,' the new sister replies, pausing at the foot of the bed with Mother Superior. 'Is it a job o' work ye'll be havin' for me to do?'

Sister Sanguinulenta glides back beside the bed, taking hold of his forearm again.

'Aye, 'tis so an' truly so, Sister. 'Tis a spot o' bodder we're havin' here wid dis young girl. She's a candidate for de scholarship dis fine mornin', but she's in no fit state to be takin' it, I'll be t'inkin', what wid one t'ing an' anudder.'

'An' de one t'ing will be, Mudder?'

Mother Superior takes the cigarette out of her mouth and gestures with it down the bed.

'Dis deformity o' hers, Sister, as ye can see. She'll be callin' it a cuck now, an' did ye ivver see or hear o' sich a t'ing as dat in all your born days?'

Still smiling, the new sister looks fully at the bed and its helpless occupant for the first time. The smile vanishes from her face in an instant and she takes a step back, clutching at Mother Superior for support with one hand while the other points shakily at his cock.

'Holy Mudder o' God! An' what is dis?'

''Twas we were hopin' ye'd be able to tell us de virry same, Sister.'

'I've nivver . . . but wait a minute.'

She makes a visible effort to pull herself together, letting go of Mother Superior and moving towards the bed.

'What is it, Sister?' Mother Superior asks.

'Jus' a minute, please, Mudder. Sister, if ye would . . .'

Sister Phallocratora gestures at his cock, making a circle of her forefinger and thumb and sliding it downwards. Sister Sanguinulenta nods slightly and reaches out for his cock with one hand, taking hold of it just below the head and tugging the skin down. Sister Phallocratora reaches inside her robes and produces a large magnifying glass, then moves forwards again, to stoop over the bed, putting the magnifying glass close to his cockhead and peering through it. He can see the individual coppery hairs of her right eyebrow, the clear white of her eyeball, the shining emerald iris of her eye and the black disc of her pupil. Her breath puffs over the head of his cock and it twitches, and he sees her pupil flex and swell. Then she puts the magnifying glass down and turns her head to Mother Superior.

'A *cuck* was she callin' it now, Mudder?'

'Aye, a cuck. Are ye tellin' me ye are familiar wid de tings after all now, Sister?'

'I suppose I am at dat, Mudder. 'Twas de shock o' de t'ing, ye'll understand. Seein' one in de flesh for de virry first time, ye'll understand.'

'Aye, an' I do, an' de Sisters too, I'll warrant.'

Silent nods from the four sisters. Sister Phallocratora turns back to his cock, raising her magnifying glass again and peering closely at it. Mother Superior clears her throat behind her.

'But ye'll be tellin' us, den, Sister, what de Divvil it is?'

' 'Tis a cuck, Mudder,' Sister Phallocratora says without looking back at her.

'An' didn't we know it already, Sister?'

'An' so ye did, Mudder. But did ye know what comes wid a cuck?

Sister Phallocratora glances back at her for a moment.

'Or ye, Sisters? Did any o' ye know what comes wid a cuck?'

Silent shakes of the head this time, and from Mother Superior: 'No, an' I didn't now.'

' 'Tis *dis*, Mudder,' says Sister Phallocratora triumphantly, and she reaches between his thighs and lifts up his balls, spreading his ball-sac and letting his balls roll visibly inside it. The touch of her warm, smooth hand and moving fingers makes him groan and his cock twitches again.

196

'An' what are dose, Sister?'

'Balls, Mudder.'

She releases them and he gasps again, more softly, with disappointment.

'Where ye find a cuck ye'll find balls, Mudder. 'Tis de rule, ye'll understand.'

Mother Superior nods, puffing smoke.

'I'll be takin' your word for it, Sister, but I'm still no closer to understandin' what a cuck is, am I now? Nor balls.'

'What dey are, Mudder? An' isn't it plain what dey are? T'ank you, Sister.'

Sister Sanguinulenta releases his cock and he groans again with disappointment.

'A curse from Heaven, Mudder, dat is what dey are.'

'An' hadn't we guessed it, Sister? Hadn't we guessed it on first laying eyes to dem?'

'But technically, Mudder, technically, what a cuck is is a *snake*.'

'A snake, Sister?'

'De virry same, Mudder.'

'An' de balls, I suppose, are de eggs?'

'Ye have it in one, Mudder. 'Tis a snake an' two eggs we are confronted by here.'

'But do ye have the cure o' dem, Sister, dat's what we're wantin' to know? Can ye rid de poor lass o' dem?'

'I have, Mudder. I have de cure by similarities, Mudder. Ye'll be knowing the Latin o' it, I take it? *Similia similibus curantur*?'

'Aye, an' 'tis familiar wid it I am. Similar t'ings by similar t'ings are cured. But what do ye mean, wid reference to a cuck and its balls?'

'Vinnim, Mudder.'

'Vinnim, Sister?'

'Vinnim, Mudder. De snake, as ye might expect, is highly poisonous and generates a fearsome vinnim under attack. As ye shall see, Mudder, ye shall see. I have read a cuck in prime condition can spit its vinnim clear across a room.'

'Spit, Sister?'

'Spit, Mudder.'

Mother Superior drags hard on her cigarette, eyes widening with wonder.

'But are we not all in mortal danger, standing here so close to de ting as it rears its blasphemous head at us? An' didn't wee Sister Sanguinulenta, not three minutes past, take hold o' de t'ing wid her bare hand?'

'She did, she did, but we are not in danger, I assure ye, Mudder. 'Twill only spit its vinnim under certain conditions, as ye shall see, an' me intention is to catch de vinnim even as it flies, so dat I might feed it to de poor wee lass an' drive de cuck an' its eggs from her body. Sister, if I might have your assistance agin?'

Sister Sanguinulenta takes hold of his cock again with her left hand, pulling down on the shaft to expose and tighten the head.

'An' if I might have a little assistance wid generatin' de vimmim, Sisters. If ye'll all jus' spit onto me hand now.'

Still holding firmly onto the shaft of his cock with her left hand, Sister Phallocratora holds out her right hand, palm flat and open, reaching over the bed to Sister Perpetua, who reaches up and lifts her veil, swinging up a little. He hears her spit onto Sister Phallocratora's hand, which swings to Sister Tormenta as Sister Perpetua lowers her veil. Now Sister Tormenta raises her hand to her veil, swinging it up, spitting on Sister Phallocratora's palm. Mother Superior has watched, puffing on her quarter-smoked cigarette.

'An' what's dis ye'll be doin', Sister?' she asks.

Sister Phallocratora is putting her palm under Sister Flagellatio's mouth now, receiving another globule of nun's spittle, then under Sister Sanguinulenta's.

'Watch me an' ye'll see, Mudder.'

She swings her right hand to his cock, holding it slightly cupped now to retain the spittle, and pauses a moment, then slaps it against his cockhead in one swift movement, trapping the spittle between palm and cockhead. She starts to rub it in, working it thoroughly over his cockhead, and he groans.

''Tis lubrication I'm wantin', Mudder. For the vinnimdrawing. Now, I'll begin.'

And she starts slowly and firmly to masturbate him, her firmly closed hand working up and down over his glowing, spittle-lubricated cockhead, grinding at it in circles, back and forth, working up and down, grinding at it in circles, back and forth. With a sigh, Mother Superior releases the smoke she has been holding in as she watches the lubrication completed and the masturbation begun.

'Radder ye than me, Sister. Radder ye than me. But how long does it take to draw de vinnim?'

'O' dat, Mudder, I'm unsure. Ah, Sisters, back! Back for your virry lives!'

There is a moment of panic: Mother Superior taking three quick steps backwards, Sister Phallocratora and the four veiled nuns throwing themselves onto the beds on either side, veils bouncing a little as they land, for his cock, excited for far too long by what has already gone on, has responded to Sister Phallocratora's masturbation after only a few strokes and grinds of her hand and begun to spurt thickly and powerfully. Jets of sperm are shooting ceilingward, pausing a moment as they reach full height, then breaking apart as they fall, splattering copiously over his body.

'Will ye look at it spit,' says Mother Superior wonderingly.

Sister Phallocratora, sprawling on her back on one of the beds beside the prisoner, nods sadly.

'Spit indeed, Mudder, an' it's an apology I'm owin' ye an' de good Sisters here, for I nivver imagined 'twould spit so soon or so hivvily. Look, 'tis not done yet.'

They watch in silence as his cock fires its final jets of sperm, then pause for a moment before slowly and carefully approaching the bed.

'Check your robes, Sisters,' Sister Phallocratora advises. 'If ye find any stray splatters o' de vinnim, 'tis vital ye get dem off de clot' at once. It can eat t'rough clot' in seconds, so I've heard, an' 'tis deadly on de bare skin o' any woman. An' I'll ask ye all to breade shallow, so as not even to take de odour o' de stuff into your lungs.'

'An' what o' de poor lass herself,' Mother Superior asks, gesturing at his sperm-soaked body with her cigarette. 'Will she nut suffer herself now from de contact?'

The nuns and Sister Phallocratora herself are examining their robes carefully for stray splatters of sperm; now Sister Phallocratora looks up, satisfied she is clean, but shaking her head.

'No, Mudder, not while de cuck is still attached to her body. Its presence immunises her, ye might say, an' de vinnim does not work its usual effect. But quick, does anyone have a spoon?'

'A spoon, Sister? An' what call would we h— ah, Sister Tormenta, ye have one.'

Sister Tormenta has produced a long-handled silver spoon from her robes. Sister Phallocratora takes it from her with a murmur of thanks and bends forwards cautiously over the contestant, breathing carefully as she begins to guide it over his sperm-splashed skin, gathering sperm in the bowl.

' 'Tis important I'm quick, Mudder,' she says without looking away from her task. 'De vinnim loses its power quickly on contact wid de air, an' cannot work half its mischief after a minute or two.'

'An' what is it ye want to do wid it, Sister?'

'Feed it to de poor lass, o' course. Dere, I have a nice bowlful.'

She moves to the head of the bed, brushing past Sisters Sanguinulenta and Flagellatio, but he turns his head away from her and she tuts with exasperation.

'Ah, an' it's plain de Divvil's still strong in her, if she doesn't want to sup it down an' rid herself o' dis cuck an' balls. Sisters, could ye not help me a minute here?'

Sisters Flagellatio and Tormenta nod silently and step forwards from opposite sides of the bed to take hold of his head. Mother Superior, puffing absently at her cigarette, hears his tendons creak as they wrench it into place, turning his face to the ceiling, then begin to force his jaw open.

'Careful o' de vinnim, Sisters,' she says, but none is splattered on his face or chin and the sisters can work without fear.

Sister Phallocratora tuts again, but this time with satisfaction, as they drag his jaw open and she can place the spoon of the sperm-filled bowl above his panting mouth, pause a moment, and then tip it neatly inside.

'Dere, honey. 'Twill taste nasty for a minute dere, but 'tis all for your own good. Close her mout', please, Sisters,' she adds quickly as he begins to cough and splutter, and the two nuns force his jaw shut.

Sister Phallocratora looks down on him, smiling, reaching up to stroke his sweat-damp forehead.

'Dere, me girl, 'tis all for your own good, nasty dough it may seem at de time. Now, if de vinnim is fresh enough, we should see de cuck departin' her body at any moment.'

Mother Superior's and Sister Phallocratora's eyes swing to his cock, as do, beneath their veils, those of the four silent sisters. It is still stiff despite his orgasm, and stands harder as the nuns stare at it, beginning to throb a little. Ten seconds pass. Twenty. Thirty.

'Well, Sister?' asks Mother Superior.

'Ah, 'twas insufficiently fresh,' admits Sister Phallocratora. 'We'll have to try again, but I'm t'inkin' de vinnim sacs will be drained considerably after dis recent discharge an' 'twill need some considerable encouragement.'

'How long, Sister? She's booked for an examination dis morning, as ye'll know.'

'How long, Mudder? Another twenty minutes for de vinnim to have chance to weaken, then another twenty minutes o' handwork.'

'Can ye no use gloves?'

Sister Phallocratora looks back at his cock, musing.

'Aye, well, maybe. I can try, for sure, but you can add ten to dose twenty minutes o' work, for reduced sinsitivity.'

'Well, does it have to be by hand at all?'

'But how else, Mudder?'

'Could we not get her climbin' the Stairs of Torment on her hands an' knees, bare arse whipped by rosaries every t'ird tread? I'm t'inkin' if dat cuck's not spitting vinnim again by de fifiet tread, dere's somethin' badly wrong wid her.'

Sister Phallocratora pauses, eyes widening, as she looks away from his cock at Mother Superior.

'Set her on the Stairs of Torment and whip her arse every t'ird tread, is dat what ye're sayin'?'

' 'Tis dat, Sister.'

'Wid rosaries, Mudder?'

'Wid rosaries, Sister.'

'Den I believe ye have it, Mudder. We'll have de t'ing spittin' vinnim again in no time. If I have your permission to supervise her removal to de Stairs, Mudder?'

'Gladly, Sister.'

'T'ank ye, Mudder. Sisters, if ye'll untie de wee lass an' lift her off de bed an' set her on de floor for me. Don't mind de vinnim – it'll be weakened enough by now so dat ye'll not need to worry, dough a quick wash won't come amiss at de end o' de mornin'. Dat's right, Sisters.'

The four silent sisters are untying the rosaries, loop around their wrists, then seize him and lift him off the bed. Sister Phallocratora moves away from the bed, standing with Mother Superior in the middle of the aisle as she watches the four sisters work.

'On de aisle on all fours, Sisters, if ye please. Den we'll whip her on her way to de Stairs o' Torment.'

Nods as the sisters manoeuvre his body off the bed and lower him to the cold stone dormitory floor, turning him so that he lands on it on hands and knees. Task completed, they let go of him and move back a little, shaking the strings of their rosaries loose from their wrists.

'Would ye not like first swipe, Sister?' Mother Superior asks.

'Ah, 'tis kind of ye to ask, but no. I'll reserve mine for binding her hands behind her back when she starts de climb. But why do ye not set her on her way yourself, Mudder?'

'I'm askin' meself de same question, Sister, I'm askin' meself de same question. An' do ye know?'

She slips her nearly finished cigarette into her mouth and draws on it hard, so that the tip glows angry red in the gloom of the dormitory, then removes it and blows out smoke.

'An' do ye know, I can see no good reason why nut?'

She takes a stride towards the kneeling contestant's arse and stubs her cigarette out on his left buttock. He yelps and bounds forwards, and all at once the rosaries of the four silent sisters are descending on his arse in relentless synchronised rhythm, forcing him along the aisle of the dormitory towards the door. In seconds he is passing through it, oblivious to the gruesome crucifix and shadowed text that hang above his head. Mother Superior and Sister Phallocratora stroll after him, but Mother Superior pauses a few feet from the door to look upwards.

'An' what is it, Mudder?' Sister Phallocratora asks, turning her head, then taking a few paces back to join her.

'I nivver did git de translation from de poor soul, Sister.'

'An' what is it, Mudder? Dis light is murder on me eyes.'

Mother Superior laughs, takes Sister Phallocratora by the arm, and begins to walk after the diminishing screams of the rosary-driven contestant.

'Freely translated, Sister,' she says as they pass together beneath the crucifix and through the door. 'It says: "Ye'll find wisdom on de lips o' de wise, an' a rod on de arse o' de foolish." '

'A blessed sentiment, Mudder.'

'I'll not be disagreein' wid ye dere, Sister. Nut at all.'

Eleven

For a moment he keeps his eyes closed and lets his head stay slumped on his chest as he explores the aches in his body, remembering where and who he is; and then Mother Superior's lighter clicks and flares almost directly in front of him. He hears her suck on her cigarette, then sigh luxuriously as she blows smoke out over him. He opens his eyes, still looking down, and sees a haze of smoke expanding over his chest.

'Top o' de morning to ye, Brudder Philip.'

Looking down, he can see the tips of her black stilettos and the hem of her black silk robes on the floor. Now he shakes his head and looks up, his eyes passing up her body, past the purple silk rope around her hips to the mounds of her breasts, but her head is veiled for the moment in another cloud of cigarette smoke, blown at him from her red-painted lips. He coughs involuntarily, eyes stinging for a moment, and then there she is again, emerging through the smoke, her cigarette poised at her lips, her green eyes surveying him coolly, sardonically from the pale oval created by her coif.

'Ye are awake den, Brudder Philip?'

Behind her he can see Sister Tormenta and Sister Perpetua. He swallows, blinking uncomfortably for a moment as he feels his cock respond to her voice, slowly beginning to climb upright, and says, 'Yes, Mother Superior.'

She slips her cigarette into her mouth, draws on it deeply, slips it from her mouth, then jets smoke in twin streams from her nostrils as she opens her mouth and sucks it in. His cock jerks fully upright but her eyes do not drop to it. Now she's no longer jetting smoke from her nostrils, just sucking it into her mouth, clearing the air in front of her face, closing her mouth. Then, her eyes still fixed on his face, she lets her mouth come open again in an O through which she blows a long streamer of smoke, but not at his face, downwards, at his groin. He follows it down, watching as his cock is enveloped in smoke, veiled for two or three seconds, then unveiled as the smoke drifts upwards. He raises his eyes to hers again.

'Ye've not larned your lesson, have ye, Brudder Philip?'

He shakes his head.

'I said to ye: "Have ye, Brudder Philip?" '

'No, Mother Superior.'

'Dat's a good boy ye are, Brudder Philip, but so slow. Too slow. An' we cannut be havin' it, nut in a boy of your age. So it's anudder lesson ye'll be needin', an' another lesson ye'll be havin' today, me boy. Sisters Perpetua an' Tormenta, are ye ready wid de chair?'

She turns and now he sees that two nuns have been standing behind her – the silent Sisters Perpetua and Tormenta.

Mother Superior continues, 'Den let's be havin' him in it.'

She slips the cigarette back into her mouth and draws on it, stepping to one side with a rustle of silk, and he can see that the two Sisters are standing to either side of something made out of glass. It's so transparent that for a moment he can't make out what it is, and then he sees that it's a wheelchair. A glass wheelchair. Sister Tormenta steps behind it, putting her black-gloved hands to the handles, her rosary swinging from her right wrist, and Sister Perpetua comes forwards to him as he hangs splayed against the wall, balls dangling beneath his jutting cock, wrists and ankles and upper thighs, knees and elbows and shoulders clamped firmly into place. She looks down at his cock and then looks sideways at Mother Superior, but Mother Superior shakes her head.

'Leave it stiff for de good ladies who are awaitin' him,' she says.

Sister Perpetua silently nods, turns back to him and begins to open the locks on the steel clamps holding down his left ankle and knee and left wrist and elbow. He can smell the musk of her leaking pussy, and as she steps across him to unlock the clamps on his right leg and arm her robes brush the head of his cock. He groans a little, staring ahead of him at Sister Tormenta as she stands waiting behind the wheelchair. The steel locks on his right side click open, and Sister Perpetua is ready to release him.

'Forward wid ye, Sister Tormenta,' says Mother Superior.

Sister Tormenta pushes the wheelchair forwards, its wheels turning in perfect silence on the stone floor as she positions it to his left, leaving clear space ahead of him, as though she knows he's going to fall from the wall as soon as he's released, crashing face down on the floor. Now that the chair's closer he can see the tread on the transparent wheels and the narrow spokes, the little horn-and-bulb of transparent plastic sitting on the backrest, the transparent straps hanging loose on either side of the seat and backrest, and the transparent plastic cushion on the seat. But the cushion seems to have a hole in the centre of it, leading down to a hole in the seat. It's a *chaise percée*, a pierced seat. Sister Perpetua steps across him again, her robes brushing at the head of his cock, and begins to lift the clamps on his right arm, first his wrist, then his elbow. He groans again as his arm drops, swinging on the pivot of the clamp at his shoulder. It hangs slackly down his right flank. Now she steps across him again, the head of his cock brushed by her robes, and begins to lift the clamps on his left arm, first his wrist, then his elbow.

He groans again as his left arm drops. Now the upper half of his body is held up only by the clamps at his shoulders. If they were released he would slump forwards at the waist, his head hanging between his open thighs, his stiff cock poking into his bare chest, its head glowing against his skin. She steps across him again, left to right, and he knows she's deliberately tormenting him with the slight repeated brushing of her robes on the head of his cock. She kneels and begins lifting the clamps on his right leg, first ankle, then knee, then upper thigh, the cool beads of her rosary brushing his skin. He can smell that she's started to sweat slightly with the effort of lifting the clamps. The scent of it rises to him, mingling with the sweetness of her perfume and the musk of her leaking pussy, and his cock is stiff and solid as she steps across his body again, her robes gently brushing the head of his cock again.

But it's never going to be enough, never going to be repeated quickly or firmly enough for him to come, and the thought of that, the frustration of that, *is* enough, and he starts coming, his cock jerking even higher and beginning to spurt long shafts of white sperm. He hates the waste of it, the way it's firing into empty air, not against the black robes of the veiled woman who has tormented him. This was why Sister Tormenta didn't stand with the wheelchair right in front of him, why Mother Superior is standing to one side. They knew he was going to come. Sister Perpetua is lifting the clamp around his ankle, but Mother Superior coughs gently behind her and she turns her head, still stooping with her slim hands on the clamp.

'D'ye not see what he's gone and done, Sister Perpetua?' Mother Superior asks.

Her cigarette sweeps away from her mouth, indicating the shining patch of sperm on the floor. Sister Perpetua rises from his ankle, turning in the same movement and gliding forwards. The scents of her – sweat, perfume, menstrual blood – are folded in disturbed air and reach his nose stronger than ever for a moment. She stoops over the patch, examining it carefully, then turns and looks towards Mother Superior, who nods, drawing on the cigarette. She releases smoke and then speaks through it, her face still veiled by it, Goddess speaking from a cloud.

'Yes, Sister. He's come, merely while ye were settin' de poor wee feller free. Dere's gratitude for ye.'

Sister Perpetua lifts her right hand, swinging the rosary that hangs from the wrist, and Mother Superior nods again.

'Aye, ye may. An' Sister Tormenta too.'

Sister Perpetua turns and glides back from the patch of sperm as Sister Tormenta glides from behind the wheelchair. They stand facing each other on either side of his cock, two or three feet back from it. Mother Superior says from behind him, 'Six strokes ye'll deliver, Sisters. Three each on me count.'

Their right hands swing up against their right shoulders and he sees that they've let their rosaries slip down into their hands, clutching at them firmly by the crucifix so that the string of beads hangs free.

'Ye first, Sister Perpetua. One.'

Sister Perpetua's hand lashes down and forwards, pivoting at the elbow, and the dangling string of her rosary whips across the shaft of his cock, leaving a burning track of pain. Her hand swings back to her shoulder and Mother Superior says, 'Two', and Sister Tormenta's hand lashes down and forwards, pivoting at the elbow, and the dangling string of *her* rosary whips across the shaft of his cock in the same place, reawakening and heightening the sting of Sister Perpetua's stroke.

'T'ree . . .' says Mother Superior. 'Four . . . Five . . . Six . . . An' dat'll be enough, Sisters.'

Sister Tormenta turns and glides back to the wheelchair and Sister Perpetua glides back to the clamps on his left leg, kneeling to the ankle, lifting the clamp there, raising a little to lift the clamp on his knee, then on his upper thigh, the beads of her rosary dangling from her right wrist, gently brushing and tickling his skin. He looks down, seeing her black robes and the bright red track that divides the white shaft of his cock in two. The clamp around his upper left thigh is free and now he's held up against the wall only by the clamps around his shoulders.

'Sister Tormenta, if ye please,' says Mother Superior and Sister Tormenta glides towards him from behind the wheelchair as Sister Perpetua steps across his body again, her robes brushing against the head of his cock for the final time as she lifts her hands for the clamp on his right shoulder.

Sister Tormenta reaches him and lifts her hands to the clamp on his left shoulder.

'Ye may release him, Sisters,' says Mother Superior. 'But careful wid him, mind. We don't want to deliver him damaged to Balsonnalyne.'

What was that? Balsonnalyne? Was that an Irish town? Was he leaving the Heart of Darkness today? Sisters Perpetua and Tormenta swiftly tug open the clamps on his shoulders, catching him by his upper arms in the same deft movement as he topples forwards from the wall, holding him up, then pulling him towards the wheelchair, his legs nearly useless beneath him. As they reach it they turn him and guide him into the seat. He slumps into it gratefully.

'Balls,' says Mother Superior.

Sister Tormenta has moved round to the handles of the wheelchair again and it's Sister Perpetua who slips a hand under his buttocks, feeling for his balls. They're

210

trapped between his thighs and the transparent plastic cushion. She pushes him more firmly back into the seat and then slips her hand beneath his buttocks, tugging at his balls until they drop neatly through the hole he saw while he was still clamped to the wall.

'Good,' says Mother Superior 'Now cuck.'

Sister Perpetua adjusts it between his thighs, allowing it to jut forwards ahead of him.

'Good,' says Mother Superior. 'Now sthrap him in.'

Sister Perpetua sets to work with the body straps, tightening them across his thighs, stomach and chest, then with the arm straps, tightening them across his wrists and forearms, fixing him into the chair. She steps back, job done.

'Good,' says Mother Superior, then, to Sister Tormenta, 'Take him on his way, Sister.'

Sister Tormenta turns the chair neatly on the spot then pushes him to the door. He feels his cock and bruised buttocks respond to the memories of the previous day, twitching and tingling, but the stairs have changed: a long ramp has been laid down the middle of them and he can see two black figures waiting at the foot. Is it Sisters Flagellatio and Sanguinulenta? Yes, he can see the coloured veils they are wearing, yellow and blue. Sister Tormenta pushes him to the head of the ramp, then lines him up facing down it. He feels her let go of the right handle of the wheelchair, raising her arm as though to signal; and yes, far below Sister Flagellatio or Sanguinulenta has raised her right arm in reply, the cloth of her robe glistening oddly to the movement, as though it's made of plastic or vinyl instead of silk. Sister Tormenta puts her left hand back on the handle, pushes him forwards, lining him up down the exact centre of the ramp, small front wheels rolled a little down it, big back wheels just on the brink, and then gives him a firm, measured shove.

He picks up speed fast, wheels beginning to hum at a higher and higher pitch on the wooden surface of the ramp as he feels the air slide over his shaved skull and the still-swollen head of his cock, fright suddenly powering his hands and fingers so that he can grip the armrests of the chair hard. Ahead of him he can see the robes of both the nuns glistening as they turn their backs on him and glide away from the foot of the ramp. When he reaches the halfway point, they're fifteen or twenty feet from it and turn back to watch him again. He wonders, his cock stiffening further at the thought of it, whether the wheelchair is going to smash when it reaches the foot of the ramp and has to roll on the level again. Will Sisters Flagellatio and Sanguinulenta have to glide back to drag his bleeding body from the wreckage, their hidden feet crunching on shards and splinters of glass?

He closes his eyes and bows his head to his chest, waiting for the crash of breaking glass, the impact as his body is hurled against the floor, slashed and torn by shards of glass. But the wheelchair hits the foot of the ramp with no more than a slight thump and rolls on, so that he opens his eyes to see the two nuns coming up fast at him, black pillars on the white marble of the floor. The wheelchair is slowing, like his heart and breath, so that when he reaches the two, the wheelchair stopping almost exactly between them, he can count his heartbeats again and his breath is coming almost silently. Now they move, closing in behind him, and he can hear their robes squeaking faintly. They *are* made of plastic or vinyl, black shiny plastic or vinyl.

They start pushing him, Sister Sanguinulenta-or-Flagellatio's right hand on the left handle of his chair, Sister Flagellatio-or-Sanguinulenta's left hand on the right handle of his chair, but as they approach the large bronze doors at the end of the hall, Sister Sanguinulenta-or-Flagellatio releases the handle for a moment and works the little horn. He quivers as it honks underneath his left ear, and then hears a voice through the doors, hugely amplified but coming from many yards away, so that he can't distinguish the words. The doors swing open ahead of him, spilling bright, almost intolerable light and a confused, gossipy buzz of women's voices. He's pushed through them in the glass wheelchair by the two nuns, his aching balls dangling through the hole cut in the seat, his cock jutting between his splayed and strapped-apart thighs. As he passes through and enters the vast chamber that awaits him, a sudden ironic roar of welcome goes up, sweeping away from him into the far corners of the crowded seats that face the stage, overwhelming the gossipy buzz of women's voices that was there before. Two cameranuns are waiting just inside the doors, lightweight white TV cameras swung over the shoulders of their black vinyl robes. They move in eagerly, trotting backwards as the wheelchair rolls down the black marble aisle, their lenses, shaded by deep visors, trained on his cock and dangling balls, and the huge screen standing between the two raised contestants' seats on the stage suddenly snaps on in merciless detail: sweaty, dangling balls and blue-veined cock, thirty or forty times lifesize, filmed from two constantly shifting angles and transmitted to an audience of three or four thousand women.

Another roar goes up from the crowd as the image appears, this time of laughter and contempt, and he notices the dark vertical shape cutting into the lower half of the screen. It's the compère, standing and watching him come in. The outline of her shoulders shifts as she raises her microphone to her lips, and speakers mounted above the stage crash out above the ribald comments that are being hurled at him.

'Ladies! Pelting may now commence!'

Now the women are standing on their seats as the wheelchair passes, hands tugging at their skirts, lifting them up, and the smell of menstruation that he noticed as soon as he passed through the doors is suddenly stronger, coming over him in waves. His cock throbs and in the same instant something warm and wet slaps across his face and falls into his lap, bouncing from the jutting shaft of his cock. He barely has time to note that it's a used and oozing tampon before the air is suddenly full of them, arcing through the air, flung at him eagerly, mostly clumsily, sometimes expertly, by the thousands of women in the audience. They strike each other in midair and fall short or wide or directly on top of him or the nuns pushing him or the nuns filming him, piling up in his lap, splattering and streaking his body with fresh, musk-blaring menstrual blood. The women are chanting as they hurl, continuing to chant once they've hurled, bouncing up and down on their seats to the rhythm of it, clapping their blood-streaked hands, and the sound of their voices and hands beats on his ears the way the hail of tampons is beating on his body.

'Rat-dick! Rat-dick! Rat-dick! Rat-dick!'

He can see what is happening more clearly on the screen ahead of him: the blizzard of tampons coming at him from all sides, thudding across his chest and head and shoulders, bouncing off the wheelchair, littering the aisle for yards behind and on either side and in front of him, so that the wheels of the chair rock and bounce as the nuns push him forwards over them, their shoes squelching beneath the chant as they tread the wet tampons into the marble.

The shoes of the cameranuns squelch too, and he wonders at their powers of balance, for they're both trotting backwards, feet stumbling and twisting in the carpet of tampons, but still managing to keep the lenses of their cameras steady on his cock and balls, feeding the huge screen on the stage ahead of him. His cock is almost buried in tampons now, but his balls are still on full display beneath him, swinging as the wheelchair rocks and bounces. There are spots on the image projected on the screen: stray splatters of menstrual

214

blood that have found their way under the visors of the camera-lenses, and he thinks one or both of the cameras is going to be blinded by a direct hit soon. But now the compère, her dark shape cutting higher into the screen as he gets nearer the stage, is lifting her microphone back to her lips, and the speakers above the stage crash out again.

'Ladies! Ladies! Please, ladies! Please cease pelting and prepare to welcome our first contestant!'

For two, three, four moments there's no difference and he thinks the audience has ignored her, but then he realises that tampons were still in the air or just on the point of being hurled. Only a few women are too excited to obey or even to hear the command, and their neighbours are grabbing them by the arms, shouting the compère's instructions into their ears. In another second the blizzard has thinned, coming in threes and fours, then ones and twos, and then it's stopped and only the clap-buttressed chant of 'Rat-dick!' is still being hurled at him.

All over the hall he can hear women sitting down again, still gasping and panting from the excitement of the persecution, their voices strained as they join in the chant. The squelch of the four nuns' shoes in the carpet of tampons is almost drowned in it, but the carpet is thinning underfoot too. They're nearly at the stage. He can't see the lower half of the screen any more and the compère's shape cuts through the upper half of it all the way to the top. Then the wheelchair reaches the foot of the ramp that rises to the stage and the cameranuns trot backwards on it without a glance behind them, filming him as he's pushed onto it. The pile of tampons in his lap slides against his chest as the chair tilts and two or three bounce clear to the surface of the ramp. He hears one of them squelch as Sister Sanguinulenta-or-Flagellatio's shoe lands on top of it.

'Ladies!' cries the compère above the chant of 'Rat-dick!'. 'Please welcome our first contestant.'

Whistles and jeers shrill out at him, laughter and cat-calls, then the wheelchair is being turned to take him across the stage to his waiting seat. Now two cameranuns move back, filming from a wide angle, and as he passes the compère she lifts her microphone to her lips again. It sounds odd to hear her voice reach his ears directly from her lips and then, a fraction of a second later, much louder, from the speakers above his head.

'Giselle and Anthea, if you can do the honours.'

As the two sisters push the wheelchair up to his seat he hears four or five pairs of shoes and a rumble of small wheels on the stage behind him; and as the two Sisters turn the wheelchair, facing him out over the audience, he sees two young women in white vinyl smocks and trousers coming briskly towards him, one of them pushing a small cart, black and blonde hair bouncing in two neat braids down their backs, their slim hands in white vinyl gloves. Behind them he can see four more young women, identically dressed, with neat braids of red or blonde or black hair bouncing down their white vinyl backs, striding down the ramp, the lower halves of their bodies already cut off by the edge of the stage, but he thinks they're carrying shovels. Sister Flagellatio-or-Sanguinulenta crouches to put the wheelchair's brake on, then straightens and he hears her shoes retreating behind him with Sister Sanguinulenta-or-Flagellatio's. The young woman pushing the cart stops it two or three feet short of him, then trots to join the other young woman, who is already stooping over his lap, deftly untombing his cock from tampons, which she throws left and right to the floor of the stage.

The first young woman bends and begins picking them up, gathering a double handful before trotting to the front of the stage and throwing them out over the audience. The speakers crash out again, and this time he hears the compère's voice directly from her lips a fraction of a second afterwards.

'Re-insert, ladies!'

The young women who marched down the ramp have come into view again on the aisle. They reach the edges of the carpet of tampons and he can see that they're stooping to them, two on either side of the aisle, scooping the tampons up in light shovels, then straightening to throw them back into the audience. Then they stoop again, taking two or three steps forwards as they shovel up more tampons, then straighten to throw them back into the audience. Ahead of him on the stage the first young woman throws her third and final double-handful of tampons back into the audience, and his cock is fully uncovered now. He can see women in the audience pulling up their skirts again, opening their legs, re-inserting the tampons that have been thrown or shovelled back to them. But they must be re-inserting other women's tampons, and his cock throbs and twitches. On the stage Giselle-or-Anthea turns and comes back to the cart, pushing it up to him. She swings the cover open and he can see that it's full of make-up gear. She reaches inside, tugging at a triangle of cloth sticking up through a hole in a steel plate. The cloth slides out of the hole, lengthening, and then she tears it off with a deft flick of her wrist and he sees that it's a disposable wipe. As she moves towards him Anthea-or-Giselle turns to the cart too, tugging at the new triangle of cloth sticking from the hole.

Giselle-or-Anthea reaches him and begins to wipe briskly at his blood-splattered face with the cloth, cutting off his view of the hundreds of women in the audience re-inserting other women's tampons into their oozing pussies. The cloth is moist and cool, soaked with rose-scented cream, making him feel dizzy for a moment. Another cloth, wielded by Anthea-or-Giselle, lands on his chest and starts to wipe the blood off there, and he shivers as it passes across his peaked nipples. Giselle-or-Anthea finishes with his face and turns back to the make-up cart, throwing the soiled cloth away in a little bin and hauling up and breaking off another. She turns back to him, working on his ears and neck now, then scrubbing at his shaved scalp. The speakers above him crash out again.

'Thank you, ladies! Now, allow me to introduce you to our first contestant, little Philip Tyndale!'

Anthea-or-Giselle is scrubbing briskly at the shaft of his cock now, but as she hears this she flicks the cloth free and she and Giselle-or-Anthea step away from him, allowing the cameranuns to move in close, pointing the lenses of their cameras directly at his cock and balls. He can imagine them swelling on the screen in the middle of the stage, his balls dangling pathetically beneath him, the shaft of his cock still glistening with Anthea-or-Giselle's scrubbing, his cockhead purple and swollen.

'Little Philip is a postgraduate student of European literature at the University of Northchester and his specialist subject tonight will be . . .'

The compère pauses, as though consulting something, and then continues with mock awe. 'His specialist subject tonight will be themes of female domination in the work of the Victorian poet Charles Algernon Swinburne, eighteen thirty-six to nineteen-oh-nine.'

An ironic 'Oooooh' goes up from the audience and he feels his cock twitch and jerk, then jerk again as the audience, watching it on the screen, roars with laughter.

'As you can see, ladies,' the compère continues, 'Philip is a very excitable little boy. Aren't you, Philip? But we may be able to put a stop to that.'

Then, dropping the microphone from her lips, she adds, 'Giselle, Anthea, please', and the two make-up girls move in on him again. Anthea-or-Giselle completes her work on his cock, scrubbing at the head now, pulling the skin of his shaft down so that the head is fully exposed. He hears the compère draw in breath as she puts the microphone back to her lips.

218

'So, ladies, on the count of three, I'd like a big Balls-on-the-Line welcome for little Philip. Are you ready?'

There are a few cries of 'Yes' from the audience. What has she said? Another intake of breath. Balls-on-the-Line?

'I said, "Are you ready?" '

More and louder cries, another intake of breath.

'I *said*: "*Are . . . you . . . ready . . .?*" '

The whole audience roars 'Yes!' this time and he shivers with delicious dread, his cock jerking between his thighs. Giselle and Anthea have finished scrubbing him down and turn back to the cart to drop their soiled cloths into the bin there. The cameranuns move in again as his body is exposed.

'Then on the count of three. One . . . two . . . three!'

And here it comes, shrilling in on him from the four thousand throats of four thousand menstruating women.

'Hello, little Philip!'

His cock, the lenses of both cameranuns fixed on it, jerks and stands almost upright, and into the echoes still ringing in his bruised ears comes the needling surf of gleeful female laughter.

'Thank you, ladies!' the compère cries.

Giselle and Anthea move back in on him, shielding him again from the cameranuns' lenses, rattling inside the make-up cart. Giselle-or-Anthea picks up what looks like a huge gold lipstick container, twisting the base so that a dark purple head of lipstick glides from it. Anthea-or-Giselle is taking the cap off a transparent container filled with what looks like tightly packed ginger hair and reaching inside, but Giselle-or-Anthea cuts off his view as she moves forwards and takes hold of the shaft of his cock just below the head with her free hand, tugging it forwards and setting to work with the purple lipstick. She's adjusting the colour of his cock-head, making it suitable for the cameras, her lips pursed

219

and professional as she works with quick, practised strokes, gliding the dickstick over the dome and around the rim of his cockhead.

Then she's finished, moving back so that he can see what Anthea-or-Giselle is holding ready for him. In her left hand is a tiny wig of ginger hair. In her right a small bottle. She moves forwards, stooping over his lap, and he can feel her breath brush over the head of his cock as she applies glue in two quick curving sweeps to his groin, then hands the bottle back over her shoulder to Giselle-or-Anthea and takes hold of the tiny wig in both hands. It's a pubic wig, he realises. He can't remember the special name for them. Anthea-or-Giselle slips it over his groin, stroking it deftly into place, then tugging at it a little to check that's it's firmly in place. Merkin, that's it. She fluffs the hair up with both hands, tilting her head first one way, then the other, then leans back and turns away from him, allowing Giselle-or-Anthea to move in on him again.

She's holding a large dusting brush in one hand and an open tin of pink face-powder in the other. His nose tickles with the dusty perfume of it. Only it's not face-powder. Anthea-or-Giselle has moved behind his wheelchair and he feels air move on the back of his head as she stoops, then feels the wheelchair shudder faintly as she takes hold of something and tugs. Suddenly he feels the two sections of the seat between him move upwards, lifting his thighs and raising his balls from the hole in which they are dangling, exposing them to the dusting-brush and the tin of not face-powder but of ball-powder.

He restrains a sneeze as Giselle-or-Anthea coats the brush in powder, twirling it quickly in the tin, and sets to work on his balls, dabbing at them, working the powder into the wrinkles and down the seam that divides his ball-sac. She recharges the brush and he can't restrain a small sneeze this time as the soft brush begins work on his balls again. He hears another intake of breath on the speakers.

'Bless you,' the compère says, and the women in the audience roar with laughter again.

Then Giselle-or-Anthea moves back and turns away and the wheelchair shudders again as Anthea-or-Giselle releases the lever she has tugged and lowers him back into the seat. Giselle-or-Anthea is putting the brush and tin of ball-powder back into the make-up cart, then swinging the lid shut again, and he feels Anthea-or-Giselle take hold of the handles of the wheelchair. They've finished. Anthea-or-Giselle pulls the wheelchair backwards two or three feet, positioning him directly in front of the contestant's seat that he knows is waiting behind him. His cock twitches nervously.

Anthea-or-Giselle stands and moves up beside his left arm, beginning to undo the straps as Giselle-or-Anthea moves up beside his right arm and begins to undo the straps there. They work with the same brisk, calm efficiency and both his arms are quickly free. Now they bend forwards to undo the straps on his thighs, their hair swinging in front of his face, their combined breath tickling the head of his cock. Now his thighs are free. They bend further, slipping hands and forearms under his thighs, swinging his freed arms over their shoulders, and hoist him from the wheelchair, lifting him clean over the back of it with faint, cock-twitching feminine grunts, and lower him into his new seat. Cold steel touches the skin of his back and pain spurts in his buttocks as they let go of him and his full weight settles into the seat.

And now, as Anthea-or-Giselle pushes the wheelchair off the stage and Giselle-or-Anthea busies herself with strapping him in and noosing his balls so that they dangle into the glass box below the seat, the second contestant arrives. First he hears a murmur at the rear of the audience, from the women closest to the doors, then, to his left, the compère lifts the microphone to her lips and says, 'Doors please.'

The murmur in the audience has spread and he can see women turning to watch the doors. The two cameranuns on the stage, who have been filming him as he's strapped into his contestant's seat, turn and begin running for the ramp. The roar that greeted his own entrance trembles into early life as the doors to the set begin to swing open, increases suddenly in volume, then crashes out in full as another glass wheelchair with another naked man strapped into it comes rolling in, pushed again by Sisters Sanguinulenta and Flagellatio. He can see a few white tampons still scattered down the black marble of the aisle, missed by the shovellers, and he hears the clatter of the cameranuns' shoes as they run down the aisle towards the wheelchair. As they reach it and begin filming, the compère raises the microphone to her lips again and says, 'Ladies! Pelting may now re-commence!'

He has a full view this time: the women lying back in their seats, skirts hoisted, tugging wet tampons free of their oozing pussies, then standing on their seats to hurl them at the wheelchair and its helpless occupant as they begin to chant 'Rat-dick!' again. But then his view is suddenly cut off and he looks up, startled, to see the compère standing in front of him.

'Everything all right, Anth'?' she asks through the chant of 'Rat-dick! Rat-dick! Rat-dick!' from the audience, and not Giselle-or-Anthea, just Anthea, looks over her shoulder from where she's crouched in front of him, still adjusting his balls.

'Yes, thanks.'

He can smell the compère's perfume, see her large breasts swelling in her black dress, and, when she looks up from Anthea and smiles at him, the head of his cock bounces gently on his stomach as it responds. Her smile is the smile of a shark and she might be the dominatrix of his dreams: 35 or 40, dark-haired, big-breasted, her face rounded, cheeks smooth and fleshy and dimpled, and wearing bright red lipstick on full lips.

'Everything all right, Philip?' she asks, and then, without waiting for a reply, she steps to one side of him and turns to watch the new contestant being wheeled down the aisle. He's so aware of her breasts hanging at just the level of his face that he doesn't notice her hand move out and drop to his cock, and when she takes hold of it and begins to wank him slowly and luxuriously he groans and shudders. Anthea stands up in front of him and turns away to the cart. The compère glances at him for a moment, then glances down at his cock, then looks back at the audience.

'We play it backwards, you know,' she says conversationally.

Anthea is pushing the cart across the stage, ready for the newcomer.

'Over the closing credits, so it looks as though the wheelchair is spouting tampons into the audience as it rolls back down the aisle. Like a tampon fountain.'

The wheelchair is two-thirds of the way to the stage now and under the blizzard of tampons still being hurled from the audience he can see it bouncing and shuddering over the carpet of tampons already on the aisle. The compère's hand squeezes and tugs, moving more slowly, more luxuriously, moving to the rhythm of the women in the audience who are standing on their seats, and clapping to each syllable of 'Rat-dick! Rat-dick! Rat-dick!' Then she reaches over with her other hand, still holding her microphone in it, and starts to scratch delicately at his left nipple with a long, sharp fingernail. Her perfume has enfolded him and his balls are straining to lift in the noose tightened around them by Anthea. She switches to his right nipple.

'Do you like that, Philip?'

He opens his mouth to start gasping with orgasm, feeling sperm beginning to boil up in his balls, ready to

223

spurt from his cock in torrents on the next expert stroke of her warm, soft, smooth hand, and she lets go of his cock. He groans with frustration, sucking eagerly on the sensation of her scratching fingers on his right nipple, trying to force himself to orgasm with that, because he's on the brink, he's practically over, and she couldn't be so cruel as to deny him it, she couldn't, she *can't*, because his balls are going to ache like buggery.

She lifts her finger from his nipple and strolls away from him, lifting the microphone to her lips again. The newcomer is at the foot of the ramp now, still being pelted with tampons from the crowd, and he can smell the wave of menstrual blood that comes with him. His balls are aching fiercely and he strains to lift one of his arms free from the armrest of his seat, clenching and relaxing his fingers impotently.

'Ladies!' the compère cries. 'Ladies! Please cease pelting and prepare to welcome our *second* contestant!'

The newcomer is on the ramp now and the last tampons are arcing up out of the audience at him. First the two cameranuns come into view, walking backwards as they film the newcomer, then the vinyl-covered heads of Sisters Sanguinulenta and Flagellatio, rising above the floor of the stage, then the shaven skull of the contestant, glistening with sweat, then his face and the black domino across his eyes, then his shoulders and body, then the blunt, purple head of his erect cock peeping through a wobbling pile of soiled tampons, then the glittering armrest of the wheelchair, one of its wheels, and then he's reached the head of the ramp and the Sisters are turning the wheelchair to push him to his seat and the waiting make-up cart. Anthea is waiting for him and Giselle appears again, trotting from the side of the stage to reach the newcomer. He hears shoes on the surface of the stage and turns his head to see the four young women who shovelled the tampons running across it. Two of them have shovels in their hands again but the remaining two are each pushing a white wheelbarrow.

He hears the intake of breath as the compère raises her microphone to her lips again. Giselle is collecting a double handful of tampons from the newcomer's lap, re-exposing the full length of his cock, but she's not turning to throw them into the audience this time. No, she's taking a step to one side, stooping to spill the handful to the floor of the stage, then turning back to the newcomer's lap.

'Ladies! Now, allow me to introduce you to our second contestant. I'm afraid we can't reveal his true identity, so we're just going to call him Little Willy!'

Giselle hasn't uncovered the newcomer's cock fully yet, but she's uncovered enough and she moves back now. The cameranuns move in on the newcomer, filming between his legs. An appreciative murmur runs through the crowd.

'Only, as you can see, he isn't such a Little Willy, is he? Now, Little Willy is an Anglican priest and his specialist subject tonight will be . . .'

As before she pauses, and now Philip can see that she's dropped her microphone and lifted a small card to her face, her lips moving silently for a moment as she reads what's on it. She drops the card and raises her microphone again.

'His specialist subject will be . . .'

She raises the card again as though not quite sure she has remembered right. Giselle is spilling a third double handful of tampons to the floor of the stage.

'Will *be* . . . the subordinate position of women as preached in Pauline Epistles of the New Testament!'

The murmurs in the crowd alter in pitch and he hears the first boos. The four young women have appeared on the aisle, two on each side, one with a wheelbarrow, one with a shovel. They're collecting the tampons this time, not throwing them back into the audience.

'Yes, that's right, ladies! The *subordinate* position of women as preached in Pauline Epistles of the New Testament!'

More boos. The cameranuns move back and Giselle and Anthea move in.

'That's what it says on my card!' says the compère through the boos. She moves to the front of the stage, holding the card by one corner and lifting it high into the air.

'The divinely ordained subordinate position of *women* – as preached in the Pauline Epistles of the New *Testament*, no less.'

A few tampons, fallen under seats while the pelting was under way and now retrieved, suddenly arc out of the audience, thrown hard at the newcomer. They land wide or short with wet slaps, and Giselle and Anthea, who are scrubbing at the newcomer's body with the scented clothes, don't pause to look over their shoulders. The boos are continuous now, coming from all sections of the audience. The compère flips the card contemptuously into the audience and walks backwards from the edge of the stage, pleased with the reaction she's provoked. She lifts her free hand, gesturing for silence, raising the microphone to her lips again.

'Well, ladies!' she cries. 'Let's hope Little Willy has seen the error of his ways before he leaves here tonight, shall we? That is –' and she pauses, turning her head theatrically to stage-right '– if he *does* leave here tonight.'

There's a rumbling from both sides of the stage, and Philip's head turns one way, then the other. Stage-left: two young women in jeans and T-shirts are pushing forwards what looks like a circular children's swimming-pool made of glass and resting on a wheeled platform. Stage-right: two more young women in jeans and T-shirts are slowly pulling forwards a cart piled high with what looks like thin planks and struts. He can see three more young women in jeans and T-shirts behind the cart, quickly and efficiently pulling the planks and struts off the cart. Two of them set the struts upright; the third lays the planks on top of them. It looks like a ... yes, like a model railway, and it's heading directly for him.

The women pushing the children's pool stop in the centre of the stage. Now he can see that the pool has short, downward-pointing pipes sticking from its sides. Two of the women take hold of the pool on opposite sides and lift it off the wheeled platform, before lowering it carefully to the floor of the stage, then open a narrow, rectangular box still sitting on the platform, take up a handful of its contents and move briskly around the pool laying them one by one beneath the mouths of the downward-pointing pipes. Wineglasses. Ten long-stemmed, narrow-mouthed wineglasses.

The compère walks forwards to the front of the stage again, lifting the microphone to her lips. Behind her Giselle and Anthea have finished their make-up work on the newcomer's cock and balls and are tidying the make-up cart, before swinging its lid closed, getting ready to move away and leave the newcomer to the lenses of the cameranuns.

'Is that enough, girls?' the compère asks, looking down the aisle at the women with the wheelbarrows and shovels.

They look back at her and he hears one of them shout in reply, her voice sounding thin and reedy after the blast of the compère's voice over the speakers: 'Yes, probably, Domineta.'

For a moment he thinks she's said 'Domina', and the ache in his balls suddenly flares, as though wrenched higher by the sudden upward jerk of his cock, and he releases a stifled groan. But no, it was 'Domineta': 'little Domina'. Just as he was little Philip. The ache in his balls subsides, throbbing dully at him, not piercingly. The Domineta raises the microphone to her lips.

'Then bring what you've got back. We're running a little late.'

As she turns from the front of the stage and walks over to the newcomer, she glances across the stage at Philip for a moment, an amused smile on her face. She shakes her head almost imperceptibly, and the ache in his balls flares again. She heard his groan. She knows what he thought. Now she reaches the newcomer, Little Willy, the man in the black domino, standing beside him on the opposite side to Philip, and he watches as, watching the wheelbarrows return up the aisle, she reaches in front of him. He hears the newcomer gasp as her hand takes hold of his cock, her long fingers not quite meeting around the shaft, then hears him gasp again as her hand begins its slow, luxurious cycling. The cameranuns are down on one knee in front of the newcomer, filming the masturbation, and he hears the crowd murmur. Some of the bolder women start to shout advice. He sees the Domineta smile. She lifts the microphone to her lips with her other hand, having to bend a little to one side as she continues to masturbate the newcomer, her hand moving slower and slower.

'What do you think, ladies? Should I take him to orgasm?'

He suddenly hears a voice on his right and reluctantly turns his head away. The women setting up the model-railway line are only a few feet away, and the line is definitely going to run up to him. What did the voice say? The women pulling the cart have stopped and one of the women laying the track moves out from behind it, trotting over to him, kneeling beside his chair. What is she doing?

'Well, ladies? Shall we vote? All in favour of my taking Little Willy to orgasm and not leaving the poor dear with a *terrible* ache in his balls, please shout "Aye"!'

Philip feels his seat vibrate under him, then gasps with surprise as light suddenly blazes down on him and he feels himself rising smoothly into the air. He feels air on his dangling balls and looking down he sees that the seat is being lifted on four narrow steel poles. The woman who kneeled beside his seat rises and turns back, before trotting back behind the cart.

'No?' says the Domineta.

Brilliant white lights have sprung awake in the ceiling and floor, blazing directly at him, making him blink away tears for a moment. He realises that the audience has been silent: no one has been in favour of bringing the newcomer to orgasm. The women pulling the cart move again and his seat stops rising, then tilts back a little, making his balls swing beneath them.

'OK. Then all in favour of my *not* taking Little Willy to orgasm, thus leaving the poor dear with a *terrible* ache in his balls –'

He's about three feet off the stage, balls swinging a few inches off the model-railway track that is now going to pass directly beneath him – directly beneath *them*.

'– please shout "No"!'

The entire audience screams 'No!' and he turns his head back to watch the laughing Domineta let go of the newcomer's cock and step forwards. He can't see the women with the wheelbarrows and shovels, and his ears are still humming with the unanimous verdict of the crowd, so he can't hear them on the ramp. But now their heads appear, the heads of the shovel girls, their shoulders, arms, hips, legs, trotting ahead of the wheelbarrow girls, whose heads have appeared now too. The women setting up the railway track are only a foot or so away from him. One of the women pulling the cart looks over her shoulder, then laughs and nudges the other one, who looks over her shoulder too and laughs. They're looking at his balls, dangling beneath his seat. They turn the cart, ready to pull it round him while the track-layers lay the track underneath him.

The shovel girls and wheelbarrow girls reach the top of the ramp and turn up the stage for the children's pool. And now the track is being laid beneath him, the track girls reaching between the steel poles that hold his seat up. One of them pauses a moment and pokes at his balls with a cool fingertip, setting them swinging, before carrying on with her work, and he hears a laugh go through the audience. One of the cameranuns is filming him again, down on one knee on the stage about twelve feet away, camera raised and fixed on his balls. The shovel girls and wheelbarrow girls reach the pool and start to tip the contents of the wheelbarrows into it: fat, blood-soaked tampons whose smell reaches him as he hangs in the air with his balls a few inches above the track of a model railway.

One of the shovel girls is taking her shoes off and rolling up her trousers, revealing slim, tanned calves and slender, delicate feet that make his cock twitch. Now the other shovel girl is doing the same, and the first one is climbing into the pool, stroking a lock of hair out of her eyes. As the second one joins her, and the wheelbarrow girls scoop up the last tampons from the wheelbarrows and throw them into the pool, then bend to take off their shoes too, the first shovel girl starts to move her feet up and down, left, right, left, right and he sees the first rill of menstrual blood pour down one of the pipes and into a wineglass. The second shovel girl joins her, starting to tread the tampons too, her feet moving left, right, left, right, and menstrual blood is rilling into more wineglasses. He hears an intake of breath on the speakers above him.

'Well, ladies! I hope you have provided a good vintage for our two lucky contestants. Have you, do you think?'

The Domineta pauses for a moment, listening to the shouts of 'Yes!' from the audience, then puts the microphone back to her lips.

'Oh, come on, that's feeble. Let's hear it again. Do you think you've provided a good vintage for our two lucky contestants?'

'Yes!' comes the cry, much louder this time. The two wheelbarrow girls have climbed inside the pool now and all four women are treading vigorously.

'Still feeble! Do you think you have?'

'Yes!' comes the cry again, and he feels his balls shift and try to climb towards the fork of his thighs.

'Good!' says the Domineta. 'Then let's make sure we get every last drop of it.'

She turns and moves across the stage, heading directly for him. The track-laying has nearly reached the newcomer's seat now and he sees one of the track-layers moving out from behind the cart, starting to trot to the newcomer's chair to operate the mechanism that will raise it. But then the Domineta is standing underneath him, lifting a stiff finger to poke at his balls.

'Repeat after me,' she says into her microphone, and as she begins to sway it she sets his balls swinging. ' "Left, right, left, right, my balls are swinging from left to right." '

Some women in the audience are laughing too much to repeat the words for a moment, but they manage to recover and join in, so that the words are being repeated much more loudly at the end than at the beginning.

'Left, right, left, right, my balls are swinging from left to right.'

The Domineta has stopped swinging his balls; now she starts again, lifting the microphone back to her lips. The tanned calves and paler feet of the tampon-treaders are stained purple with blood now.

' "My cock is aching, my pubes are a fright, left, right, left, right." '

'My cock is aching,' the audience chants, 'my pubes are a fright, left, right, left, right.'

'Good!' says the Domineta. 'Now, on the count of three, from the top. One, two, three!'

She starts his balls swinging again as the audience begins to chant the words once more.

'Left, right, left, right, my balls are swinging from left to right. My cock is aching, my pubes are a fright, left, right, left, right.'

'Again!' shouts the Domineta, and the audience begins again. The tampon-treaders have started to tread to the rhythm of it, and he sees that several of the glasses are nearly full.

'Left, right, left, right,' the audience chants. 'My balls are swinging from left to right. My cock is aching, my pubes are a fright, left, right, left, right.'

The Domineta moves away from him, motioning for the audience to continue.

'Left, right, left, right, my balls are swinging from left to right. My cock is aching, my pubes are a fright, left, right, left, right.'

The Domineta reaches the pool and bends to begin turning tiny stopcocks in the pipes above the glasses that are full. Women in the audience have started to stamp in time with their chant and he can feel the stage shake faintly through the steel poles holding his chair up. When he looks to his left he can see that the newcomer's chair has been raised and the track has already been laid beneath him, passing a few inches below his large, dangling balls.

'Left, right, left, right, my balls are swinging from left to right. My cock is aching, my pubes are a fright, left, right, left, right. Left, right, left, right, my balls are swinging from left to right. My cock is aching, my pubes are a fright, left, right, left, right. Left, right, left, right, my balls are swinging from left to right. My cock is aching, my pubes are a fright, left, right, left, right.'

The Domineta is turning the last stopcock and all the glasses are full. She straightens up, lifting the microphone to her lips, and the four young women treading the tampons notice that the glasses are all full and stop treading.

'Thank you, ladies!' the Domineta cries into the chant. 'Thank you. We've had a bumper harvest, ten brimming glasses of menstrual blood that our two lucky contestants will have to drain to the last drop here, in front of you tonight!'

Cheers from the audience burst through the last stamps of the chant. The Domineta turns away from the pool, saying quietly to the treaders, 'Clear it away, dears.'

They start climbing out of the pool, lifting first one foot, shaking it as dry as they can, placing it on the stage and repeating the process with the other foot before stepping fully onto the stage. But he can see that they leave uneven footprints of menstrual blood as they walk on it. Three of them take up positions around the pool, bending and taking hold of it as the fourth treader trundles the wheeled platform to them. The three women lift up the pool with soft grunts and take short, shuffling steps sideways, swinging the pool over the platform, then lowering it carefully on top of it, leaving the ten wineglasses of menstrual blood sitting in a perfect circle on the stage behind them.

Then two of them wheel the pool away, stage left. As he watches it go he sees that the track has been laid completely under the newcomer's chair and is disappearing into the shadows on either side of the stage. Two of the treaders have trotted stage right and now return, pushing short wheeled stepladders with circular tray-holders at the top of them. One pushes her stepladder up beside Philip, then turns and trots off the stage again, while the other pushes hers up beside the newcomer, Little Willy, then turns and trots off after her companion, who is already trotting back onto the stage carrying a silver tray. She squats on the stage on the edge of the circle of menstrual glasses, lifting five of them one by one and laying them on the tray in a smaller circle. As she straightens, before turning to walk

233

across the stage to Philip, the second treader has reached the remaining crescent of menstrual glasses with her tray.

The treader reaches Philip and climbs the stepladder. At the top she slips the tray into the holder waiting for it and climbs down again. Philip can smell the menstrual blood in the five glasses, see it sitting dark and thick in them, and his stomach rolls with disgust at the thought of having to drink it. The other treader is carrying her tray across the stage to the newcomer, and the track of the model railway is laid fully across the stage from right to left, emerging from shadow, disappearing into shadow. His balls are still aching and he can still feel the Domineta's hand on the shaft of his cock. The treaders have all disappeared off the stage now, and only the Domineta and the two cameranuns are left. The Domineta glances left and right, checking that everything is ready, nodding as she receives some signal from the shadows on stage left, then strolls into the centre of the stage.

The audience has started talking among itself again and she looks out over it for a few seconds. Then she turns her head left and right as two new cameranuns come gliding onto the stage on motorised cameras. When they're positioned right, she nods and raises her microphone to her lips. The speakers above him are humming as though they've been switched fully on.

'Ladies and our two gentlemen!' she cries, and he can feel the whole stage shaking beneath him with the thunder of it. 'Welcome to Balls . . . on . . . the . . . *Line*!'

The theme music starts flooding from the speakers, a jaunty, sarcastic pastiche of a 1940s or 1950s holiday melody, with drums and trumpets and flutes cleverly imitating the rhythm and sound of a steam train. A high-pitched whistle cuts unexpectedly through it, seeming almost real, and he jumps, then sees a movement out of the corner of his eye and turns his head to see a model train come steaming from the shadows stage right, heading along the track towards him. Literally and lusciously steaming towards him, because he can see smoke curling up from its black funnel and another plume of steam rockets above it as the whistle sounds again. It's travelling fast and he feels hot air whisked across his balls as the engine passes beneath him, then cooler air as the four carriages and guard's van follow it.

He turns his head to the other side, watching the train fly across the twenty or thirty feet of stage separating him from the newcomer's seat. Then he sees the newcomer jerk and his mouth open silently in a scream as the whistle sounds again just as the engine is passing under his seat, the plume of hot steam rocketing directly against his balls for a moment. He can hear the laughter in the audience even through the theme music of the show. Then the guard's van is vanishing under the chair and the whistle is sounding again as the train disappears into the shadows stage left. What will happen now? The theme music is starting to quieten and the Domineta has her microphone ready at her lips again, looking out over the audience.

But then the whistle sounds again and he looks stage left to see the train coming out of the shadows again. The track must loop offstage so that the train can turn back on itself, and the music is quiet enough now for him to hear the wheels turning and track rattling as it passes beneath the newcomer's balls and comes on towards him. He waits for the whisk of hot air as it passes beneath him again, and screams as the whistle sounds just as it did under the newcomer, and hot steam blasts against his balls for a second. The last seconds of music are lost in the roar of laughter from the audience as the train rushes beneath him and back towards the shadows stage right.

'And have we got a show for you tonight, ladies!' the compère cries.

His balls dangle, aching from *masturbatus interruptus*, damp and stinging from the hot steam blasted against them. Again the train rushes out of the shadows stage right.

'Two contestants must battle it out to avoid some agonising pain. 'On my right –' she transfers her microphone into her left hand, holding out her arm, pointing to him '– we have little Philip Tyndale!'

Cheers and laughter.

'Little Philip is a postgraduate student of European literature at the University of Northchester and his specialist subject tonight will be themes of female domination in the work of the Victorian poet Charles Algernon Swinburne, eighteen thirty-six to nineteen-oh-nine.'

'Ooooh,' goes the audience, then dissolves into laughter.

'And on my left –' the compère's arm comes out, pointing '– we have our mystery guest, Little Willy!'

Cheers and laughter. He flinches as the train passes beneath him, the puff of air from its passage feeling cool now on his steam-blasted balls.

'Little Willy is an Anglican priest and his specialist subject tonight will be . . . the *subordinate* position of women as preached in the Pauline Epistles of the New *Testament*!'

Boos and ironic cheers. He hears the whistle of the train again from stage left and flinches. It's coming back again, steaming out of the shadows.

'Both of them are here tonight, ready and unwilling to play –'

The Domineta jerks both hands into the air and the audience yells: 'Balls on the Line!'

The train passes beneath him as the Domineta turns away from the audience for a moment, nodding stage left. Philip feels his seat shudder and start to sink and cries out for a moment, thinking his balls are going to be lowered onto the train as it rushes beneath him, but the train has passed and is steaming back into the shadows stage right. His balls touch the surface of the track and settle, sitting fully and fatly across it, waiting for the train to return. He looks stage left and sees that the newcomer's balls have been lowered to the track too.

'Yes, ladies! Only one contestant will have his balls lifted off the line tonight before the *Flying Cocksman* comes steaming back at the end of the show. Isn't that a shame?'

'No!' scream the audience.

Laughing, the Domineta takes a sheaf of question cards from a young woman who has just trotted onto the stage, then turns and prepares to start the game.

NEXUS NEW BOOKS

To be published in July 2004

THE PLAYER
Cat Scarlett

Carter, manager of an exclusive all-female pool tour, discovers Roz in a backstreet pool hall. When he sees her bending to take her shot, he can't resist putting his marker down to play her. But, when he signs Roz up to his tour, she discovers that the dominant Carter has a taste for the perverse, enforces a strict training regime, and that an exhibition match is just that.

£6.99   ISBN 0 352 33894 6

THE ART OF CORRECTION
Tara Black

The fourth instalment of Tara's series of novels chronicling the kinky activities of Judith Wilson and the Nemesis Archive, a global network of Sapphic corporal punishment lovers dedicated to chronicling the history of perverse female desire.

£6.99   ISBN 0 352 33895 4

SERVING TIME
Sarah Veitch

The House of Compulsion is the unofficial name of an experimental reformatory. Fern Terris, a twenty-four-year-old temptress, finds herself facing ten years in prison – unless she agrees to submit to Compulsion's disciplinary regime. Fern agrees to the apparently easy option, but soon discovers that the chastisements at Compulsion involve a wide variety of belts, canes and tawses, her pert bottom, and unexpected sexual pleasure.

£6.99   ISBN 0 352 33509 2

To be published in August 2004:

THE PRIESTESS
Jacqueline Bellevois

Gullible young solicitor Adam finds himself attracted to Megan, his beautiful fellow employee, and dominated by worldly-wise workmate Donna. The owner of a slinky, City-based fetish club finds she is being defrauded by a mysterious regular, known as The Priestess, and the three of them must learn to serve their client well. Submitting their own sexual tensions to the rules of the club, and discovering its association with a bizarre 'sanatorium', the trio discover that their lives will never be the same again.

£6.99   ISBN 0 352 33905 5

TICKLE TORTURE
Penny Birch

Jade, confident but submissive, is struggling to come to terms with the demands of her lesbian lover, AJ, to become her lifestyle slave. Matters aren't helped when her participation at a wet, kinky cabaret goes too far, bringing its shifty management after her, intent on sexual revenge. With the added distraction of her lewd friend Jeff Bellbird, and extra toppings from Doughboy the pizza man, Jade looks less likely than ever to resolve her dilemma.

£6.99   ISBN 0 352 33904 7

EMMA'S SUBMISSION
Hilary James

This fourth volume of Emma's story finds its very pretty heroine back in the thrall of the sadistic Ursula, who is now supplying well-trained young women as slaves and pleasure creatures to wealthy overseas clients. Having been trained by Sabhu – Ursula's Haitian assistant and slave-trainer – Emma is hired out to the cruel wife of an African dictator who uses her in the most degrading ways. Emma soon discovers that the woman has acquired a painting which has been stolen from Ursula. Ursula wants it back at any cost and, if Emma fails in her mission to retrieve it, she may never see her beloved mistress again.

£6.99   ISBN 0 352 33906 3

If you would like more information about Nexus titles, please visit our website at www.nexus-books.co.uk, or send a stamped addressed envelope to:

Nexus, Thames Wharf Studios,
Rainville Road, London W6 9HA

NEXUS BACKLIST

This information is correct at time of printing. For up-to-date information, please visit our website at www.nexus-books.co.uk

All books are priced at £6.99 unless another price is given.

- - - - - - ✂ -

Please send me the books I have ticked above.

Name ....

Address ....

....

....

.... Post code...................

Send to: **Virgin Books Cash Sales, Thames Wharf Studios, Rainville Road, London W6 9HA**

US customers: for prices and details of how to order books for delivery by mail, call 1-800-343-4499.

Please enclose a cheque or postal order, made payable to **Nexus Books Ltd**, to the value of the books you have ordered plus postage and packing costs as follows:

UK and BFPO – £1.00 for the first book, 50p for each subsequent book.

Overseas (including Republic of Ireland) – £2.00 for the first book, £1.00 for each subsequent book.

If you would prefer to pay by VISA, ACCESS/MASTERCARD, AMEX, DINERS CLUB or SWITCH, please write your card number and expiry date here:

....

Please allow up to 28 days for delivery.

Signature ....

Our privacy policy

We will not disclose information you supply us to any other parties. We will not disclose any information which identifies you personally to any person without your express consent.

From time to time we may send out information about Nexus books and special offers. Please tick here if you do *not* wish to receive Nexus information. □

- - - - - - ✂ -